THE ADLON
BERLIN—1939

Gone were the days of Imperial Germany, but the splendor remained as the aristocracy of the new Reich played out their private passions in the lavish suites of the fabled Hotel Adlon. . . .

ED RAINE. The American journalist looked for the truth in high Nazi circles. Until he learned a devastating secret in the arms of a beauty he could neither trust—nor resist.

EMMA FELSER-GRIEBE. High priestess of the silver screen, and Goebbels' chosen consort, she was the ultimate Aryan, guilty of the greatest infidelity: treason.

OTTO SCHELLEN. Himmler's man at the Adlon, he used the sweet persuasion of sex to uncover the traitors within.

BEA GOODPASTURE. A saucy British blonde with a message, a mission, and some undercover tricks very much her own.

All of them were players in a game of power and death—while the whole world hovered on the fiery brink of war.

By Zachary Hughes
from Jove

HOTEL DESTINY SERIES

THE ADLON LINK

Next to come in the series:
FORTRESS LONDON

THE ADLON LINK

ZACHARY HUGHES

Hotel Destiny 1 Berlin

A JOVE BOOK

First Jove edition published July 1981

First printing

Printed in the United States of America

Jove books are published by Jove Publications, Inc.,
200 Madison Avenue, New York, NY 10016

DISCLAIMER

Obviously, real people, places, and events are a part of this book. However, while based on historical events, the happenings herein are fictional. There is no intentional resemblance between the fictional characters and persons living or dead.

1

EDGAR RAINE STRODE briskly through the airport, trying to make up for lost time. Or rather, time well used—he had wanted to explore Zürich during his brief stopover and had set out for some hasty sightseeing. But he had wandered the streets of the old part of the city longer than he intended, awed as any other greenhorn American by the age of things here in Europe, the palpable sense of history; now he was barely able to catch his flight to Berlin, the last leg of his journey.

As he joined the line of passengers boarding the Swiss Air Lines DC-3, he recognized Hans Blumenthal a few places ahead of him. Blumenthal, with his graying hair and sweeping mustache framing a square, Germanic face, bore an extraordinary resemblance to the late Chancellor Hindenburg. In his radio commentaries, which were often highly critical of the New Germany, Blumenthal was fond of saying, "No one knows the squareheads like a squarehead."

As luck would have it, once they had boarded, the seat next to Blumenthal was vacant, and Ed took the place, anticipating an informative conversation. The aircraft's twin engines roared in preparation for takeoff, and Ed noted that Blumenthal's hands were clenched.

"It always makes me want to pray a little," Ed said.

"I pray a lot," Blumenthal said, in his distinctive voice so familiar to millions.

Safely in the air, with his ears popping as the plane gained altitude, Ed said, "Mr. Blumenthal, I'm quite a fan of yours. I'm Edgar Raine of Allied News."

Blumenthal favored the lanky young redhead with an appraising glance. "Business or pleasure, Mr. Raine?"

He had to smile. It was still hard to believe he'd landed the choicest assignment of all, Berlin. "I am the Allied News Organization's new man in Berlin. I'm still a little overwhelmed."

"Speak the language?" Blumenthal asked.

Ed answered in flawless German. "We're both square-heads, Mr. Blumenthal. My mother was born in Dresden, and she's back there now, running a gift shop. Came over several years ago to help out her aging aunt for a while, and liked things so well she decided to stay."

Blumenthal grunted. "Might be a good idea if you talk her into leaving."

Ed didn't rise to the bait. He knew Blumenthal's views, and some of them were reasonable. Hitler was making things a bit too hot with his propaganda attacks on Poland, but Ed Raine happened to feel that there was some justification for them. He'd read everything there was to read on Germany, and not just because he'd been given the Berlin post. He liked Germans. They were a wondrously logical people in both action and speech, in spite of what Mark Twain had said. Ed was sure that Hitler would settle for Danzig and the Polish Corridor, the coastal strip that would connect Germany to East Prussia, just as he was sure that if a plebiscite were held, the largely German people of this corridor would vote to be part of the New Reich. But you didn't argue such points, for they were already unpopular, and especially so with a man like Blumenthal. Saying a kind word for Germany would be waving a red flag in the man's face, and Ed was not so egotistical that he felt he couldn't learn from an old German hand like Blumenthal.

So, as the plane droned on, as it dipped for stops at Stuttgart and Halle-Leipzig, he kept Blumenthal talking about Germany. Blumenthal had been in Berlin during the crisis of 1938, through the bloodless seizure of Czechoslovakia. His predictions of war had proved to be groundless then; Ed was sure that his new predictions that, this time, France and England would finally be forced to declare war on Germany were made in ignorance of the true situation. Hell, every thinking man realized that Germany had been given a rough deal at Versailles. You just don't do to a proud and vital nation what the victorious Allies did to Germany at the point of a gun. An if there was such dictatorial censorship in Germany, how had Blumenthal's critical broadcasts been released during the Czech crisis? But though Ed disagreed with Blumenthal's conclusions, he listened raptly to the older man's stories, his pungent characterizations of the Nazi leaders, his wealth of background information. The four-hour flight was quickly over.

From the air Berlin was a neat and colorful collage of red-brick factories and precise areas of residential and business blocks. The two rivers, the Spree and the Havel, twisted and turned to connect with a network of canals. Only New York, London, and Tokyo had more people. Only Rome, London, Rio, Los Angeles, and Brisbane sprawled over more area. Templehof airport rose to meet them; the pilot made a flat, smooth approach and touched down with a jar scarcely felt by the passengers.

He was there at last, a tall, red-haired Midwesterner of twenty-nine with a chance to make his name as well known as Hans Blumenthal, Bill Shirer, Ed Murrow. He retrieved his briefcase from under the seat, stood to join the crush of people impatiently pressing to get off the plane. Blumenthal kept his seat.

His gabardine suit wrinkled by travel, Ed Raine would have looked at home in, say, Milwaukee, or at a Junior Chamber of Commerce dinner in Des Plaines. In spite of sharing the vices to which newsmen are prone—booze, broads, and odd hours—he looked wirily fit. His brown eyes were alert and clear, his nose a bit sharp but pleasantly so, his mouth shaped to make a smile come easily.

When he reached the doorway he hesitated. He could see only the tarmac and the terminal and aircraft parked nearby in front of huge hangars, but Berlin was out there. He could spout the statistics and history of the city that had been capital of the Reich since 1871, and of Brandenburg and Prussia for centuries before that, for he'd done his homework. The Berlin assignment was a plum, and he was not going to blow that chance for lack of a proper background of researched knowledge. He had already roughed in a couple of color pieces that he would flesh out after getting impressions through his own eyes, nose, ears.

As he stood there, blocking the way for those behind him, he knew a feeling of great anticipation laced through with a modicum of dread lest he fail. Hell, he was a small-town boy, not a world traveler like Lowell Thomas or Bill Shirer. His knowledge of Germany and Germans had come to him secondhand, through his mother and from books. He felt very much an American—an American who, in his own vast country, had space and distance enough without traveling to some foreign country to see old buildings, art museums, artifacts of history salvaged from the long European past, which made the United

States seem to be exactly what it was, a new country. He was traveling abroad for the first time, and just the sight of Berlin from the air had given him a thrill. He was an untraveled American, but that was now being remedied. He would take full advantage of old Europe's culture, not be ashamed to gawk, to question, to absorb what Europeans had lived with and taken for granted for centuries.

A leadline ran through his mind: *Berlin is a northern city, on a latitude with Newfoundland or lower Hudson's Bay. Even in August there is a different feel in the air, a residual coolness, a comfort so different from a muggy August in New York. Here the summer days are long, the sum coming up before it seems decent for it to be light—*

"If you don't mind," a man behind him said testily.

He walked down the steps, followed the line of passengers toward the passport and customs officials, still composing his color piece in his mind . . . *At Templehof, sleek airliners land on what was once a parade ground for the goose-stepping hordes of Frederick the Great.*

He knew well the sternness of the German character, saw it reflected in the serious but courteous passport officials. "You speak our language well," one of them said.

"With good reason," Ed said. "My mother is German."

"Ah, then welcome home, Herr Raine. Your address is correct?"

"Yes."

"And you are a news reporter?"

"That I am," he said.

"Perhaps, being German, you will not color your reporting as some do."

"I'll do my best," Ed said.

Cleared, moving along to claim his luggage, he turned at the sound of a commotion. Hans Blumenthal was being escorted, not in silence, away from the passport check area by two men in dark suits. Ed pushed his way back to the desk. "May I inquire what is happening with my friend, Mr. Blumenthal?"

"For that answer you will have to ask the Gestapo," the official said.

"I don't understand," Ed said. "He's an American citizen." The official shrugged and reached for the next passport. Ed followed the loudly protesting Blumenthal down a hallway. One of the men holding onto Blumenthal's arms saw him, halted the trio.

"May I ask what is the problem here?" Ed said.

The two Germans looked at him coldly.

"It's all right, Mr. Raine," Blumenthal said. "These gentlemen are merely going to keep me company until six o' clock, when there is a flight for London."

"But you just came from there," Ed said.

"It seems that I am no longer welcome in Germany," Blumenthal said.

"Is there anything I can do?" Ed asked lamely, not quite believing the situation.

"If you gentlemen don't mind." Blumenthal shook the hands from his arms and reached into his pocket. "I promised Bill Shirer I'd bring him these." He held out a small packet of Havanas.

"*Nein*," said one of the dark-suited men, seizing the cigars.

Ed addressed the men in German. "My name is Edgar Raine, and I'm a correspondent for ANO. May I ask why you're detaining Mr. Blumenthal?"

"We do not take it lightly when a guest in our country insults the Führer." And with that the two bustled Blumenthal on down the hall and into a room.

Before the door closed behind him, Blumenthal yelled over his shoulder, "Tell the boys at the Adlon I said hello, and give 'em hell!"

Ed felt a little less buoyant, his splendid feeling of arrival and anticipation slightly dampened. But Blumenthal's criticism of Germany and of Hitler was, after all, a bit extreme. And Germans weren't the only ones who had a low opinion of often arrogant Jews . . . He claimed his luggage, noted that the contents had not been overly disturbed, and went to seek a taxi.

The drive into the city made him feel better. The streets were impeccably clean, lined with lush linden and plane trees. The driver, finding that he spoke German, was like taxi drivers everywhere, seeking to enlarge the tip with friendliness and an informal travelogue.

"*Ja,*" he said, as they crossed a bridge, "more bridges than Venice. Bridges over the rivers and canals. And barges on the canals to bring us the fruits of the countryside, the apples, the pears, the peaches. And the coal and steel for our factories."

Flags. Flags everywhere. Ed had seen pictures taken during the Olympics, when the entire city was draped in red and black, with flags that made huge, brilliant slashes of color. Now they were smaller, but almost every house, almost every building, was decorated with the red and black and the swastika.

He felt even better when, stalled in traffic, he heard the clop-clop of horses' hooves and a horsecab drew up alongside. The cab was just as described by his mother, iron-shod wheels, top folded down in the beautiful weather, the driver in a sort of uniform, a pleated jacket and battered top hat with a white band. The horse, Ed noted, was a roan; he recalled his mother saying that Germans thought it was bad luck to ride behind a white horse.

"Things are going well?" Ed asked.

"In Berlin, good. In all of Germany, good," the stolid driver said firmly. The traffic still didn't move, so he looked at Ed. "You are an American?"

"Yes."

"You are visiting?"

"I'm a newsman."

"Good." The driver eased the cab into motion. "You write this. You will write that things are never better in Germany. You will write that we are one country, that we have one great leader, that once again we have our pride and can hold up our heads."

"And if war comes?"

"Bah, there will be no war. Why will there be war? The Führer demands only what is rightfully ours, is it not true?"

Ed didn't answer. Earlier, he would have quickly agreed, but now he remembered how Hans Blumenthal had been hustled away by two grim men. Perhaps . . .

And then it was not necessary to answer, for ahead lay the symbol of the greatness of Germany, the Brandenburg Gate, and beyond, the grand boulevard, Unter den Linden. The boulevard itself, planned by Dorothea, wife of the Great Elector, was once adorned by the huge linden trees she herself planted in 1681. In front of the gate was a broad plaza with green lawns and a fountain with sparkling water. And on the corner of the plaza was the Hotel Adlon, his destination, its light-colored roof marked with dormers like half-eyes over the five-story facade. Roman arches decorated the first floor, balustraded balconies on the second, smaller wrought-iron balconies the next—an imposing building, the hostelry of kings.

"Don't stop yet," Ed told the driver. "Drive on down to the palace and come back."

"You like our Unter den Lanternen?" The driver chuckled. "A bit of German humor, you understand?"

"Yes," Ed said. The ancient lindens had been cut down during construction of the subway, but Berliners loved their trees, so new saplings had been planted down the center of the wide boulevard. "The street lights are taller than the trees, eh?"

"A bit of German humor," the driver repeated.

Unter den Linden was lined with hotels, clubs, cafés, high-priced shops, was choked with cars, double-decker buses, trucks, people, heads high, eyes alert, busy, busy, busy. Because of the traffic, it took a while to drive the relatively short length of the boulevard and back. Ed took it all in— sights, smells, sounds, and the driver's spiel.

At the Adlon, the driver stated the price of the ride; Ed paid and tipped him well: part of the unstated bargain. Uniformed porters swarmed from the wide entrance. Above him were the tiny wrought-iron balconies, the high windows, behind him Pariser Platz. A good address, the Adlon— Number One Unter den Linden. It was the best place in Berlin to stay—it housed everyone from visiting royalty to resident newsmen in its luxurious, soundproof rooms—and had been the best ever since it opened in 1907.

Now, thirty-two years later, Ed Raine was treated like visiting royalty at the reception desk, his reservation swiftly and efficiently processed. He followed the porter through the lobby with its Oriental carpets and square pillars of ocher-streaked marble, into the bronze-encrusted elevator to the third floor. There he had to leap aside to keep from being bowled over by a young woman who was turning acrobatic flips down the well-carpeted hall. She did one final flip, left the floor completely, turned over in the air, and landed lightly on her feet, smiling broadly at him. She was dressed in slacks and her long, ash-blond hair was knotted at her neck.

"Sorry," she said, and then fled, laughing, down the hall.

The porter made a circle at his temple with his forefinger. "Norwegians," he said, as if that were a total explanation.

The room was no disappointment. The view was excellent, looking over the lawns and the fountain of the Pariser Platz toward the Brandenburg Gate and the busy boulevard. The carpeting in the room was so thick that it felt like deep grass, the bath spacious and modern. The porter opened doors, turned on a light, stood with hands behind his back until Ed brought out a tip.

"If you need anything, sir, you have merely to signal."

Electric-light signals, not old-fashioned bells.

Then he was alone. The first thing he did was to open the travel case of his typewriter and place the machine on the desk, with paper, eraser, blue pencil beside it. He was hanging up his rather wrinkled clothing in the closet when he thought he heard a knock on the door connecting to the adjacent room. He paused, listening. The knock came again, and this time he thought he heard a voice saying his name. He fumbled with the locks. The door opened and he looked into a smiling face—cupid's-bow lips, extravagant green eyes heavily made up, dark blond hair tightly curled to a beautifully shaped head.

She was the most sensuously glamorous woman he'd ever seen. "Welcome to Berlin," she said.

2

COLONEL WOLF VON STAHLECKER strolled, leisurely but sternly upright, swinging his walking stick in his left hand. His habitual afternoon walk along the boulevard invariably led to the cellar bar of the Adlon. There he tucked the walking stick under the stump of his right arm, nursed his one glass of the white beer that was Berlin's specialty, and gave thoughtful, always correct answers to the newsmen who used the wood-paneled bar as their hangout. However, on the afternoon that Edgar Raine was approaching Berlin, he did not leave the hotel immediately, but made his way into the bustling marble-pillared lobby and, with no observable glance to see if he were being watched, into an elevator.

In a hallway on the third floor he did look—first to one side, then to the other, seeing only an expanse of carpets and the quite good pictures on the walls—before he knocked lightly on the door at the turning of the hall. When the door opened he entered quickly and satisfied himself that he was alone with the woman. In contrast to the old-

11

fashioned opulence of the rest of the hotel, the sitting room of this suite was sleek and modern; it looked as if it had been designed by a film decorator for a glamorous star. It had.

Emma Felser-Griebe wore an ornate dressing gown. Her blond hair, clinging closely to her well-shaped head, was immaculate, her makeup complete, giving her a slightly theatrical appearance. Even without makeup she would have been beautiful. With it she was a vision to gladden von Stahlecker's heart.

"Ah, lovely as always," he said.

"And you, my dear Count, are looking well," she said, showing him to a stark Mies chair—done in white leather, not black. She sat on the pale satin sofa and poured him a cup of coffee. "Did you have a pleasant walk?"

"The weather is quite accommodating," he said. "I took time to have a coffee at a sidewalk café, to read the papers and see the handiwork of the office of Herr Goebbels in the headlines. You've seen them?"

"I saw something about the 'utter Polish madness,' " she said. "And large headlines that read, 'POLAND LOOK OUT.' "

"The newspapers seem to bear out our fears." He sipped coffee from a delicate cup, lifting it from the chrome-and-glass table near his chair. With only one arm he was unable to balance the cup and saucer on his knee. His right uniform sleeve was flat and empty, pinned neatly to his side. "You were with him last night?"

"Yes," she said, looking away.

"And?"

"As you suggested, I told him that I wanted to get started on the updated version of *The Blue Angel*; we've discussed it before. He said that it might have to wait."

"For how long?"

"He told me, 'Be patient, my dear.' " She had mimicked

the peculiar voice perfectly, and they both smiled. "A year, perhaps less,"

"Madness," von Stahlecker said. "Before I met you, I would have said that remaking a classic film would be madness, too, but if anyone can make the world forget Marlene's performance it would be you."

"Thank you," she said.

"So. A year. Yes, it is, in their minds, a good estimate. Poland will fight, but horse cavalry will be no match for tanks. The demands for the Danzig corridor are, of course, not the real purpose."

"He said as much, once," she said musingly. "Hitler has no intention of settling for the corridor without Posen and Upper Silesia."

"And then, when he reduces Hungary, Rumania, and Yugoslavia, the Reich will be self-sufficient, with oil, coal, all the vital raw materials and nations of slaves to produce them and our food. A self-sufficient Germany, immune to an Anglo-French blockade, will not be tolerated, of course."

"Of course," she said.

"You go to Dresden soon."

"The weekend."

"There you will, no doubt, see Herr Deler."

"It could easily be arranged."

"Not with obvious intent."

She nodded.

He put down his cup and reached for his briefcase. "This is for Herr Deler," he said, handing her a letter. "I do not have to tell you that you must not be caught with it." Again, she nodded. "You do, of course, have a right to know what you carry. It is a letter from Mr. Churchill, carried home to us by von Schlabrendorff after his July visit in London. In it, we are assured that your friend's estimate of one year to swallow Poland and the others is not realistic. Britain and France will go to war if Hitler goes into Poland.''

As he spoke, he was fumbling inside the briefcase, rearranging contents that had been displaced. A photograph fell out, and Emma quickly picked it up. He laughed. ''Do you recognize that handsome young lad?''

The faded photograph was of a teenage German soldier of World War I, rifle sling and gasmask strap making a cross over his upper chest. He was standing slumped in utter exhaustion, his coal-scuttle helmet tilted to one side not rakishly but tiredly, his eyes burning coals in an ash-gray face. The only thing that held him erect, it seemed to Emma, was the dim awareness that he was not one of the almost two million Germans who were dead, that he was alive with a knowledge of life palled by the bitter and everlasting gall of defeat.

''Are there more?'' she asked.

He nodded. ''Why does one save such things?'' He handed another photograph. This time he wore the neatly tailored uniform of a Reichswehr cadet, brass gleaming, the pleated pockets of his tunic pressed to perfection, the coal scuttle clamped rigidly straight by its narrow chinstrap. She saw his young face alive again, his lips set in determination, eyes burning and impersonal but no longer dead, flashing the fire that had been concealed in the 1918 study of a defeated teenager. It was a face so handsome, so provoking, that she sighed, for it was the face of young Germany, a face she now saw in the uniforms of Hitler's new horde. The Reichswehr, the peacetime defense force allowed Germany under the Versailles treaty, had been the cadre, supplying superb, fully trained officers for the rearming. This face, in a million of forms, would state, had stated in the Rhineland and in Czechoslovakia that Germany was sick of defeat. It was a face of pride, courage, honor.

"If I had met you then I would have immediately fallen in love with you," she said with a mock-flirtatious smile of her cupid's-bow lips. "Such a patriot!"

"Ah," he said.

"When did you change?"

She did not have to explain her question. "Don't encourage me to ramble," he replied. "But I suppose I changed when I became mature enough to ask myself, Was it such a terrible price to pay for taking the world into a war that became the most deadly war of history? We lost only the Sudetenland and the Saar. After all, the Austro-Hungarian Empire was the real loser, reduced to just Vienna and a few provinces, having to give up Czechoslovakia, Hungary, Yugoslavia, Rumania. And the Russians lost most of all—Finland, Latvia, Estonia, Poland, and the Balkan strip to the Black Sea."

He sighed, handed her two more photographs. One showed a crystallike cluster of Fokker biplanes, engines gone, tails knocked off, tilted onto their noses to be burned. The other was a French farmer using an abandoned German tank to pull a harrow, his stolid face peering from outfolded hatch doors, his women sowing seed behind, tired faces expressionless.

"Good Lord," he said, "how many times have I said it? How many times have I told anyone who would listen? If you want to know war, dig a trench shoulder-deep in your garden, fill it half full of water, and sit in it for days on an empty stomach while hired lunatics shoot at you from close range with machine guns."

"I can't remember the war," she said.

"Not many do, even those who experienced it. They remember only the shame of defeat. They remember the Allied blockade that went on until March of 1919. They remember the eight hundred thousand who starved."

"I remember once going shopping with my mother

when I was about seven," she said. "She had a basket full of money and put it down for a moment. Someone poured out the money and stole the basket."

"If Hitler is allowed to lead us into war," he said, "it will be worse next time."

She shuddered. "Time is growing short."

"It is almost in readiness," he said. "Lord, if only they had not gotten cold feet in 1938! It would be a different Germany now."

"And this time," she said. "Will they get cold feet this time?"

He shrugged with his good shoulder, rising. "Please tell Herr Deler that his support is vital, that he is being relied upon to bring General von Witzleben with him. Tell him that it must happen before the twenty-sixth or, as it was last year, it will be too late."

"So soon? Two weeks?" she asked sadly.

"Yes." Beneath his air of firm determination, she caught a glimpse of the underlying fatigue, the near-despair. "Tell him that we must have the troops of the Wehrkreis III."

"Yes," she said. "By the twenty-sixth." She escorted him to the door and checked to see that the hall was empty before he slipped quickly out.

At a side entrance to the hotel a moment later he squinted, stepping into the sun, looked right and left, then set off with a businesslike stride. There were times when he had little faith. They had all failed so miserably before, and now it was imperative for them to succeed. He could not walk down the boulevard without remembering how it had been and imagining how it would be again. Ah, the German people. Not content with 1,563 days of fighting foreigners, they had fought among themselves in 1918. When he had come home in November as the Communist uprising was being put down, dead horses lay under the linden trees. There, just there, a boy had started to butcher a horse. He was stopped by a portly businessman with an army rifle.

"You don't even know the animal is dead," the man had said. "Wait until a veterinarian arrives."

"He's dead. You can tell by the eyes," said the boy. He was soon joined by flat-chested and sunken-cheeked women who sawed and hacked at the meat with any implement at hand. A diet of nothing but turnips had turned them into scavengers.

Yes, there was much to remember, and often he felt that he was the only one who did remember. There was no underwear, no towels, no soap. In 1923, when the value of the once-solid mark dropped to more than four trillion to one American dollar, two eggs would buy more than a wheelbarrow full of money, if you were lucky enough to have eggs. A generation of children grew up on a diet of bread, ersatz coffee, and boiled turnips. In the Hundekeller, where it took huge piles of paper money to buy one beer, an American threw a handful of small change on the floor, then, laughing but somehow threatening, said that only naked women could pick it up. At first there was snickering, and then a middle-aged, heavy *hausfrau* began to take off her blouse. Soon several other women joined her, one angrily telling her protesting escort that one American quarter was worth more than all of the paper marks in the beer cellar.

He had fallen into a bad habit of talking to himself. As he walked his lips moved, words being formed silently. Was it any wonder, he thought, that we all went on a binge when things began to get better? We all fancied ourselves to be like Anita Berber—beautiful Anita, the darling of Berlin, dancing in the nude at the White Mouse Cabaret while slowly committing suicide with cocaine and morphine and lovers of both sexes, painting the town with pugs and drunks, burning as brightly as a candle and extinguished as easily. Along the Kurfürstendamm you saw the rouged young men, courted by the barons of finance, escorted to transvestite balls . . .

And so, he thought, looking up to note his progress back toward his office, for the mass of Germans, the moral and decent Germans, outraged and bewildered by the wildness, Hitler was welcome. He was no killjoy, when he jailed and shot the homosexuals and herded the whores into officially run brothels, but a means for returning Germany to decency.

Von Stahlecker shook his head, for even he had stood in the crowds—not dressed in a brown shirt, but nonetheless extending his hand in the Nazi salute, feeling himself to be comfortably allied with the good, knowing that here, at last, was a leader. No longer, he thought, would he and the other members of the Reichswehr, only a hundred thousand strong, play at defense with guns of wood, with tanks made by placing cardboard silhouettes on automobiles, with toy balloons whirled on the end of a string to act as targets for the wooden antiaircraft guns.

"This man Hitler," the commander, General Hans von Seeckt had said, "has ideas. Under Hitler, German factories will turn out real guns, and you will be the crack professionals who will train a new German army—not a hundred thousand but eight hundred thousand, a million, two million men." And he had felt pride and strength and purpose. Then . . .

"When did you change?" Emma had asked him.

But there are things a man can't say. He can think them, remember them, remember the early heat of April not much more than two years ago in the Basque country of Spain, the drone of the Heinkel's engines, the quick little lift of the aircraft as each five-hundred-pound bomb dropped away, a glimpse below of women and children being lifted high into the air, as high as twenty feet, starting to break up, legs, arms, heads, bits and pieces engraving that fleeting image on his mind. One small town of seven thousand people, a road and rail junction, and eight waves of bombers. Well, he had told himself, it is, after all, war. There were the two munitions plants and the bridge—legitimate targets. But then there were orders to all members of the Condor Legion to hush up the bombing of the small place called Guernica, to say that it was Basque dynamiters who leveled the town during their retreat from the victorious Fascist forces. And then one read: sixteen hundred civilians dead, nine hundred wounded.

The sole German casualty of the raid was the right arm of a German bomber pilot named Wolf von Stahlecker, and that was not the issue, as the medal pinned onto his tunic by Hitler himself was not the issue. The issue was what had happened at Guernica, the devastation, the death, the lesson it should have taught the world, the simple and elemental lesson that the world could no longer afford to use war as an instrument of diplomacy.

"Sir," he had said to Hitler, who had put a comradely arm around his shoulders and pulled him to one side for a private word of praise. "We can no longer afford war."

"With brave men like you," Hitler had replied, "we need not anticipate war, for our strength will be evident. Thanks to you and your brave comrades who fought in Spain, we have a new ally. And we will not forget you." The Führer was in one of his more elated moods. "But that Franco! Do you know, Colonel, that I talked with him?"

"I did not know, my Führer."

"Ach," Hitler had said, "what an hour! I would as soon have three or four teeth pulled as to try to get anything out of that man."

And so he had spoken with, had been embraced by Hitler. And now he was a traitor, at least in his mind. For in spite of what George Orwell had written on his return to England, this time England and France would march. Orwell described a complacent land: "England, with railway cuttings smothered in wild flowers, the deep meadows with great shining horses, men in bowler hats, pigeons in Trafalgar Square, the red buses, the blue policemen, all sleeping the deep, deep sleep of England." But England would be awakened by the roar of bombs—not in London, but in Warsaw, if Hitler had his way. The stupidity of the countries to the west had limits. When Hitler marched into the Rhineland in 1936, the London *Times* said, "He is only going into his back garden," and France filed a futile protest with the League of Nations. No one, it seemed, had read Hitler's own book, in which he stated openly that he considered all of Austria, Czechoslovakia, and Poland as much his back garden as the Rhineland.

Von Stahlecker was as sure of it as he was sure that his missing right arm ached. This time England would awaken from her deep sleep. The lesson would have been learned. No more easy victory, as in Czechoslovakia, where Sudetenland Germans met the troops with flowers, women weeping in happiness. This time the English and the French would remember another picture, the entrance into Prague, with stolid Czech policemen holding back grim crowds from which men shook their fists and wiped passion-wet eyes with twisted handkerchiefs. This time they would realize that the Nazi battle cry, "*Ein Volk, ein Reich, ein Führer*," could easily grow to a military monster in the heart of Europe. This, and the logic of it enforced by the words of Churchill, could not be tolerated. This time the thing Hitler feared most would happen. Once again the mistake would be made. Once again England would march.

And against this bleak prospect stood a one-armed former bomber pilot now serving in the information service, a girl with fantastic legs who, in her films, played the perfect German woman, the Aryan goddess, with just a hint, at times, of the beautiful female demon. She was the only one he could definitely count on, although others paid lip service. In the end who would risk all to save the world from war? Only God knew.

3

"WELCOME TO BERLIN." Emma Felser-Griebe struck a pose she knew was quite effective. She saw the American's eyes widen in surprise, then narrow to begin that inspection of her person with which she was so familiar. She stood in silence. She was not blasé enough to be totally bored with admiration, and she also, out of a sense of pure mischief, enjoyed imagining his startled thoughts. In the hotel only a few minutes, he was suddenly accosted by a woman in an ornate lounging gown. What else could he think?

He was obviously at a loss for words. Still enjoying his bemusement, she laughed. "Come with me," she said. Not to her surprise, he followed her into the sitting room in which, only a half hour before, she had talked with Wolf von Stahlecker. A beautiful bouquet of summer wildflowers, somehow incongruous in the ultramodern room, stood on a white marble table by the window. She picked up the vase and extended it.

"There is a card," she said.

He opened the card, "In my absence," it read, "let these be my welcome to you as you arrive in my country." He recognized his mother's handwriting immediately and felt a sense of relief. Hardly likely that his mother would engage a prostitute to welcome him. He wanted to apologize, saw her smile, felt a rising blush—Jesus, she had a nice laugh. It began low and rose to a silver tinkle.

"You know my mother, then?" he asked, finally finding his tongue.

"Very well. I was with her at dinner only Thursday last, and she asked me to greet you." Her voice was like a cool liquid, with a gentle German accent. "So, I greet you, Edgar Raine. Once again, welcome to Germany."

"How very nice of you," he said, "but you have me at a disadvantage."

"I am Emma Felser-Griebe. My parents run a shop next door to your mother's in Dresden."

Once again he was speculating. The corner suite in Berlin's most expensive hotel—he, himself, even with an American expense account, couldn't afford to live there longer than it took to find a flat somewhere. The expensive gown. A shopkeeper's daughter? Not likely.

"And your mother has told me all of your favorite German foods, so I have taken the liberty of ordering dinner for us."

"Again, very kind," he said.

"There is wine, or if you prefer, more powerful liquids," she said. "And when I have prepared a drink for you you must tell me all about America."

He accepted a glass of white Rhine wine and sat facing her. She crossed one leg casually but elegantly. Nice, nice legs.

"And tomorrow I will show you Berlin," she said.

"I will have the most beautiful guide in the city."

"So, they teach Americans the—how do you say?—the bullshit, also?"

He laughed. "Hardly," he said.

"I know," she said, "that it is so, for American girls are so wholesome and healthy and wear their hair so." She pulled her hair into a distorted pompadour and made a pout with her lips. "To German men, perhaps, I am pretty."

"Don't forget that I'm half German."

"Well then, being half pretty is better than not at all." She laughed. "But enough of that. Did you have a nice trip?"

"So-so. Long."

"Ah, but you are lucky, with your American passport and your freedom to travel as a newsman."

"Why lucky?"

She shrugged. "Such liberty is not enjoyed by all. You can come and go as you please, is it not true?"

"More or less."

"Then I will ask you, on your next trip to England, to bring me silk stockings."

"My pleasure," he said. "And how is my mother?"

"Very well. She sends her love, of course, and her apology for not being able to meet you. It is a busy time and she had no one to watch the shop."

"Yes, I know," he said. "Well, I'll pop over to Dresden soon."

"Perhaps we could travel together," she said. "I must go to Dresden this weekend."

He felt great interest, imagined them together in a nice little car or in the dining car of a train. Not bad duty for a lanky redheaded American. "That's a little soon for me," he said, with regret. "I'll have to turn in a little work first, get acquainted, get my feet on the ground. My editors want an article as soon as possible—for example, on the German Youth Movement."

"Ah," she said, with a frown. "You have merely to write that it began with endless singing to the strumming of thousands of guitars and was taken over by the Nazi movement, and that now the songs are all warlike."

He raised an eyebrow. "You sound as if you don't approve."

She laughed. "I am not one to approve or disapprove. It has nothing to do with me, after all."

Dinner arrived, served by a uniformed waiter, before he could pursue the subject; during the meal she talked of the city, its history, its society. There was something about her, an assurance, an air of command, that precluded questions. It seemed to him that a question would have been met with a blank stare. However, she did say one more revealing thing. He asked her if she'd ever seen Hitler.

"Many times," she said.

"And?"

"And what? He is the Führer." She smiled. "Perhaps we have one thing in common, Hitler and I. It is said that he practices his gestures for public speaking in front of a mirror and even has them photographed so that he can study and improve them."

"And do you practice gestures in front of a mirror?" he asked.

"Of course," she said. "Now you must try the sweetmeats."

She chatted easily over brandy and, just as he was wondering how long it would go on, what would develop from the evening, she rose. "Now, my new American friend," she said, "I must bid you good night."

"I was hoping that we could, perhaps, try a bit of the city's night life," he said, feeling keen disappointment.

"Another time," she said. "You will be ready at ten?"

"Ten?"

"In the morning," she said, "for your introductory tour of my city."

"I look forward to it," he said.

Alone in his room, the day catching up with him, he discarded the idea of going down to the bar to see who was there. He made only one brief entry into his journal before drawing a hot bath and soaking until he was drowsy.

THURSDAY, August 10, 1939
Limited contact with Germans on my first day here. Taxi driver says there will be no war. People on the streets go about their business seemingly unworried. Only the incident at Templehof, with Blumenthal, to speak of the fact that Germany is supposed to be a military state. People hardly act repressed. The Adlon is all I was led to believe it would be. Too bad I can't afford to just stay on here. I am eager to be at work and will accept the invitation of this Emma Felser-Griebe to make a tour of the city, using it as an occasion for a background piece.

In her own quarters Emma Felser-Griebe bathed, scented herself, and dressed in a clinging silk dress. She sat down at her desk with pen and paper. As she wrote, she chose her words carefully.

My Dear Herr Smidt,

I have interviewed the actor we have discussed. If he is his mother's son, perhaps he will be suitable for the role you have in mind for him. I will know more after tomorrow. E.F.G.

She pushed a button to summon a hall messenger, who took the letter to the pneumatic mail chute in the hall. It would rest in the box downstairs no more than an hour or two before being picked up with Germanic efficiency— Berlin had four mail deliveries a day plus one on Sunday— and being sent forward to its destination. The next morning "Herr Smidt" would open the private box in a branch post office and retrieve her message.

Emma Felser-Griebe heard a discreet knock on the hall door. With a sigh and an expression that she permitted herself only when alone, she rose to admit her caller.

4

WITH EMMA DRIVING, the one necessary errand took only a moment. She waited outside as he made a quick stop at the American Counsulate in Bellevuestrasse to present his credentials. With nothing to detain him, they drove on.

The day was perfect—not hot but pleasantly warm. She was dressed like a dream in a soft tan suit and a floppy hat with a full veil. The automobile was a dream also, a Mercedes 500K.

"K for Kompressor," she explained, when Ed said he knew little about German cars. "Or supercharger. Five-liter engine, eight cylinders developing one hundred sixty horses."

"Am I impressed?" he asked with a grin, as she roared away from the front of the Consulate.

"You should be," she said. "It will hit a hundred."

"Not with me in it," he said.

"No," she said, "for at high speeds it rather gulps petrol."

"We call it gasoline. Or just gas." They had already established that he was to teach her proper American English.

"Ah, gasoline, gas," she repeated. "So. Now the day is yours. Have you any specific requests?"

"I bow to your knowledge of the city," he said. "But I'm greedy. I want to see it all."

"Have you six weeks to spare?"

"Compress it," he said. "Give me the two-dollar tour today and we'll save some for later."

She zoomed around a double-decker bus with a verve that had him grasping for something to hang on to. "If you're interested in scientific progress," she said, apparently unperturbed by a near collision with an oncoming truck, "we can stop at the Long-Distance Seeing and Talking Office near the zoo. For about, ah, sixty cents, you can call up a friend in Leipzig on television."

"I don't have any friends in Leipzig."

"Too bad. Then it's the zoo for you, my friend."

And so through the magnificent Zoological Garden. Emma acted the tour guide with a vengeance, driving, parking, pointing out, describing, marching him to the sites and back to the car . . . He lost all sense of direction, gave up trying to take notes, for the way she threw the sporty little car around made writing impossible. But he could store impressions in his mind, tall buildings, bridges, tugboats—*schleppers*—towing low, long barges on the canals with a family wash hanging out on one of the barges, one tug lowering its stack to pass under a low bridge. They paused at the Lustgarten, a huge square with a Grecian colonnade at one end, some bedraggled bunting and swastikas left from the last huge rally. She had heard Hitler speak there.

"How do you feel about Hitler?" he asked, when they were back in the car.

"Sometimes I go for weeks without feeling anything about him," she said with a light laugh. In other words, none of your business. "Ahead, once again, is the Spree. It is a part of the most advanced city transportation system in the world. With the canals, the rivers, the subway, Berlin is second to none in transportation and yet there are, within the city limits, thirty thousand pigs, twenty thousand cows, ten thousand goats, seven hundred thousand chickens, one hundred eighty thousand rabbits, nearly six thousand beekeepers, and twelve functioning windmills."

"You're a font of information," he said dryly. "What's the message you're trying to get across?"

"That the people remember 1918."

The bitterness was strong in her voice. He turned to study her face. He couldn't see much, only that she glanced at him, her eyes just hints through the veil, plastered against her face by the wind.

"They also have their little Schreber Gardens to grow vegetables. It's estimated that forty-six thousand tons of potatoes alone are grown inside Berlin each year. They are prepared."

"Emma?" he asked. He paused to be sure the torrent of information was halted. "Why the veil?"

She laughed, relaxed again, and sped the car around another bus. "Because I don't want to be recognized, you goose."

"You don't want to be seen with me?" he asked in puzzlement.

Her laugh was a gay peal of silver. "You honestly don't know? How stupid of me to think my fame had spread outside of Germany."

"I confess my ignorance," he said.

"I am properly chastised," she said ruefully. "Now I know that America has never heard of Emma Felser-Griebe, rising star of stage and screen."

"Now I am impressed," he said. "Tell me about it?"

"I'm too modest."

"Are any of your films showing now?"

"One or the other is always showing," she said, with a shrug as she parked the car again.

"I'll see one at the first opportunity. I had no idea you were famous."

"I think I like it best that way," she said. "If I had guessed you didn't know, I wouldn't have told you. It's nice to be just Emma."

"I'll write home immediately," he said, "and brag about being welcomed to Germany by its most famous movie star."

"No, you mustn't do that," she said.

"That's unfair," he teased. "I'm touring the city with the most beautiful girl in Germany and I can't brag about it?"

"I have to be very careful," she said. "You know the papers. They love writing about movie people."

"And your reputation would be ruined if it were known you were out with an American?"

"It's just that I guard against gossip of any kind," she said. "So, Edgar Raine, you and I shall be secret friends. It will be exciting to have our own little secret."

They walked. He found the city to be like Paris in one respect. There was an abundance of statuary, but of a stolid, Germanic heaviness, and there were open-air cafés everywhere. Back in the Tiergarten, at the Kroll on the edge of the Spree, a band played as they had tea. A cheerful and boisterous crowd sat in sleek Bauhaus-style chairs sipping their beer, coffee, tea from tables packed so close together there was scarcely walking room between them.

After yet more touring they had dinner in her pale, luxurious suite, both of them by now pleasantly tired. He was distracted, composing a background story in his mind. The food, however, drew his attention. She had selected French dishes, and they were delicious. The wine was properly chilled and of a good year. Soft music came from a concealed radio. When the meal was finished she signaled for the waiter.

"Well," he said, "I have some work to do. The office will think I'm on vacation." She would not have to ask him to leave as she'd done the night before.

"Don't go." She released the words without thinking, for her caller would not be coming. The thought of being alone came as a surprisingly painful letdown after an enjoyable day.

"I should," he said indecisively.

"You don't want me to be lonely, do you?" She gave him a teasing little smile.

"You're sure you don't have something else to do?"

"Stay with me, Ed. Talk to me."

He was easily convinced. He too, had enjoyed the day. There was something about her, in her words, her actions, her eyes, that seemed to hint of unspoken secrets. He was intrigued. "Shall I tell you the story of my life?"

"I know, you were a naughty little boy," she said.

"Oh, just the usual stuff. I put a snake in my teacher's desk."

"And dipped the braids of little girls into your inkwell."

"No, I was afraid of girls."

"You've conquered that, I'm sure."

"Yes and no." There was an indefinable note in her voice. He felt the atavistic interest, but along with it there was a sense of warning, a warning to be very, very careful. He did not know her at all, had been totally unable to get past the sophisticated facade of the accomplished actress. And yet, as she sat with one arm stretched out gracefully on the back of the couch, her dark eyes seemed to be challenging him. "I'm only afraid of girls now if they bite," he said.

"A lady would never bite." She showed her nice teeth in a smile.

Well, he thought, you can kiss a girl without really knowing her. Some thought that was the best way, avoiding a lot of complications. He stood in front of her and reached for her hand. She did not draw it away. She came to her feet easily and her eyes did not release his as he bent to find her mouth. It was soft and responsive. The clinging dress was silken, allowing him to feel the heat of her body. He broke the kiss when she made a soft sound in her throat, an "ummmmm" that could have been either approval or protest.

"Sorry," he said. "I abuse your hospitality."

She caught his arms as they sought to leave her, placed them around her waist. "Ed, just hold me," she whispered. "I'm so alone, and I'm so frightened."

Frightened. He wanted to ask her what frightened her, but her lips were upturned and inviting, and this time the kiss was deeper. It was she who broke the kiss, pushed him away.

"Emma?" he asked, letting his arms fall away.

"I'm sorry," she said. "Let me think for a moment."

"I'll go."

"No, not yet. Just let me think for a moment." She turned away from him, confused by her emotions.

In a mad world one did what one had to do. In a good cause, a noble cause, any action could be rationalized. And yet, she had never before felt that she had cheapened herself, never before had she felt guilt. And now it was there, a shame, a need to weep great, billowing waves of tears, to cry out to someone for forgiveness. What the hell was happening to her? She had agreed to meet this American for two reasons—for the sake of his mother and for the other. She had spent an evening and a day with him, and after two kisses she felt weak and she knew that if she went back into his arms she would obey any wish he might have. Had she coarsened herself so much that she was ready to fall into bed with any man?

She turned, her green eyes hooded, looking at him from behind her mascaraed lashes.

No, there was something else. There was a sweetness in him, almost an innocence. He looked, as he answered her gaze with a puzzled look, like a little boy, red hair touseled, the hint of an unknown hurt in his down-turned lips. "Why did you kiss me?" she asked.

He smiled. "You're very beautiful."

"And is that all?"

"Well, Emma—"

"Because you are a man and I am a woman," she said, with a shrug. Had she the right to ask more?

"I'm sorry if I offended you," he said.

"No, no, of course not." She sat down, wanting more than anything to go back into his arms but fearful of the consequences. He stood indecisively.

"Emma, I wanted to kiss you," he said. "I still want to."

She felt a queer little tugging at her heart. Things seemed to close in on her, to threaten. Never had her future been more uncertain. So easy to tell herself to grasp at even one moment of happiness. And so she put aside all fears of consequences and rose to go to him, to draw him into the bedroom.

It happened with a quickness that left them both breathless.

She smelled of clean, sweet woman. Only once before had he known such desire, such a tremulous need to know all of her, to experience all of her, to hold and kiss. And for a moment, as it began, he knew that old, hard pain, as the memory of the other, so young, so sweet, assailed him, as that old love rose up and reminded him that he was not a man for casual affairs.

He had not always been so. There'd been one girl in high school, and for a while he was madly in love with her—until he found that the wonders she exposed to him, the shattering opening to herself to him, were not reserved only for him. For a while he was resentful, but then came an incredible piece of luck for a seventeen-year-old—a torrid affair blossomed and exploded and expanded into an increased knowledge of women and their need. She was married, a product of the twenties, a decade that, for a time, had altered the morality of a Puritan country. And she taught him that lovemaking was not a one-way affair, that the man's responsibility was not solely to kiss, fumble, attack and sink back sated, but to encourage, abet, to lift his partner to his own height of easily achieved passion and to be patient, thoughtful, inventive.

However, they were not the cause of that bittersweet pang of momery as, with Emma's lips accepting his, he knew that it was going to happen. It was Laurel. For not since Laurel had he felt the sweetness of it, the totality of it, the need that was more than lust. And that was it. He was in a strange country, with a woman so beautiful that he could not believe it, and he was, for a few long, agonizing moments, reluctant, for he had loved Laurel as he'd never loved a woman, had explored life and love with her in a oneness that was so much greater than the educational experience that it was incomparable. Neither of them had felt they were doing wrong in anticipating, in reaching out for their love instead of waiting while two proud and anxious mothers planned a wedding. Giggling, laughing, clinging, eyes wide in the beauty of it, she a bit fearful, they had loved. And then he saw her decapitated body being removed from a crushed and broken bus outside Indianapolis.

No other woman, before Emma, had broken through the long-lasting pain of that experience, no woman since Laurel had given him that helpless, lovely feeling of need. And he felt traitorous, told himself, however, that time had passed, that Laurel was, after all, dead. This girl, this German girl he'd known for such a short while, so willing, so strangely willing, with all her silken softnesses and her trembling needs, brought back for a moment the old pain, and that pain was conquered by the joyous feeling of discovering something anew.

"My God, Emma," he murmured when it was over.

"Please don't condemn me," she whispered, tears forming. "Please don't think—"

"Hush, hush." He kissed her eyelids. "My Emma."

"Will you stay with me, just until I'm asleep? Hold me, then go. Promise me you'll go before the maids come in the morning.

He lay on his back, her perfumed head on his shoulder, her arm over him, one warm thigh across his. Things like this just didn't happen to him. But was it because, since Laurel, he had not allowed them to happen? He was no Puritan. God knew he'd been willing enough with the girl in school, and with the married woman. And still he felt a faint twinge of guilt, remembering Laurel. And for a moment he feared, remembering Emma's sweetness, that she might just have the power to make him forget, then he knew that no one could ever do that. Possibly, he would love again, but he would never forget Laurel.

This girl, what was it about her? Was she being honest? Was she really lonely, frightened? It had happened so easily, so naturally. No virgin, she. Definitely not the first time for her; but then she was a woman, a woman of fame. And there was something else. In the beginning, their love had been wilder than anything he'd ever experienced, closer to personal combat than love.

He fought the urge to close his eyes as her breathing evened out; then he carefully extricated himself from her soft warmth. When he was dressed he stood in the doorway, just looking at her. She lay on her back, arms open, trusting. She was a picture so beautiful, so desirable, that he hesitated to leave, but he had promised. Swiftly he crossed the sitting room to his own room, and silently closed the door.

As the sun began to lighten the outside darkness he was still unable to sleep. He sat up in bed and wrote in his journal:

FRIDAY, August 11, 1939
  The city of Berlin lies at the center of a system of canals begun in the eighteenth century. The canals follow the gouges of the great ice sheets of the Pleistocene, the weak spots in the low hills that ring the city. Young as European cities go, Berlin was founded only after Albert the Bear conquered the native Slavs in the twelfth century. The first known mention of the city in written records came in 1230.
  Berlin absorbed her sister city, Kölln, in 1709, the two cities having been previously conquered by Frederick II, who built a fortress in Kölln. Berlin was the permanent residence of the Hohenzollerns from the fifteenth century and was the capital of the electorate of Brandenburg . . .

And why am I writing down the dry facts of history just after dawn when I should be sleeping, or at least working on my first piece to be cabled home, he asked himself. Because, damn it, I'm a little confused. She hit me like a bomb, that woman. I feel weak, drained, too keyed up to sleep and too dizzy to think of anything but her lying there, those terrific legs against my sides, the hands in my hair, her mouth . . .

Berlin underwent a series of sackings and forced levies during the Thirty Years' War. The city blossomed under Frederick the Great, who built the opera and turned the Tiergarten into a large park. Berlin is a proud city but she has not been without periods of humiliation. Occupied by the French after the battle of Jena in 1806, Berlin came alive again, after the fall of Napoleon, as the capital of Prussia, second largest German state.

Knock this shit off. At least, if you're going to sit up and write, write something you can use. He snapped the journal shut and moved to the desk, fed paper into the platen of the typewriter.

This reporter looked upon Berlin with new eyes from a hotel that was once the center of social and official life of the German Empire. The Hotel Adlon, frequented by the famous and glamorous people of Germany and the world, is on the finest and most spacious boulevard in Europe, Unter den Linden, almost a mile of splendor running from the former palace to Bradenburger Tor, a double avenue divided by a promenade planted with young linden trees to replace those cut down during the construction of the subway.

From the Adlon, one sees what seem to be 4,332,000 happy Germans. On the surface, it seems that there is nothing but prosperity, and happiness, and yet one perceives an underlying tension—for if war should

come, this center of rails, with at least twelve lines
connecting inside the city limits, would be a prime
target.

If war comes, the British and French would bomb
the northwest section of Berlin, with its scientific and
military institutions; the north, with machine works;
the northeast woolen-manufacturing area; and the rail-
way works in the south. Not much would be left after
that.

But, damn it, there wasn't going to be a war. Hitler
would settle for bringing the Germans of the Polish Corridor back into the Reich. England and France would blus-
ter, but they would not march. He yawned, stretched,
climbed back in bed. No, no one was mad enough to go to
war.

But why was Emma afraid?

Emma. Jesus. Each time he had entered her, he felt as if
he were going to go on forever. Emma.

How the hell do you go to sleep with an erection?

Well, first you close your eyes.

5

SHE HAD LEFT before he awakened; at least there was no answer when he tapped on the connecting door. He had breakfast in the long marble-walled dining room, which was hung with crystal chandeliers and heavy bronze wall sconces. He felt somewhat shabby in his business suit, for others were dressed in morning clothes. He could hear soft hints of a half-dozen languages, recognized French, Italian, Russian, German, and the soft explosiveness of Japanese from two immaculate diplomatic types.

Then there was work to do. The first of his stories to be cabled home had been gestating since even before he arrived in Berlin. It flowed from his mind into his two forefingers, as he typed newsman style, hunt-and-peck honed into a skill which, when he was steaming, rivaled the machine-gun speed of a trained typist.

The Allied News Organization, infant of the American news services, could not hope to compete with its richer and more established rivals and to counter the odds that consisted of more money, more men, more coverage. Allied depended on a certain style of creativity in its writers. And his boss in New York stressed original points of view.

"Ed," he had said, "we're getting Berlin from a dozen old-timers, and we're getting it from Shirer and a half-dozen others via radio. What we get is Hitler this and Hitler that and war, war, war. Is that all there is? Is this man Hitler really a madman bent on conquering the world? Well, let's leave that to the Shirers and the others. I want you to dig down below the surface. Talk with the people. The way you speak German you can almost pass. Be one of them. Find out how they feel. Stay away from the Jewish problem, unless you come up with something just too hot to hold. Hell, it hasn't been too many years since seventy-five percent of the American people were convinced that a Jewish conspiracy was causing the Depression."

So his first piece was pure color. It spoke of a city, of a people that had lifted itself from the desperation of depression, inflation, near civil war, from total defeat. He did not judge. He did not editorialize. He just told about a city and its people. And when he was finished he rather liked it. He walked to the cable office and was impressed by the neat surroundings in the branch post office, the writing desks and comfortable chairs and, wonder of wonder, pens that would actually write.

The major portion of the day was ahead of him. Time to meet some of his peers, and the place to meet them was the dark, smoky Adlon cellar bar. The place was crowded, even in the early afternoon, and he immediately saw people whose faces he recognized. Ed Murrow was over from London to talk with his coworker, Shirer; they were two of the big ones. Murrow's braodcasts from London and Shirer's from Berlin and Europe had made their names household words. They were the new breed, the instant newsmen, and they had discarded the stereotyped characteristics of the old-fashioned print newsman, except for Murrow's chain smoking. They were holding court at a large table, and he made no attempt to push himself into that select grouping. He remembered Blumenthal's message for Shirer, for the boys at the Adlon, but now was not the time.

A man of the type more familiar to Ed leaned on the bar, gray hair a bit long, fingers stained with typewriter ribbon ink and nicotine, cigar in one hand, hawk face in a grimace of pain as he hoisted the first hair of the dog for that day. Ed stood beside him. When the old-timer had finished his gin-and-tonic, Ed said, "Buy you another one?"

"Best offer I've had all day," the older man said.

Ed introduced himself, got a name in return, along with a firm handshake. "It's an honor, Mr. Stanton," Ed said, and he meant it. "I really admire your work. Great stuff you sent out of Abyssinia." John Graff Stanton was an individualist, a free lancer who sold his copy to the highest bidder.

"Man who buys me a drink doesn't have to call me mister," Stanton grunted. "Damn, they're sending them out young, aren't they?"

Ed laughed. "How old were you when you went into the trenches in 1918?"

"That's different." Stanton gestured with his cigar. "Kids grew up quicker then. Had to."

"Seeing you here sort of worries me," Ed said. "People say you stir up wars yourself, just to have something to cover."

Stanton laughed, feeling a bit better after his second gin and tonic and thinking of switching to scotch. "Yep, I told the Nips to swarm over the Great Wall from Manchuria."

"I read your pieces from China, too," Ed said. "I liked that little touch, your telling about how the Japs wore white sashes over their heads so that they could be easily identified during night fighting."

"Got sick of it," Stanton said. "Pure slaughter. Six hundred thousand of the bastards, the new Samurai. Modern artillery against sticks and stones. Two million dead Chinks. I decided my stomach had had enough after Nanking. Ever smell fifty thousand dead bodies?"

"I hope I never have to," Ed said. He threw marks onto the bar to pay for Stanton's scotch. "What do you think of the situation here?"

Stanton shrugged. "Well, they think there's going to be war." He nodded toward the table where Murrow and Shirer sat.

"What about you?"

"I don't know if the English and French have the guts. We didn't, when the Japs sank the *Panay*."

"You'd go to war over one gunboat?"

"Son, what's the greatest nation on earth?"

"I'm sorta partial to the good old U.S. of A."

"Bullshit. England. Or Great Britain. They're great not because of what they are but because of what they were. Once a meddling Englishman could go fucking off into the wilds of the world somewhere, get himself slaughtered by Zulus or A-rabs or what the hell, and the whole damned British Empire would move, for one man. That's greatness. That makes the fuckers think a little. Kill one bloody limey and you got the British fleet on your ass. If we'd sent the Pacific fleet into Tokyo Bay when they sank the *Panay*—if France had mobilized when Hitler went into the Rhineland—if they'd met him in Czechoslovakia with a hundred divisions—"

"*They* think there's going to be war?" Ed asked, with a chuckle.

"I didn't say I did," Stanton said. "I said if we'd had any guts it would have been a short and dramatic and relatively painless war, but we've fucked around until Hitler and the Japs have built a war machine that will take years to stop. Listen, boy, I've seen 'em. I watched the brown-shirted bastards march past Hitler's reviewing stand for five or six hours in Nuremberg. Ain't you heard the broadcasts of his speeches? Read Goethe. Knows his Germans. As individuals, admirable; as a mass deplorable." He gave a passable imitation of Hitler's hysterical style of speech. "*Eins hundert tausend, zwei hundert tausend, neunzig million—*"

As Stanton raised his voice a silence fell. Two German field-grade officers glared at him from the end of the bar. Stanton gave a lopsided grin and raised his glass to them. "Just telling the boy about *der Führer*'s great and inspiring speech," he said. "*Heil Hitler.*"

The two officers returned the arm salute.

"Ninety million of the bastards indulging in the German's greatest pleasure. He'd rather be submerged in the mass mind, lose his individuality, play follow-the-leader, than get his rocks off," Stanton said, lowering his voice. "Will there be war? Hell, there's already a war. The Nazis in Danzig under *Gauleiter* Albert Forster are making war on the Poles there, marching in the streets, yelling *Heil Hitler*. It's a war of nerves so far, but the Poles are going to fight, mark my words. About France and Britain your guess is as good as mine."

"My guess is that Hitler will settle for the corridor and Danzig and that they'll let him have them."

"Well, might be best all around. Let Germany settle down. He's staying in power by feeding the people their own greatness and threats to the great German people from the barbarous Poles. Go ahead, let him have Danzig and the corridor. But build up an army and post it on the frontiers of France and tell the bastard that if he makes just one more attempt to gobble up Europe we're going to hit him with a haymaker that'll land him in the Dark Ages. Then he'll have to settle down and give the Germans consumer goods instead of guns and tanks. Without the threat of war he wouldn't last two years, and then maybe the good guys, if there are any in Germany, can take over.''

Stanton killed a new scotch in short order. ''Well, sonny, I've got work to do. Nice talking to you. Might warn you, though, if you're going to send out anything that can be construed to be critical of the great man and his regime, better send it by diplomatic mail or something. Don't wire it.''

''Yeah, thanks,'' Ed said. He stood at the bar until he finished his drink. For some reason he did not try to analyze, he felt depressed. He thought of Emma. She was on her way to Dresden. And he hadn't even asked when she'd be back. Jeeesus! Just the thought of her was enough to threaten embarrassment. Stop thinking of her, or he'd be like a red-faced high-school kid, walking down the hall with his hand in his pocket, trying to hide an erection.

He left the bar, stopped at the lobby desk to check for messages. None. Well, it was only his second day in Berlin. He turned away and had to sidestep quickly to avoid being run down by a dwarf woman riding a sturdy German tricycle. Her huge head was haloed by a well-coifed mane of blond hair, her rather pretty face was made up heavily. Dressed in boy's pants and a blue blouse that showed amazing breasts on a stubby, wide torso, she pedaled furiously in front of the desk and away.

He looked at the desk clerk in amazement. ''Norwegians,'' the clerk said. That seemed to be a full explanation for the staff.

Lead line: *I was almost run over by a dwarf on a*

tricycle in the Hotel Adlon today. Elevator occupied by a middle-aged woman wearing a monocle, leading a French poodle on a jeweled leash. And in front of my door, two stooge types. One on each side of the door. Dark suits, wide-brimmed hats pulled low over eyes which were not seen, hands crossed in front of their crotches, pictures of patience. Straight out of a Cagney film.

"Herr Raine?" one stooge asked.

Ed nodded doubtfully.

"You will come with us, please."

"Will I?" he asked.

"*Ja*, you are wanted. There is nothing to fear, Herr Raine."

"Why should there be?" he asked, but he was looking over his shoulder. "You Gestapo?"

A dry laugh. "No, no, of course not." A look, a grin that showed a broken tooth. "He thinks we are Gestapo, Wilhelm."

"*Ach*, so?" Wilhelm said. "You have reason to fear the Gestapo, Herr Raine?"

"Just what the hell is it you want?" Ed asked.

"Come with us, please."

He went. Not far, just down the hall past Emma's door. One goon knocked, opened the door, stood aside, and made a stiff bow.

The man seated in a comfortable overstuffed chair was small in stature, dark-faced; his hair was lank and combed slickly back. As Ed paused in the doorway he rose and took two limping steps forward, hand extended. Ed was astounded: Goebbels—Paul Joseph Goebbels, Minister of Propaganda. "Ah, Herr Raine," he said, "it is indeed a pleasure."

Ed heard the door close behind him. "The pleasure is mutual, sir," he said, wondering what the hell was going on.

"Sit down, sit down," Goebbels said, taking his chair. "I stand as little as possible, because of this." He lifted his withered left leg.

"Sorry," Ed said, not knowing what else to say.

"Ah, it used to bother me," Goebbels said. "No more. It is not what is here, but what is here"—he tapped his forehead—"that matters. Is that not right, Herr Raine?"

Ed nodded.

"There is wine." His host gestured toward a nearby buffet.

"No thank you," Ed said.

"Then we shall get to it." Goebbels reached for a paper on the table next to his chair. "I have been reading your first dispatch to your news service."

Ed tried to hide his expression of surprise.

"Excellent, Herr Raine." He chuckled. "And I am quite a judge, you know, having been a writer myself."

"Thank you, sir," Ed said.

"Yes, indeed, as a judge of writing I find your style to be informal—delightfully so—and quite informative. But the important thing is, Herr Raine, that you have captured the true feeling of Berlin. These others, pah! They search for maggots under the stones, and if there are none they invent them. May I say that if you continue to present a fair picture of The New Germany, which is all we ask, we will not be ungrateful."

"Thank you again," Ed said, thinking. Well, well, well. "Do you read all dispatches by foreign correspondents?"

There was a warning in the cold, quick look. "Not personally, Herr Raine." The dark look was replaced by a smile. "But if we do not inform ourselves of what is being said about us, how can we hope to counteract the slanders with the truth?"

"I see."

"We Germans have nothing but respect and warmth for the great American nation," Goebbels said. "We are often distressed by the distorted view of our country that is presented by some of the rabble-rousers. Why, German people make up a large percentage of the population of your country. Are they monsters, as some would have you believe?"

"As a man of half-German blood, I don't feel like a monster," Ed said with a grin.

"Exactly. It is up to us, the sensible ones, the fair ones, to present a true picture. I think you can go far in your profession, Herr Raine. You will find that the Ministry of Propaganda will be very cooperative with a newsman who does not let the lies of the German-haters influence him."

"Thank you. I'm new here, as you must know, and I'll need all the help I can get."

"Just call my office," Goebbels said. "Perhaps I will be busy myself, but there will be others to help you obtain any information you desire."

"Herr Goebbels," Ed said, thinking, here goes nothing! "We're not the largest news service in the world by a long shot, but we do try to present a fair viewpoint. I may be assuming too much, but it would be a feather in my cap and a great thing for ANO if you could arrange a personal, exclusive interview with the Führer." He held his breath as Goebbels seemed to go into deep thought.

"Perhaps," Goebbels said at last. "But not in the immediate future. The Führer is, of course, deeply concerned about the provocative actions of the Poles, and the intransigence of France and England. When this crisis is past—" He spread his hands.

"In the role of a newsman," Ed said, again smiling, "may I ask the Minister of Propaganda a question?"

"Of course."

"*Will* this crisis pass?"

"Let me say only this," Goebbels said. "We Germans are a peace-loving people. We do not want war, only what is rightfully ours. Our requests are reasonable. If war comes it will not be Germany's fault, but the fault of the warmongers in Poland, in France, in England."

"Will Hitler settle for Danzig and the corridor?"

"How many times do we have to state our purpose?" Goebbels asked impatiently. "Read the newspapers, Herr Raine. Our requests are simple. We want only that the good German people of Danzig and the corridor be allowed to be a part of their glorious homeland."

"Then it would be true if I write that Danzig and the corridor are the last territorial demands Hitler will make in Europe?"

"Quite true." Goebbels rose. "Don't forget to call upon my office for any information you may need. I understand you are interested in doing a piece on the German Youth Movement. We can be very helpful there. In fact, I have told my people to make arrangements for you to visit a model Hitler Youth Camp."

"Very kind of you," Ed said, taking the outstretched, limp hand, allowing himself to be ushered out.

In the hallway it hit him. How did Goebbels know he was interested in the German Youth Movement? He had, to his knowledge, mentioned the fact to two people, his boss in New York and a girl in the Hotel Adlon, Emma Felser-Griebe. Who had told Goebbels?

Well, it wouldn't hurt to have a man as powerful as Goebbels on his side. He knew that Goebbels had Hitler's ear. He also knew that Goebbels was not above using him to foist off German propaganda on a major press service, but he could be on his guard against that. In view of Goebbels's offer, knowing in advance that he'd be fed some pap, it might be best to send a letter in the diplomatic pouch to warn the boss that he'd be feeding some pure propaganda along with his own views. Work out a few code words to tell the boss to cut the sections between the words.

But was he just being paranoid? Old John Stanton had warned him not to criticize the regime, but others did and their dispatches went through. And here he was thinking like a spy, working up code words and secret signals. What the hell was he doing? Catching a contagious disease called suspicion?

6

FOR THE PLEASURE of its patrons the Hotel Adlon maintained a gymnasium. The Baroness Helga Gies approached the swinging doors leading into the gym with her short, deformed legs pedaling furiously. She was late. She banged the balloon tire of the trike hard against the doorway, flinging the door open, and pedaled through before it banged back. The gym housed a full range of exercise equipment—a leather-covered vaulting horse, a springboard, rings, and a climbing rope hanging from the ceiling, a wall covered with ladderlike bars, and another with pulley weights. In front of her the highly varnished floor was covered by tumbling mats, and Karl Hardraade was putting the members of the acrobatic troupe through their paces.

There were six of them, four young men and two lithe and pretty young women, all of them the best in their field. Of the six, four had participated in the 1936 Olympics, right there in Berlin, with Hardraade taking away a silver metal on the bars. Ah, Karl. To a dwarf he represented everything she would never be and never had been, agile, beautiful, strong, perfectly formed, his muscles not overly developed but smooth and powerful under his tawny skin. In tights he was spectacular, his pelvis drawing the Baroness's eyes each time he faced her. And that Margo. Six feet tall, unbelievably limber, able to twist that magnificent body into astounding shapes. To a dwarf who could not even turn her head without turning her shoulders, Margo was the object of considerable envy and a bit of hatred.

Helga wheeled her trike to a stop near the practice mats. The first exhibition performance was only days away and the troupe, newly assembled, was raw, not yet working as a unit.

"All right, children," she cried in a piping, little-girl's voice, "gather round."

Karl Hardraade completed an exercise with a soaring full aerial flip with a full twist and landed lightly on his feet directly in front of her. "Good, Karl," she said.

The others came, Margo wiping perspiration from her face with a towel. There was the healthy and almost sensuous smell of sweat, the aroma of young and heated bodies. Helga took a deep breath. Karl's bulging crotch was directly in front and just above her face. She forced herself to look higher, into their faces so far above her.

"The pyramid," she said. "Have you worked on the pyramid?"

"We have." Karl answered for the group.

"Does it go well?"

"It goes well."

"Then I will see. But first—" She paused dramatically. "There is news. Can you guess who will be among the audience on the first night?"

"We can't guess," Margo said, with a smile. She was

amused by the little Baroness who came only to her knees
when she stood and who moved, when off the trike, with a
tortured, waddling walk that was painful to watch. "Who
is it?"

"*Der Führer!*" The Baroness's voice was filled with
awe. "Herr Hitler himself. Now you see, children, why it
must be perfect, why we must work, work, work."

"We will do well." Karl, as always, was calm, unruf-
fled.

"He remembered you, Karl," the Baroness said.

"You've seen him?" asked little Eric, just fourteen, the
smallest of the men.

"No, no, he is a very busy man. I saw one of his
secretaries, who told me that the Führer was looking forward to seeing the skills of the man who had beat out a
German for the silver medal on the bars. So he remembers
Karl."

"I'm not so sure that's an honor."

"Hush, Karl," Helga said. "You must not speak so.
We are, after all, here on a tour of good will, a tour of
friendship between our two countries."

"Karl doesn't really mean that," Margo said.

"I know, I know. Now, let me see the pyramid," she
said. "Karl, if you please, lift me onto the stool."

She raised her arms and he picked her up as one would
lift a child, swinging her upward to allow her to straddle his
hip to ride there, sixty pounds of adult woman imprisoned
in a deformed body. Her rather pretty face was close to
his, her blue eyes narrowed, and as he walked across the
mat, he could feel the heat of her womanhood through the
clothing. Her breath grew jerky, slightly labored, as it
always did, but Karl pretended not to notice. As long as
she asked for no more than this, he was willing to carry his
funny little employer.

My legs aren't much good for walking, but thank God,

she thought as the movement of his walk sent thrills upward from that softness pressed against his side, they can spread outward.

They built the pyramid with Eric, the small one, atop, the two girls below, three men forming the base. Karl, being the biggest and strongest, was the catapult. With the base of three in place the girls leaped onto his cupped hands and he sent them soaring to perform a full flip and land with their feet on the supporting shoulders. Eric, light and agile, did a double before landing so lightly on the shoulders of the two girls that there was never a bruise on the delicate skin of the white and creamy Margo. Twice, three times they performed the trick, which was to be a finale to the individual exhibitions of acrobatic skills, and then it was Margo who said, "I've had enough."

"Yes, time to quit," Karl agreed. He plucked Helga off the high stool on which she had been sitting, her legs opening to straddle his hip.

"Will you dine with me, then?" she asked, as he carried her toward the tricycle.

"Sorry, Helga," he said. "We have other plans."

"Oh?"

"Marge and I. We're going out."

"Remember that you are in training."

"Of course."

So, she thought, it will have to be Eric. He is so young. "Eric," she called in her piping voice, "there are matters I wish to discuss with you about your routine. Will you come to my room at dinnertime?"

Eric cast a glance at Karl, who raised an eyebrow. They had talked of it. "She is an evil woman," the young Eric had said.

"She is not evil, but sad," Karl had replied. "And her money is paying for this little junket that will show you the great cities of Europe."

"But when I am with her I cannot keep from staring. I'm embarrassed."

"She is used to being stared at," Karl had said. Now his look told Eric to accept.

Eric gave a half-bow and held the door while she pedaled her trike through. "With pleasure, Baroness."

Other plans. Karl Hardraade was scarcely in his room when the door, which he had left unlocked, was opened. Margo carried a small case that contained a change of clothing. Her gym costume was damp, darkened with perspiration. She closed the door behind her and came into his arms.

He took her hand and led her to the luxurious bath, where he peeled away her damp costume. She was just an inch shorter than he; her body was perfect, lithe, rounded. The feel of it under his soaped hands was a delight.

On a lower floor, Ed Raine sat before his typewriter chewing on an unlit cigarette. "*The Minister of Propaganda,*" he wrote, "*does not expect war. Joseph Goebbels, in an exclusive interview for ANO, stated that war can easily be averted by the simple return of Danzig and the Polish corridor, with their German people, to the German Fatherland.*"

The article almost wrote itself, a scoop in his first week in Berlin. As he read it over he felt that Goebbels would be pleased, for he had reported the interview with total impartiality. However, as he made his daily entry into his journal he grinned, knowing that Herr Goebbels would not be pleased if he could read the private thoughts he wrote there.

SATURDAY, August 12, 1939
    Although Paul Joseph Goebbels, Minister of Propa-

ganda, exudes good will and seeks to inspire and demonstrate trust, there is in the man an element that causes doubt. Of course, Goebbels's ministry has distorted facts to meet the political plans of Hitler, but doesn't every government—even in countries like the U.S. and England, where the press is supposedly free—try to feed news into the pipeline most favorable to itself? I do, however, tend to believe the man when he says that Hitler will be satisfied with the old Germany reunited after he is given Danzig and the corridor. Foolish to go to war over such a small piece of land, largely populated by Germans anyhow.

An afternoon bus ride around the city alone did not change my opinion of the basic prosperity and contentment of the Berliners. The newspapers blared their usual anti-Polish headlines, but if this crisis is having much effect on the average Berliner, I haven't met the average Berliner. Even the flower vendors think Germany has a right to protect its own citizens in Poland, and to reunite former German territory with the Fatherland.

He considered going down to dinner and discarded the idea. He'd had a beer and wurst in the Tiergarten and wasn't hungry enough to get dressed for a formal dinner. He'd just stay put for the evening. Write a few letters. Think about a new angle for the article on the Hitler Youth. Check out the rumor that the Germans were breeding a genetically pure race of supermen through mating superior women with pure Aryan types. Go easy there, however, for it was probably just propaganda. The Germans were, basically, a puritanical people and highly moral. In fact, one of Hitler's initial appeals to the people was his promise to erase the decadence of post-Depression Germany. He rolled a fresh sheet of paper into his typewriter.

* * *

On the other side of the third floor, in the suite of the Baroness Helga Gies, the thoughts of that tiny lady were not totally moral. But then, she was neither puritanical nor German. Her fine German trike, with its ball-bearing wheels and balloon tires, its bicycle-style chain-and-sprocket action specially adjusted for her short legs, was parked in the sitting room. Helga Gies, bathed and dressed in a custom-made dressing gown that hid the squat, thick-jointed body, sat in a chair with her legs extended in front like a child, waiting. When she heard the knock on the door, she called out for young Eric to enter.

Eric, slim, small, young, was ill at ease. Why, he wondered, did she not have her dinner in her room with one of the girls? Why pick on him?

"Eric, I think I have ordered a dinner that will please you," the Baroness said.

"I'm sure it will."

"How do you think the rehearsals are going?" she asked.

"They go well, Baroness."

The talk was stilted and mostly one-sided until dinner arrived on a silver-encrusted cart. Eric offered nice compliments about her selection of foods. Yes, she thought, that is one thing I know, good food. For she could eat as much as she wanted and not add an ounce of fat to her hard, thick body. Not that it would have mattered if she had.

Ah, she did so enjoy having them near, the handsome young boys, the strong young men. It was a pleasure just to look at them, watch them move so gracefully, and more than a pleasure to . . .

Relaxed by the food, Eric became more talkative. Easily he answered her questions about his schooling at home in Norway, about his friends, his ambitions. He wanted to compete in the 1940 Olympics in three events.

"With hard work you can be," she said. "I have great confidence in you, Eric."

She also knew gymnastics, and was, in spite of her own impossible body, the finest coach in Norway. Being selected as a member of her exhibition troup was the greatest honor that had come to Eric, and he paid for it with an hour of conversation after dinner and then, at the request of the Baroness, by carrying her to her bedchamber.

Strange, he thought, the way her breathing changes when she is carried, sitting on one's hips, but perhaps Karl was wrong in thinking that she was being stimulated. To Eric, it seemed unbelievable that such a creature could have sexual feelings. And yet, as he carried her the short distance her breathing became hurried, her face gazed into his, a rather pretty face.

He put her down onto her small, stubby feet on the deep carpet of the bedroom.

"Good night, Baroness," he said politely.

"Thank you for a lovely evening," she said. She watched him go sadly, noting that he was careful to engage the lock on the door.

Then she began her preparations for bed, first by waddling back into the sitting room to mount the trike, for she needed to stand on it to reach the sink and the toothbrush. Finished there, she rode to the dresser, where, counting, she brushed her golden hair one hundred times. And then, in the darkness, she lay in her bed, feeling even smaller in the huge expanse of cool sheets, thinking the bitter, bitter thoughts.

If they only knew, she thought. Oh, if they could only know what they miss. For inside the dwarfed body there was a passionate woman, a woman reduced to taking what thrills she could by opening her short legs and clasping them around a muscular male waist, pelvis pushed hard, hard, hard, against the hip bone.

"Filthy woman," she said aloud, in her piping voice.

But she could not sleep. She thought of Lars. Oh, God, how they had laughed when he married her—the tall, handsome lad and the dwarf. And how heavenly it had been for so short a while, to be able to be a woman, to coo and giggle in silly abandon, to explore his masculine body by crawling over it like a clumsy, loving little puppy, showing him that in spite of her smallness and the rigidity of some joints, she was fully a woman. Oh, Lars, Lars, how could you have done it to me?

Oh, she'd known, or at least suspected, from the first, that he wanted her money more than he wanted her, but she'd been willing to pay. Five generations of industrious ancestors had piled up much money; and since she, like the mule, was sterile, there would be no heir. After her, nothing—the state would take most of the money; the rest would go to charities that studied birth defects and dwarfism. She had no qualms about spending her money on him so that he could live well, very well. She granted his every wish; she asked in return only that she be allowed to love him, and to show him that she was woman, that she could be wild and abandoned, loving and sensuous, capable of taking all he could deliver.

"But darling," an unfeeling acquaintance asked. "You're so tiny. Doesn't he, ah, hurt you when . . .?"

"There I am normal," she'd said smugly.

But it was not normal to use the excuse of her deformity, the fact that walking was painful and laborious, to be carried by the young men and to sneak a little movement now and then to accentuate the warm, warm feeling.

"Fool, fool, fool," the little piping voice said.

For she could buy them. She could buy anything. And yet there was her pride. She was a Gies. She could trace her ancestory in an unbroken line back to Margaret, daughter of Waldemar IV of Denmark, the woman who had united all of Scandinavia and ruled it for twenty-five years. Such a one does not hire male prostitutes, nor woman prostitutes. Nor does such a one go on the market for a new husband after she hears the first purchase saying, "God, how she sickens me with her slobberings and her lust."

No, one lies in a huge and empty bed and asked the eternal question, "Why me, oh God? Why me?"

On an upper floor another member of the Norwegian troupe was having trouble sleeping, for similar reasons. Unlike the Baroness, she had been loved, and quite forcefully, but like the Baroness she was unsatisfied.

Margo lay with her hands over her head, her long, lithe legs relaxed and open, savoring the memories of the evening and regretting the frailness of males, their inability to match her strong desires. At such times she had a favorite fantasy. Once again she was back in the German Youth Camp where she'd spent the summer of 1938, an exchange student who had chosen to stay during the summer holidays. Ah, it was lovely. The marching, the rigid exercise, the discipline, all were meat and bread to her, for she enjoyed working that superbly tuned body to its limits. She had also enjoyed the young people, the youth united by a vision. She had sung with them in her almost unaccented German; she had been accepted, for, although she was Norwegian, she was as blond, as pure in Aryan descent as any of them.

Margo loved all things German. The summer had been the time of her greatest joy, to be a part of such a thrilling enterprise, to share the vision of making a new world in which the pure, the strong, the beautiful would have their rightful places. Only her desire to compete in the 1940 Olympics had kept her from staying, for she had been offered the greatest of honors. She could, if she chose, bear a pure Aryan child for the Fatherland, a child of the finest heredity, a child implanted in her by one of the magnificent, hand-picked German boys, blond, glorious of body, boys who would soon claim the world and, in the process, share it with the golden girls who would bear Germany's future warriors.

It was all so simple, once one understood. Untainted by the mongrelization that bedeviled most of the races of the world, the golden ones, the Aryans, were the only fit instruments for making a perfect world. They were above morality, above the petty dogmas of the Church, the old-fashioned ideas that had made the world an unclean place. And the world, weakened, unwilling to defend itself, was being plundered, being continually mongrelized by the arrogant Jews. But in that camp, the microcosm of the world to come, where the golden ones honed their bodies and their minds for the tasks ahead, she had been at home. She had known there the joys of sharing her own perfect body with the glorious German sons of the Fatherland, and there she had willingly not lost, but eradicated, her viriginity, and for the first time in her life she had found almost total happiness.

But they had made her leave it.

"Fräulein," she was told by the director, "we value you, of course, and you are most welcome here. You are one of us. However, you will be of far greater value to the cause living and working in your own country. You must not, of course, be indiscreet about divulging your sympathy for our cause. You can understand that."

"Yes, sir," she said.

"Germany needs friends outside her borders."

"I will do anything I can to help."

She was willing, but in an entire year there had been no contact. In desperation she had agreed to accompany the disgusting dwarf and the simpering teenagers of the exhibition troupe, just to be back in Germany.

7

THE APPEARNCE OF Admiral Wilhelm Canaris
at the Adlon did not cause a stir, precisely, although the
fact that he was a very important man could have been
gauged from the quiet reactions of the staff: the doorman
opened the door just a bit more quickly and saluted more
crisply than usual, the pages stood straighter, the clerk at
the desk prepared to be more efficient than ever. But the
Admiral stepped out of the Mercedes limousine, swept
through the lobby, and entered an elevator without pausing
at the desk. The Adlon, old and sophisticated watering
place that it was, was above actually bowing and scraping
to anyone, even the head of the High Command of the
Army's Intelligence Service, but it was capable of a slight
heightening of its already superlative service.

Upstairs, a servant opened the door of Ingo Selmer's
suite for the Admiral before he arrived; the desk had called
ahead. Selmer was a thin and frail-looking Norwegian
whose silver hair was brushed smoothly back over his
skull, giving him a commanding and ascetic air. Although

his face would not have been recognized by one out of a million Germans, he was well known in the higher circles of wealth and power, for his was a fortune second to none in Norway and rarely matched throughout Europe.

Canaris knew Selmer as an idealist, and, although it was necessary to work with him, he had scant admiration for a man who could not recognize the harsh realities. Oh, Selmer was trustworthy enough. In his idealistic desire for peace he could hold his tongue, otherwise the Admiral would not have been risking his neck in coming to talk with him. Canaris thought cynically that Selmer's main interest was in keeping up the trade ties between his Norwegian firms and the good German market and, perhaps, in winning a Nobel Peace Prize. If Canaris had his way there, the necessary deeds would be done with such secrecy that no one would get enough recognition to win such a prize. Canaris himself, although he realized the necessity of swift action, wanted no part of the credit. He did not choose to go down in history as a traitor to his government, not even a government dominated by that rug-chewer Hitler.

It was not unusual for Canaris to choose the Adlon as a meeting place. Everyone who was anyone stayed there, and the visit was relatively safe, for the high Nazis looked upon Selmer as a well-meaning idiot who could be twisted to their own ends. His usefulness was illustrated by the fact that he had access not only to the Reich Chancellery but to Ten Downing Street and had, in fact, just returned from London and a personal chat with Lord Halifax, Chamberlain's Foreign Minister.

As an intelligence man himself, Canaris was sure that the room in which Selmer was staying was secure—not that he'd put anything past the Gestapo, but he knew that it was policy to treat visiting diplomats with courtesy and to avoid unnecessary spying on them. Ingo Selmer simply was not worthy of the Gestapo's attentions. Thus, once he was seated alone with the Norwegian, he could speak freely. But first he listened.

"I have been summoned to the Reich Chancellery," Selmer said, with great self-importance, "to give an account of my meeting with Lord Halifax. However, I see no harm in briefing my old friend in advance."

"I think I can anticipate what you have to say," Canaris said. "I have read transcripts of Chamberlain's speeches in the House of Commons, in which he promises, but not in specific terms, to aid Poland in case of German attack."

"Yes, sadly, you have anticipated me," Selmer said. "In private, the British are quite firm. In fact, I have been asked to pass along to Herr Hitler the determination of the British Empire to protect the sovereignty of Poland by any necessary means."

"And do you personally believe them?"

"I fear that I do," Selmer said.

"Then you may depend on war beginning on or about the twenty-sixth of this month," Canaris said glumly.

"I am shocked," Selmer said. "Surely—Herr Hitler himself has assured me—"

Canaris waved him into silence with an imperious hand. "I know, Herr Selmer, that you are a man of peace. My question is, how deep is your dedication to that ideal?"

"I would do anything honorable, sir."

"What I am about to tell you puts my life and the lives of others directly in your hands," Canaris said. "Shall I speak?"

"That is a heavy burden," Selmer said, secretly pleased and flattered. "One which I can, however, bear with honor. You have my assurance that anything you say will be between the two of us."

"There are those of us who see as the only solution the overthrow of Hitler," Canaris said.

Selmer went pale and covered it by coughing. "I have, of course, heard rumors of such a plot, but I thought it had ended with the occupation of Czechoslovakia."

"That was not a plot," Canaris said in contempt. "Merely a game for children. This time the urgency is much greater. This time there are serious and dedicated men involved."

"I do not wish to know their names."

"You will know only mine. Now, without divulging any more information than necessary, I will brief you on the situation, and then when I ask for your aid you will not be asked to give it blindly."

"I will listen," Selmer said doubtfully.

"According to our best information, it is planned to invade Poland on the morning of the twenty-sixth. We will make our move before that date, the intention being to seize Hitler, and to occupy the Reich Chancellery and other ministeries run by members of the Nazi Party and close supporters of Hitler."

"But that was the plan in 1938," Selmer said.

"That was the *talk* in 1938. Unfortunately, the men involved did not have the strength of will to carry through."

"But it was Chamberlain himself who foiled that plot," Selmer protested, "by giving Hitler everything he was asking for in Czechoslovakia. He defused the conspiracy by agreeing to the Munich Conference. It would have been madness to go ahead with the plot then. Hitler was the hero of the hour, accomplishing his will by peaceful means."

"Ah, you know more about 1938 than I suspected." Canaris said. "Good. That makes the explanations easier. Yes, you are to some extent right. Both Hitler and Chamberlain came out of the Czech crisis with good marks. I am told that Chamberlain's announcement of the Munich Conference caused wild and joyous shouting in that staid body, the English Parliament. But they were fools. They did not know that they were merely adding fuel to the fire. Hitler lusts to rule the world. By giving in on Czechoslovakia, they made the invasion of Poland a certainty. And the so-called conspirators were fools to think it would end with Czechoslovakia. They had the men and they had the tools to do the job. Generals Halder and von Brauchitsch were ready to move, with the full weight of considerable troops at their command.''

''I said I would not ask for names,'' Selmer said, ''but since you have mentioned Halder and von Brauchitsch—''

''Forget them,'' Canaris said. ''Halder is in his glory. He is in command on the Polish front, and like a small boy with his first army of tin soldiers, he is now a confirmed fan of Hitler, champing at the bit to be turned loose with his new toys. Let me say only that we will have the troops in Wehrkreis III, which, as you may know, makes up the city of Berlin and its surroundings. We have the strength to do the deed quickly. We will not kill Hitler, for that would make him, in the eyes of many, a martyr. Instead, having disposed of his henchmen —Himmler, Goebbels, Göring and a few others—we will put Herr Hitler on trial as the criminal he is.''

Selmer, shocked to hear talk of cold-blooded murder, was becoming uneasy. He knew the affable Göring, had dined with him and admired his collection of art. To think of that likable and slightly fatuous man being killed in cold blood made him uncomfortable. Surely, he thought, there was another way. Hitler seemed to him to be a reasonable man, and yet he knew Canaris, too—knew him as an eminently logical and reasonable man. Frankly, he was confused.

''It is vital to our plan to have the cooperation of both England and France,'' Canaris said, ''but especially of England, for France will not move without a prod from the English. We must know in advance that England will support us, will recognize our interim government immediately, and, above all, will not seize the moment of confusion to make war. There, sir, is where you come in.''

"I see." Selmer nodded, somewhat tentatively.

"Nor do we trust the wishy-washy Chamberlain," Canaris said. "Our sources tell us that it is quite likely that the present government in England will fall, and will be replaced with one headed by Churchill. Do you agree with that analysis?"

"I think that if war comes Chamberlain will be deposed, and that Churchill is the logical replacement. To deal with Mr. Churchill is another matter, however. He is, as you must know, ready at this moment to fight."

"He is a sensible man," Canaris said. "We have indications that he would not fight if Hitler were overthrown and if Germany gave up demands on Poland."

"He wanted to fight in 1938," Selmer said.

"But England didn't. Therefore, we must conclude that the English people don't want war any more than we do—. Will you work with us? You have freedom of movement. You have access. We must have the word of Churchill that he will back us to the utmost, that he will use his influence to have our government recognized."

Silent for long moments, Selmer fiddled with his gold watch chain. "I can't give you an answer now, my friend," he said at last. "I am torn. I have had long talks with Göring, with Hitler. And I have been assured that they do not want war. To become a part of conspiracy that interferes with the internal affairs of a great nation is a serious thing."

"I know, I know. Why do you think I would become a traitor to my government?" He sighed and stood up. "Well, think about it. But you may take my word for it. The plans for an assault on Poland are drawn. There awaits only the word from Hitler to set the panzers in motion. If that happens, and you have not tried to help us, Herr Selmer, a part of the blame will be on your head.''

Selmer felt he must promise something. "I will speak with you again after I have visited the Chancellery. Perhaps you will be pleasantly surprised by the basic good sense of Herr Hitler.''

"I would give an arm and a leg for such a surprise,'' Canaris said moodily. His farewell was weary and brief.

A few minutes later, the Admiral entered the cellar bar of the Adlon. It took a moment for his eyes to adjust to the darkness. Looking for a table, Canaris saw Colonel Wolf von Stahlecker and nodded. Von Stahlecker rose and clicked his heels. "Sir, would you care to join me?'' he asked politely. The meeting, despite its appearance, was not accidental.

"Very kind of you, Colonel, ''Canaris said.

Von Stahlecker had chosen the table carefully. Without seeming to speak in whspers, without leaning forward, they could speak without being overheard. "What of Selmer?'' von Stahlecker asked, when a drink had been served to the Admiral.

"He wet his pants in fright.'' Canaris snorted with great contempt. "We will not be able to count on him, of this I am sure.''

"Too bad,'' von Stahlecker said. "Time grows short.''

"It's time to explore the alternate you have suggested.''

"I will proceed at once. However, it will be impossible before Monday.''

Canaris raised a questioning eyebrow.

"The contact is not available until then,'' von Stahlecker explained.

"Could you not make the approach yourself?''

"I'm afraid that is not, as yet, advisable. After all, we don't know his feelings. We must approach him through the contact.''

"So be it, then," Canaris said. "The contact is—?"

"In Dresden, to reaffirm the determination of the Mayor."

"A waste of time," Canaris grumbled. "A civilian."

"We will need civilian support. We have agreed on that, sir," von Stahlecker said. "Herr Deler is an influential man, one of the few in public position who is not tainted with Nazism."

"Oh, you're right, of course, but, God, time grows short. I will not be remembered in history as history will remember those who failed in 1938. I *will* not, do you understand, Colonel?"

"Nor do I choose to be," von Stahlecker said.

"We must have all in readiness by the morning of the twenty-fifth. Remember that." And with that Canaris finished his drink, rose, left without a backward glance. As he left the bar and entered his limousine he once more reviewed the statistics. He was a Navy man to the bone, gallingly aware that once again the fools in power were taking Germany into a war they could not hope to win; they ignored the columns of figures that told the hopeless story to anyone familiar with history. Herr Hitler, apparently, had not read a history book. But the figures haunted Canaris always: battleships—British, twelve; French, eight; the United States (for hadn't the American cousins always come to the aid of an embattled Britain?), fifteen. Cruisers—British, sixty-four; French, eighteen; United States, thirty-six. And on and on, vast armadas of ships. Germany—with three pocket battleships, two battle cruisers, two cruisers, a meager twenty-two destroyers, and sixty submarines—was left with only one choice, the doubtful honor of showing that the German Navy knew how to die.

SATURDAY, August 12, 1939
Admiral Wilhelm Canaris was pointed out to me

*today in the cellar bar. He is big stuff, Chief of the
Abwehr of OKW. (Translation: Abwehr is Army
Intelligence. OKW is High Command of the Army.)
No chance to speak with him. Was introduced, however, to Colonel Wolf von Stahlecker, who has lost an
arm. Von Stahlecker, a minor officer in the Abwehr's
information service, seems a decent sort. I spoke with
him about my plans to visit a German Youth Camp
and he made suggestions. Could not get him to voice
an opinion on political matters nor on the possibility
of war.*

*I met and spoke with Bill Shirer, and he was quite
helpful. The man knows his Germany, I must admit
that. He has, however, what seems to me to be an
almost irrational fear of German military strength. In
talking with others I am encouraged to believe that
Hitler must know that he would be outgunned by
France and England, that he could not hope to win a
war that might, just might, become a world war with
the entrance of the U.S., in spite of Roosevelt's promises not to send American men into foreign battle-
fields.*

*I am considering asking Emma to join me in my
field trip to the Youth Camp. It seems to me that my
welcome would be greater if I were in the company of
a German movie star. True, she says she wants our
friendship to be secret, but maybe . . .*

SUNDAY, August 13, 1939
   *A day of loafing and seeing the town, alone. Saw
Mutiny on the Bounty; it was amusing to watch the
German subtitles with that good old American speech
rolling out of the loudspeakers.*

8

ON MONDAY MORNING, his fourth full day in Berlin, Ed Raine began his work in earnest. There were bases to be touched, functionaries to meet, the usual government officers who handed out prepared material to newsmen. He paid a call at the Ministry of Propaganda and was pleased to find that Joseph Goebbels had indeed prepared the way for him. He was courteously referred to one Frau Sittenrichter, an efficient, rather plump lady of some forty years, who served him coffee and promised the full cooperation of the Ministry. With the efficient woman he made tentative plans for his visit to a Youth Camp, but, still thinking that he might still persuade Emma to accompany him, he set no date until he could talk to her.

He felt rather pleased with himself. A cable that morning from the home office had congratulated him on his exclusive interview with Goebbels. He knew that each newsman has his pet sources and he felt that after such a

71

short stay he had developed a top source in attracting the attention of so powerful a man.

That day he spent a lot of time on the streets, intent on absorbing all of the feel, the color, the subconscious knowledge that, to a good newsman, seems to seep in through the pores and become a part of him.

Actually, it was a slow period. The tension was there, but with the weekend just past there had been no events, either in Berlin or elsewhere, to make big news. The newsmen who gathered at the cellar bar in the Adlon were commenting on the lack of activity when he dropped in for a late-afternoon drink.

John Graff Stanton was there, besotted as usual, and he seemed to express the general feeling. "You're young and have most of your brain cells left," he said to Ed. "Give me a phrase that would express the same feeling, without being trite, as 'the calm before the storm.' "

"A breathless hush," Ed said, with a wry grin.

"Jesus," Stanton said, gesturing broadly with his cigar. "I'm in the presence of a literary genius."

"John," Ed said, "isn't it that we've gotten used to expecting huge and dramatic events? Hell, things have been popping for so long that when a few days go by without something to make chills run up and down your spine, you think something is wrong. Couldn't it be that things are really cooling off?"

Stanton snorted, then gazed at Ed in mock pity. "That's what I like about you, kid—that youthful optimism." He shook his head. "No, they'll cool off when hell freezes over. Not much before."

"Sounds like you're getting jaded, John."

"Oh, jaded, hell yes." Stanton took a deep swig of his scotch. "Happened to me long ago. Manchuria, Spain, Abyssinia—someplace like that. Happen to you, too, soon enough."

Nettled, Ed shook his head. "I don't think so. I've got to keep faith in—"

"The basic goodness of mankind and all that bullshit? Idealism, too! Jesus! Ed, my boy"—Stanton tapped him in the chest with a heavy forefinger; since his cigar was clamped beside the finger, Ed got a good dose of the strong smoke— "either you're crazy or you're in love. Who is she?"

Blinking at the smoke, Ed felt himself blushing. He shook his head again, but only blushed the more.

"Aha! I knew it. I'll buy you a drink if you tell me her name."

"No, John, it's nothing like that . . ."

"Oh, sure. Okay, I'll buy you a drink anyway."

In order to live down Stanton's imputation, Ed had to accept the drink, but he managed to keep the conversation away from women in general and Emma in particular. As soon as he could, though, he left the bar and went for another stroll along the boulevard. Twilight came late in August, and the streets were still light, though no longer sunny.

All the details of the city, the local color and shapes, were lost on him this time. As he walked, he found himself thinking more and more about Emma, wishing he'd found out when she'd be back, wondering why he wished it so strongly. At the bridge over the Spree, he started back toward the Adlon. He heard a strange sound approaching; far ahead, he saw a small artillery unit. It was like something out of the past, huge guns on caissons behind teams of matched horses. Strange, he thought. The German army had the reputation of being the most mechanized in the world. The swiftness of the movement of armor and guns into Czechoslovakia had, in fact, coined a new word, *blitzkrieg*, lightning war. And yet, here on the streets of Berlin, there was an artillery unit moving as artillery had been moved for centuries, drawn by horses. Old-fashioned and therefore faintly laughable, but the sound—the sound of rolling caissons—is unlike any other. There is a heaviness, an ominous, rolling, muted thunder that lingers in the mind. Ed was hit with a queer little pang of dread, as if the guns, the horses were eternal, inevitable.

The sound echoed in his ear as he dressed for a solitary dinner. But in the muted but gay atmosphere of the ornate dining room there was no hint of the dread he'd felt seeing the big guns, hearing the rumble of the wheels. Here, at least, the universally accepted truth that German women were among the world's least attractive was belied by shimmering gowns, gleaming jewels, immaculate hairdos. At a table near him a group of young people chattered, a table for five headed by a tall young giant of a man, with an almost equally tall blond goddess at his right. Musingly, he recognized the other girl as one who had almost cartwheeled into him in the hallway. The laugh of the tall blond girl reached him, with a hint of words in a Scandinavian language.

He felt better. Here in the Adlon there was a mixture of peoples, a feeling of good will. How could firebrands and cynics speak of war when people everywhere were so much alike? The best thing that could happen to tired old Europe was a healthy and vital Germany to lead the way into a future that had no limitations. With German scientific and mechanical know-how, with German industry and sheer love of work, the German nation could lead the way to a better life for all, if only the diplomats would not fail, would not let petty national pride and minute considerations influence them. My God, think what an alliance between Germany and Great Britain could bring! If a united Europe faced the enigmatic and repressive Stalin, Russia would be forever neutralized; in the face of Western prosperity and freedom the Russian people would, sooner or later, realize the mistake of Bolshevism. Combine Germanic energy with British inventiveness, and deserts would bloom all over the world and the sleek ships of commerce would pass to the most desolate places, carrying the better things of life. Moreover, a peaceful Europe could pressure the Japs to stop seeking empire.

All so simple. All that was required was for Hitler to realize that he had already achieved his goal of making Germany a great nation again. Ed resolved to push his new friend, Goebbels, into getting him an interview with Hitler . . .

And so the red-haired American newsman, dreaming dreams of glory, phrasing his leading questions to Hitler in his mind, signed the check and, well fed and amply wined, made his way to his room. There he spent an hour going through the German publications he'd gathered during the day, made a few notes, smoked thoughtfully, and was thinking of a bath and bed when he heard a soft knock on the connecting door between his room and the rooms of Emma Felser-Griebe. His heart leaped, and in the brief seconds that it took to cross the floor to fling open the door, he realized how much he had missed her. There was a smile on his face, a greeting on his lips, a preparation and an anticipation of taking her into his arms.

"Do you open the door so quickly for all strange women?" asked the woman who faced him. She was a head shorter than he, slim—quite un-Germanic in that respect—and her clothing showed the good taste, the neatness so familiar to him. A woman in her early fifties who looked no more than forty, in spite of her silvered hair.

"Mama," he gasped, and his smile turned into a laugh of delight as he swept her into his arms.

"Edgar," she said, as he whirled her, "you'll break my corset stays."

He set her down again, suddenly unable to speak coherently, saying things like "Why? How? Where?"

She took his hand, stepped back to gaze at him. "You look more and more like your father each year." It had been two years since she'd seen him on her last visit to New York.

"I was going to come this week," he said. "Had to get my feet on the ground first."

"I know, I know."

"Mama, it's great! How long are you staying?"

"Only a day. It won't hurt to leave the shop closed for one day, but I can't leave it longer."

"One day? I was hoping you could stay for a while. It's been a long time. There's so much to talk about."

"There will be time for that," she said, drawing him into Emma's suite.

"No, come to my room," he said. "I have a bottle of that wine you like, and I want your opinions on the stuff I've written so far, see if I'm catching the real Germany."

"Later," she said, closing the door behind them. "It will be safer here."

"Safer?"

"I have reason to know that the rooms in this suite are not wired for sound," she said.

"Hey, Mama, what is this? Wired for sound?"

"Edgar, I have only a little time. I must return to Dresden tonight. And there are things we must discuss."

"Well, sure, Mama," he said. He led her to a chair. He sat opposite and grinned at her fondly. They'd always been close. When his father died, it was only three-year-old Ed and Clara Raine against a pretty tough world. Together they'd faced the anti-German prejudice that was a part of the hysteria of World War I. Although Clara Bergdorf Raine had almost eliminated her German accent, there were still those who knew her nationality; even though she had left Germany when she was a teenager, long before any hint of the war, the business she carried on after the death of her husband suffered.

"What's the big mystery?" Ed asked.

She crossed one leg and looked quite comfortable, but he knew her well enough to see the lines of tension in her still-handsome face. "Tell me," she said, "how do you find Germany?"

"Exciting," he said. "Interesting. Not at all what I'd been led to expect by the news that comes out of Berlin for U.S. consumption." He smiled. "I haven't been accosted by the Gestapo a single time."

Her smile was twisted. "I suppose I am responsible," she said. "I remembered a different Germany, Edgar. When I first came back, Hitler was not in power yet. I saw only what I wanted to see—Dresden as I remembered it from my childhood. And of course I was busy taking care of both Aunt Thyra and her shop. Then when she died and the shop was mine, I had to look around me and see what was really there. Things had changed, were changing every day. The reality has come as a total shock to me."

"In what way?" He was puzzled. "You've said nothing in your letters."

"One doesn't," she said.

"Oh, come on, Mama," he said. "You're beginning to sound like the professional German-haters. A dictator under every bed."

"I see that my task is to be a difficult one," she said. "How shall I begin?"

"Tell me what's bothering you," he said. "We've never had to mince words with each other."

"You know the term *Kristallnacht*."

"The night of broken glass," he said. "Of course."

"In Berlin alone, thousands were arrested, synagogues burned, many people killed. When the insurance companies paid for the damage the payments were confiscated by the Government.''

"Mama, this is not a perfect world. Negroes are still lynched in the American South. Race riots do damage in the cities.''

"But in America there is not a systematic plan to eliminate a race," she said.

He was suddenly concerned. "Mama, you're not involved in anything, are you?''

She shrugged. "We are all involved in the human race," she said.

"Mama, Mama—you, the practical one? You chose to live here. I didn't want you to stay after your Aunt Thyra had died. But you had to stay; things were better for you here. And now—look, I know there's reason for concern. The Jewish persecutions are a crime, but is it all as bad as we're led to believe?''

"It is much worse than you can imagine," she said sadly. "But I came here to talk to you about a different problem. A larger one." She uncrossed her leg and leaned slightly toward him. "You are my son. I know that you have a fondness for things German, as I do, but you must understand that those who are in power in Germany are beasts, worse than beasts. It is the *duty* of decent people to oppose them. If we do not, Germany will never be able to face the world again. Perhaps she will not even rise from the ashes of the war that this madman Hitler is trying to start.''

"Mama, you're involved in something. My God, don't you know? Hell, I know enough about the situation to see that it would be insane to oppose the Government.''

"I am only one small unit in a greater effort," she said. "There are powerful men on our side. The chances, this time, are quite good, but there are needs. This is why I have come to you. We need your help.''

"I don't want to hear it," he said. "I don't want any part of it. I am a guest in this country. I will not abuse the hospitality of Germany by plotting against the Government."

She looked at him carefully for a moment. "Edgar, if you had a chance to say yes or no to a war, what would you say?"

"Now that's a silly question."

"It is not in the least silly, my son." He sobered under her level gaze. "You have that opportunity. You are needed. Tell me that you will help."

"I don't even know what you want of me," he said weakly.

"Certain high officials, in the Government and in the Army, will, before Hitler can unleash the bombers on Poland, depose him."

"Oh, God."

"The internal planning is complete. Where and how is no concern of yours at the moment. What we need is a man with freedom of movement, with access to Government leaders."

"I have no access to Government leaders," he said, "other than Goebbels. And I have that limited access only because the first two dispatches I went out were not unfavorable to Germany."

"Your press credentials would get you into Number Ten Downing Street," she said. "If you carried a letter from a very powerful man in Germany."

"So that's what you want? You want me to go to London, to carry a letter?"

She nodded.

"And if I get caught, can I expect to become acquainted with the Gestapo?"

"Along with dozens of others."

"Mama, you're crazy. You're tilting at windmills. There's

not going to be a war. Hitler will settle down after the corridor issue is determined.''

"You may not mention this, nor write of it, but we have irrefutable information that the blitzkreig will roll on the morning of the twenty-sixth.''

"Damn, damn, damn,'' he said. "Look, all I want to do is be a good newsman, to present a fair and complete picture. I'm not one of those who has access to top sources. I'm just a small fry. I write color pieces that are run on the back pages of newspapers; the headlines on the front are from the AP and UP boys. I don't agree with you that the danger is so great. Mama, go home to Dresden. Or back to Indianapolis. Forget this spy business. Break away from whoever it is who has you so stirred up.''

Again she gazed at him, just barely shaking her head. "Tomorrow, August fifteen, a quarter of a million men will receive mobilization orders,'' she said. "Already the pocket battleships *Graf Spee* and *Deutschland* and every available submarine are under sailing orders, preparing to put to sea to take up Atlantic stations.''

"How do you know that?''

"From a man who could not be wrong.''

Ed felt less sure of himself, but was still not convinced. "Let's assume, for the moment, that the information is correct. It could be only a precautionary measure. It could be a part of Hitler's bluff. After all, such tactics got him Czechoslovakia. But even if he's prepared to risk war, what good can your group do? *Depose* Hitler? That's a large order. It would take an army.''

"Which we have.''

"Jesus,'' he said. "You're serious.''

"Deadly serious. Your part will not be too dangerous. We simply must be in contact with the British Government. As the crisis approaches, it is expected that that Government will be under the control of Winston Churchill. It is he whom you will see. If you agree, and since you are my son I'm sure you will, you will melt the man whose word will be accepted by the British." She smiled. "Not to mention the fact that you will have the scoop of all time."

"Damn it, Mama."

"Now you will take me to the restaurant in the garden. We will smile and talk of old times and listen to the whispering fountain and have cake and coffee before I catch my train back to Dresden. You will be contacted when the time is right."

"Hold it! I have not said I'd become a part of this."

"Haven't you?" she asked, with a fond little smile.

"It's crazy. The whole damned world has gone crazy."

"I would agree with that assessment," she said, rising.

"Now wait just a minute. I haven't said yes. I have some questions. First, if I say yes, who will contact me, and how?"

"You would hear a knock on the door, as you did tonight."

He was stunned. Emma. Was that the explanation for her total willingness, for the rapidity with which she'd teased him into her bed? "Emma?" he asked. "Not Emma."

His mother said nothing, but her silence was confirmation. He felt the beginning of a slow burn, a muted anger that threatened to come out in harsh words, but he kept his silence. What the hell did they think he was, some kind of snotnosed kid, who could be lured into a deadly conspiracy just because a beautiful woman had opened her personal bag of goodies to him?

9

WHEN HE AWOKE on Tuesday morning he dressed quickly, then knocked on Emma's door. When there was no answer he spent the balance of the morning working, then went to the cellar bar for a beer and a sandwich. There was talk and laughter and life there, a direct contrast to his bleak mood. He couldn't shake the mood, for he couldn't forget the things his mother had said the night before.

John Graff Stanton, with his usual morning hangover, was at the bar. He nodded slightly, as if more movement would cause a severe but not quite imaginable dislocation in his neck. Ed bought him a drink.

"John," he said, "you've been here longer than I have. If the Germans were about to mobilize a large number of men, would you be likely to hear about it?"

"Depends whether they want us to hear about it. If he's doing it for propaganda purposes, the old boy would spread the word. If not—" He shrugged. "Let me tell you this, boy. You hear about some secret troop movement or the like, you be damned careful."

"So you haven't heard any scuttlebutt?" He sipped his beer. "What would it mean if the *Graf Spee*, say, and the *Deutschland* and, oh, maybe a few subs put out to sea to take up Atlantic stations?"

Stanton put down his glass and looked at Ed closely. "You trying to tell me something?"

"Scuttlebutt." Ed smiled blandly.

"From where?"

"Naughty, naughty!" Ed waved a warning finger at him. Stanton was hooked.

"Bullshit! I'm not asking for your source." There was no sign of the hangover anymore.

"I thought you were."

"Reliable?"

"Maybe."

"Hot damn." He drank deeply, then looked back at Ed. "Gonna write about it?"

"No, not yet, at least."

"That kind of source, huh?"

"I told you it was scuttlebutt."

"Well, they might go that far. How many men would you say?"

"Oh, a quarter of a million or so."

Stanton grunted. "More than propaganda. Glad I've got my bags packed."

"If it were true, if a quarter of a million men had been mobilized secretly and the Navy were going to sea, you'd think it was more than just an attempt to convince the French and British that Hitler wasn't fooling?"

"I'd be ready to shit my pants, and I'd start looking up to see the bombers so's I could find a hole." He grinned. "When do you think you can confirm this scuttlebutt?"

"John," Ed said, "you'll be the second to know. Right

after all the Americans who read ANO news releases.''

"Thanks for nothing," Stanton said.

"But I'll make a deal with you. You help me confirm or deny it, and I'll give it to you in time for the afternoon papers.''

"After you hit the morning papers.''

"Reet," Ed said.

"You're all heart. I'll check my sources. I'll be in touch." And he was gone, leaving the glass of scotch and water half full. Nice to see, Ed thought, that work took precedence over booze, even with an old-timer like Stanton.

Back in his room he had a lot to think about, and just thinking of the things his mother had said made him want to look over his shoulder. He felt silly as hell when he made the rounds of his room, checking lamps, furniture, heat grills for hidden microphones. Of course he found nothing. And Emma was still not answering his knocks on her door. That girl had a lot of explaining to do. Why, double why, was she mixed up in something like that? People went to prison, or worse, for plotting the overthrow of a government. And the thought of Emma in prison was not a pleasant one.

The thought of Ed Raine in prison was even less pleasant— that he had to admit, with a certain amount of selfishness. Such is the strength of love, he thought wryly. But that just proved it wasn't love that he felt for Emma, just a desire so strong that he could almost tremble, anticipating her face, her smell, as he tried once again to get an answer from her room.

No answer. He sat again at his typewriter, stared at the blank page. *There is a conspiracy afoot* . . . No, he couldn't write that, of course.

As for his part in the plan, he was about ninety-nine

percent certain that he'd have no part of it. He had the best chance he'd ever had in his life. He was *the* man in Berlin for ANO. He wasn't about to blow that chance because some people were misinformed.

But what if they were right? What if Hitler *was* amassing troops and tanks on the Polish border with the intention of rolling over the Polish horse cavalry with a blitz of the Czech type? How would he feel if he woke up one morning and found the world at war and had to face the realization that he could have helped prevent it?

Unable to write about what was on his mind, he tapped his fingers nervously on the desk. Finally he ripped the blank page from the typewriter, crumpled it, tossed it toward a wastebasket, and reached for his room key. He paused long enough to straighten his tie and put on his jacket; even in August, shirtsleeves were too informal for Berlin.

When he turned the corner in the hall, he saw the woman, the dwarf, at the elevator doors. She was beginning to climb to the seat of her trike to push the call button. When she saw him coming, she sat down again.

"May I?" he asked.

"Yes, thank you," she said in her high, piping voice.

"Down?"

"Yes, please." As he pressed the button, she observed, "You are not German."

"American." He felt his courtesy was a bit forced and monosyllabic, but didn't really know how to talk to a woman who didn't quite reach his waist.

"I am Norwegian," she said.

He remembered how the hotel employees, on two occasions, had seemed to think that saying "Norwegians!" said it all. After they boarded the elevator, he said, "My name is Edgar Raine. I am a newspaperman."

"Oh, that's wonderful! Oh, but excuse me for being

rude. I am the Baroness Helga Gies. I am excited at hearing you are a newsman. Perhaps you would like to write something about our acrobatic troupe.''

"I'd like to hear about it," he said.

"I was going down to have tea. Would you be my guest?"

He felt rather queer, walking alongside the dwarf, whose legs pumped furiously, moving the trike along at good speed into the dining room. He watched, somewhat embarrassed for her, as she dismounted and climbed laboriously into a chair, where her arms barely cleared the top of the table. As they ate, he listened to her enthusiastic talk about the touring group and agreed that it might make a sidebar story, a human-interest piece. He found the Baroness to be quite friendly, with a sharp wit and a fine mind, fluent in both English and German, willing to discuss the situation in Germany as well as affairs in her own country. A pleasant hour went by before she looked at the watch on her thick wrist.

"Oh, dear," she said, "I'm keeping you from your work."

"Not at all," he said. "As a matter of fact, I was thinking of going for a walk."

"The weather is lovely. I envy you," she said.

He smiled. "You seem to get around quite well on your three-wheeled steed. Would you care to join me?"

"Oh, I am too much trouble," she said. With only her face and shoulders showing she looked quite normal— pretty, nice hair, full lips, a pleasant smile. "I'll have one of my young men help me down the stairs later."

"I'd be honored to help you," he said. "And I would enjoy your company. I'll pick your brains about Europe. I'm still a tyro, you know."

"If you're sure you don't mind, I'd love to take some air."

At the stairs, she told him what to do. He lifted her from the trike and carried her to sidewalk. The impassive doorman brought her vehicle and she tipped him. Ed set off beside the Baroness, letting her set the pace—a comfortable walk. The grand boulevard was moderately busy, the sidewalks not too crowded, the pedestrians strolling leisurely. It was, indeed, a lovely day, bright and sunny, the heat not severe but enough to make one feel it.

The little Baroness talked more about the troupe as she rolled along beside him, and he, to hear her, was looking down. He looked up into the faces of a matronly woman and a prosperous-looking middle-aged man to see their eyes glued on Helga, a look of frank disapproval on their faces. As they passed there was a silence and he turned to see the woman looking back, shaking her head.

"I am used to it," the Baroness said.

He felt something akin to shame, for he knew the almost irresistible urge to stare. It was a human characteristic, to stare at the odd, the unfamiliar.

"It's harder for those who do not know me well," she said. "You see, I told you I was a bother."

"Nonsense," he said. But there was a crawling feeling of discomfort in him as they met a group of young women who stared, and then turned to stare from the rear.

"As I was saying, Herr Hitler himself is coming to our performance."

"Then I will surely be there," Ed replied. "I've yet to see the great man."

He tried to ignore the stares, the mutter of comment as people passed. A young boy in a passing car pointed rudely. The Baroness seemed oblivious to the attention she was getting until the sidewalk ahead seemed suddenly filled with black uniforms and shining boots. They came six abreast, leather spotless, cloth without a wrinkle and tailored to young, strong bodies. Ed's first reaction was one of admiration. There, he thought, was Germany, young, vital, strong, proud. He felt a bump at his leg and looked down to see the Baroness trying to get to the curb on her three-wheeler. He stepped aside and she scrambled from the seat and tried to lift the heavy tricycle into the street.

"What are you doing?"

"Waffen SS," she said.

He was puzzled. The six young men, broad chest and swinging boots taking up all the sidewalk, were quite near. Strong faces, pure Germanic features, blond hair clipped short under the smart headgear, arms swinging. He nodded, smiled, still admiring them. No wonder Hitler had had so easy a time with Czechoslovakia, if these were typical of the SS troops headed by Hitler's man, Himmler.

Helga was having trouble with the trike, unable to lift it off the curb. Ed stood beside the curb. He would step aside for them, but he'd be damned if he'd step into the gutter, even for the SS. The six SS Blackshirts broke the straight front and curved around him, arrogant blue eyes burning into his.

"Good afternoon, gentlemen," he said. Meeting their arrogance, his own admiring civility was getting a bit strained.

A black boot lashed out, pushed the tricycle into the street, where it overturned.

"Hey," Ed said, in English. Then, in German, "What the hell?"

"Let it be, Herr Raine," the Baroness said. Then, to the Blackshirts, "He is newly arrived, an American newsman."

A tall young corporal pointed a finger at Helga. "Such should not be allowed in the street to insult good German eyes."

Another grinned tauntingly at Ed. "So, being from a race of mongrels, you mongrelize yourself further by associating with freaks."

"Now see here," Ed said angrily.

"She must be a Jew," the corporal said. "Only a race of pigs could produce such."

"Are you a Jewess, sow?" asked another of the handsome, young men.

"By God," Ed said, "this has gone far enough."

A hand hit his chest, shoved him into the street. He saw red, came back. He got in one good punch; then there were three of them and he felt the jar of one blow followed by another, saw white stars, started to go down. Out of the corner of his eye he caught a glimpse of the tricycle rolling, kicked into the path of a truck, which squealed its brakes but nonetheless crushed it. And then he had more than he could handle, felt one eye bruised, was fighting blindly.

Colonel Wolf von Stahlecker, taking his afternoon stroll, saw the commotion, ran to thrust his walking stick between the three Blackshirts and the flailing American, saying, in a firm voice, "Order, let's have order here."

Ed stood back, panting, wiping his bloody nose with the back of his hand. The SS troopers, although they ceased belaboring him, looked at von Stahlecker with open contempt.

"It is a shame," von Stahlecker said, his voice trembling with indignation, "that during your training you were not taught basic decency and a regard for visitors to the Reich."

"You do not give us orders," the corporal said. He spat. "Luftwaffe."

"This Luftwaffe officer," von Stahlecker said, "is giving you a direct order, and I assure you that I have the authority and the influence to make it quite difficult for you if you do not obey. Go. Take your ill manners and your arrogance from my sight or, by God, I swear I will take your names and report you directly to not only your master but to the Führer himself."

"Come, Kurt," said one of the troopers, pulling on the corporal's arm. Two uniformed policemen were approaching on the run.

"Stay, then, and protect the Jewish freak," the corporal said to von Stahlecker.

They marched off, six abreast. Panting, angry, hurting, Ed saw that everyone in their path stepped off the curb into the street.

"Are you hurt badly?" von Stahlecker asked, extending a handkerchief to Ed with his good arm.

"My pride, more than anything, I suppose," Ed said.

"They are taught arrogance," von Stahlecker said. "It is Herr Himmler's ambition to have his Waffen SS at the forefront of any battle."

"Are they taught hatred as well?" Ed asked. He remembered the Baroness. She was standing on the curb, small, her face pale.

"I'm so sorry," she said.

"Good God, it's not your fault," Ed said, wiping his nose with the Colonel's handkerchief and coming away with more blood.

"Come," von Stahlecker said. "I'll help you back to the hotel."

Helga Gies saw the wreckage of her tricycle, looked down the sidewalk at a distance which, for a normal person, was nothing. For her, with walking so awkward and painful, it seemed like miles. And yet she would not further embarrass the American by asking to be carried. She waddled along, fell behind before Ed noticed it. He turned. Her face was contorted by effort.

"Walking isn't easy for you, is it?" he asked.

"It's all right. I'll make it."

"Look, I'll carry you," he said, bending.

"Oh, no, please," she said, but she extended her arms almost automatically and, when he lifted, swung into the most practical position for being carried, legs open, sitting on his hipbone. And then she looked into his face, saw the swollen eyes, the blood around his nose and mouth. For the first time in years she allowed herself the luxury of tears.

Ed's battered face brought curious stares in the lobby. He glared back furiously, carried the little Baroness to the elevator. Von Stahlecker followed and when Ed put her down in front of her door he said, "Herr Raine, may I buy you a drink, as a sort of apology?"

"You have nothing to apologize for, Colonel," Ed said.

"They were German."

"Well, I hope all Germans are not like that." Ed was still a bit angry, his eye was beginning to hurt. "But I think I'd better clean up a little, maybe get something for this eye."

"I will send my personal physician, if I may," von Stahlecker said.

"Hell, I'm not hurt that badly."

"He can give you something for the eye, something to help prevent the swelling as much as possible."

"Well, that's kind of you, Colonel."

"Again, my apologies," von Stahlecker said. "When you're feeling better perhaps you will accept my invitation for a drink."

"With pleasure."

He had not been in his room more than a quarter-hour when the knock came on the door. The distinguished-looking visitor introduced himself as Dr. Hans Arback. There wasn't much to be done. He inspected the cut on Ed's lip and said it wasn't deep. The doctor told him what he already knew, to put cold compresses on the eye, and then departed.

He had to squint a little as he wrote the story. He burned away his anger in a first draft that bitingly condemned arrogance, then he mellowed. After all they were only young men, proud of their uniforms, proud of The New Germany. There was a different tone to the story when it was finally finishd. the six young SS troopers as an example, he specualted on Germany's traditional preoccupation with things military, with power, with pride, with arrogance.

Bathed and changed, he took the elevator down to the luxurious lobby. Dispatch in hand, he headed for the street doors, then halted, looking ahead. His heart seemed to stop for a moment, a moment of sheer pleasure and wonderful surprise, for Emma was sweeping into the lobby. She wore travel clothes that showed her lovely body to good advantage. A broad smile hurt his sore lip. He stepped toward her, for she had paused just inside and was looking over her shoulder. He changed his broad grin into a lopsided one that did not hurt the swollen lip; he was about to call out to her as she turned and looked directly into his face.

His smile faded, for her eyes were cold, distant, looking blankly at him for a moment before they seemed to see directly through him and shift away. Strange, the girl who had been so ardent in his arms looked at him as if he were merely one of the millions she did not know. And then she extended her arm and smiled at a small, limping man who came up from behind her. They walked into the lobby together, her eyes once again sweeping over his face and past.

"Ah, good afternoon, Herr Raine," said Paul Joseph Goebbels, as he strutted, limping, beside the most beautiful woman in Germany. Confused, Ed murmured a greeting as they passed; then there was just the lingering scent of Emma's perfume.

At first he felt only unreasoning jealousy, but that swiftly changed, as he went out into the warm and pleasant late

afternoon to a realization that something was seriously
amiss. His mother had said that Emma Felser-Griebe would
speak to him of the plot to overthrow Hitler, but there she
was hanging to the arm of one of Hitler's most trusted
henchmen, in public, unashamed. Was she a double agent,
a stooge? If so, did she know of his mother's activities?
Obviously, a word to Herr Goebbels would land Clara
Raine in serious trouble. On the other hand, if Emma were
a true conspirator and had such an obviously amiable
relationship with a man so high in the Nazi Party, then the
conspirators must be better organized than he'd thought.

The beauty of the day, the splendor of the avenue were
lost on him as he walked slowly to the branch post office.
There he sent his cable containing the probing piece based
on his encounter with the Waffen SS. He decided, as he
came out, that he was a bit resentful. He resented being
shoved around and pounded upon, of course. But most of
all he resented being dragged kicking and protesting, into a
plot that could get a lot of people thrown into a Gestapo
prison, himself included. They had no right to ask him to
do it. His mother, his own mother, should have had more
sense. If she didn't like the way things were in Germany,
she could always go back to the United States.

All he wanted was to be a good reporter. He had no
desire to be a hero, was not convinced—although his
doubts about Germany were growing—that it was necessary to make the effort. The only secrecy he was interested
in was keeping a beat to himself until it was safely distri-
buted over the wires of ANO. He often felt that he was
living in a paranoid world, and he didn't like feeling that
he had to struggle to keep his sanity.

A note handed to him by the desk clerk upon his return
to the hotel did not improve his frame of mind. It was
short: *Please don't try to contact me tonight. I will contact
you. Emma.*

Contact. Contact. He sighed as he shut the door to his room, undressed, slumped onto the edge of the bed. He did not even feel like making an entry in his journal. After all, in spite of his personal encounter with the SS, it had been a day without great events. He lay down, but had a bit of trouble going to sleep. His eye ached, and he had sore muscles. He decided, before his eyes finally closed, to have a serious talk with his mother, to urge her to stop her activities with the conspirators and to think about returning to the United States. This last bothered him a bit. He knew his mother's pride in the old Germany, in the cultural and scientific gifts the Germans had given to the world. Just because he'd run into a group of bullies, he shouldn't change his own high opinion of the German people.

10

OTTO SCHELLEN WAS a reasonably contented man. Still a year and a half shy of his thirtieth birthday, he held one of the more important positions in one of the more important organizations within the Nazi labyrinth of interlocking and often competing groups. But an unexpected summons from the Reichsführer SS was likely to unsettle even the most secure man. The appointment was for ten o'clock.

In his private bathroom, just off his office, Schellen brushed his blond hair, examined his eyebrows, showed his white, even teeth, brushed a suspected fleck of dandruff from his collar, and concluded that his appearance was acceptable.

And yet. And yet.

He stepped back into his office, which was built and equipped like a small fortress. He looked at his new desk, saw the carefully hidden flaps that covered the muzzles of the two machine pistols that he could fire from his chair at the push of a button. As he cleared his throat he knew that the sound was being recorded on a wire recorder; any noise caught by the microphones hidden in the walls, under the desk, in lamps, would set the reels of wire moving. The innocent-looking office was, in fact, a superbly equipped, soundproof interrogation room.

But what could the Reichsführer want of him?

He went back over the past few days, trying to find a reason for Himmler's sudden interest. His conscience was clear, his record clean. In fact—ah, that was it; he'd come up with a plan that, although he had not received word, might just win him favor with the Reichsführer. Perhaps, even with someone higher—and there was no one higher than the Reichsführer until one stood in the august presence of the Führer himself. A spring of hope, of happiness, of optimism, welled up inside him and then faded. Damn, thirty minutes of wondering lay ahead of him. It was only nine-thirty.

His intercom buzzed. He growled a yes.

"Herr Schellen," his secretary said, "there is word from our operative in Warsaw. It is being decoded."

"Bring it to me at once," he said.

It was there within minutes. The Warsaw operative was a good man, with sources high in the Polish Government. The message was, on the surface, not exciting, unless one was aware of the underlying tension. An order had gone out to all Polish troops to fire on anyone trying to cross the Polish border. The order had, it seemed, resulted from the death of a Polish soldier on the Danzig frontier.

He felt better. Yes, his plan was the reason for his summons. Quickly he removed his own copy of the plan from his safe, read it through, glanced at his watch. Ten minutes to go.

He exchanged salutes with the guards outside the Reichsführer's imposing office. Himmler sat behind his ponderous desk, bespectacled, stern, looking very much like a country schoolmaster. Schellen saluted with a mighty click of his heels, took the straight-backed chair toward which Himmler gestured. Himmler did not look up.

"I have been looking at your record," Himmler said.

"Sir," Schellen barked.

"You have come a long way in six years."

"I am grateful for this opportunity, Herr Reichsführer."

Himmler made a vague humming sound, looked at the papers in front of him over the top of his glasses. Schellen had the irreverent thought that if he were a good boy the schoolmaster might give him a high mark.

"You joined the SS fresh from Bonn University, at the age of twenty-two," Himmler said.

"Yes, sir." And a lucky thing it was, too. His marks at university hadn't been that high. It was almost by chance that he'd met Reinhard Heydrich, the man with the iron heart, almost sheer luck that he was given a job that he found was made for him, in Heydrich's SD, the Sicherheitsdienst—the Security Service of the SS. But it was not luck that he'd been instrumental in uncovering a Communist cell, while the groundwork that broke up a Polish spy ring in Berlin. He'd earned his desk in the SD.

"I see that Heydrich speaks highly of you," Himmler mused.

"I am grateful." Yes, he was not there to be reprimanded, but to be praised.

"We will go with your plan in Poland," Himmler said.

"Sir, request permission to lead the party."

Himmler looked up in disapproval. "Now, you know better than that," he chided, in his schoolmasterish tones. "I will, however, listen to your suggestions as to who should lead."

"In that case, sir, I would recommend Alfred Naujocks."

"Yes, yes," Himmler said. "Quite a good choice. I'm

sure that Heydrich would agree. Do you anticipate any problem in obtaining the necessary Polish uniforms?''

"None at all," Schellen said.

"It will be called Operation Himmler," the Reichsführer said. "Do you have any objections to that?"

He almost laughed. Objections? None at all. Let the Reichsführer take the credit. He knew, Heydrich knew, all would know—all those who were important—where the idea had originated.

"And the Polish soldiers to wear them?" Himmler asked.

"From the prisons," Schellen said. "We will tell them that those who survive the attack will be given their freedom."

Himmler laughed dryly. "Few will profit."

"None, sir," Schellen said calmly. "The defenders at the Gleiwitz radio station will kill most of them, and the rest will meet their fate by other means." He shrugged. "There will be only dead Poles to speak of the Polish attack on German property."

"At the risk of making a good young man too proud," Himmler said, with a wry smile, "I must tell you that the Führer himself has reviewed this plan and calls it good."

Schellen felt a surge of elation. Soon, soon, he could expect the honor of being head of all foreign intelligence. "I am overwhelmed," he said.

"There is to be another opportunity for you, Schellen," Himmler said, all business again. "Read this."

He took a slip of yellow paper. It was a report from a Gestapo operative. It was puzzling, incomplete. It said merely that an anonymous informer had called the Gestapo's attention to possible "actions against the security of the state" based in a famous Berlin hotel. Schellen looked up with a frown on his face, which soon faded as he gazed briefly into the cold, hard eyes of Himmler.

"I will, of course, do anything you ask, Reichsführer,"

Schellen said. "But is this not Gestapo business?"

Himmler made a motion with one pale hand. "Soon," he said, "all security forces will be in one command, SIPO, Gestapo, SS Sicherheitsdienst. I find talent where it grows, Schellen. It is you I want."

"Then I am at your command, sir," he said. "Is there any other information?"

Himmler shrugged. "We will, when we have the chance, teach the great and feared Gestapo proper procedure. No, there is no other information. Perhaps you will be chasing phantoms. And as for my reasons for chosing you, you have shown your worth in the handling of foreign intelligence assignments. As you must know, the Hotel Adlon is a favorite place with all foreigners. You, having dealt with non-Germans so often, can, I trust, handle an investigation with more finesse than the Gestapo, who are used to dealing mainly with Germans and Jews."

"I understand," Schellen said.

"Do not underestimate the importance of this assignment," Himmler said. "There is one good reason why I am interested in this anonymous tip. The Führer is to make an appearance at the Hotel Adlon on the night of August twenty-fifth."

Schellen paled. The very thought of some lunatic threatening the Führer shocked him. And yet, although Himmler did not say as much, that seemed to be the message.

"You may depend on me, Reichsführer."

Himmler nodded curtly. "Dismissed. You will report directly to me. Don't try to judge whether your findings are important. Let me judge that."

"Yes, sir."

The office of Otto Schellen was busy within minutes. Schellen sat at his fortress desk, musingly turning the gold signet ring with a large opal, under which was hidden a gold capsule filled with cyanide. He had had it made for foreign assignments as a measure of insurance to supplement the artificial tooth he inserted before each mission. The tooth contained enough poison to assure that he would be dead within thirty seconds if captured.

By midafternoon, Otto Schellen knew the history of the Adlon from the laying of the cornerstone, had lists of guests from years back and a complete list of present guests. A careful check of the background of the guests gave him what he wanted. He issued orders.

The continuing investigation of the background of the hotel's guests would be pursued by his staff. On that list were the names of newsmen from half a dozen countries, diplomats, businessmen, a Norwegian acrobatic troupe, tourists, two internationally known writers, a famous conductor. He took special interest in the list of permanent residents of the Adlon. He knew the place, and knew the cost of its rooms. Anyone who could afford to make the Adlon a permanent residence was rich, and often the rich had powerful connections. He did not want to ruffle any feathers. A man did not get ahead by causing complaints from influential citizens.

But one name on the list held his attention. It rang a bell without his being able to identify it totally. Herr Doctor Professor Johannes Welke. It took some time for his secretary to check the files. Ah. There it was. Welke, Johannes, former professor of philosophy, Bonn University. He thought he had recognized the name. And it was very interesting to note that the Gestapo had a file on the good Herr Doctor. Age, it seemed, had forced the retirement of the Herr Doctor just before the Gestapo moved against him for talking anti-Nazism in his classes. Strange, indeed, that a university professor had enough money to live in a two-room suite at the most expensive hotel in Berlin. Interesting, too, that an anti-Nazi was living in a place where antistate activity was being brewed.

11

Margo had finished toweling her slim, tall, smoothly muscled body when she heard the knock on the door.

"It's open," she said.

It would be Karl. The daily workout and rehearsal had gone well. She hadn't really wanted to be with Karl afterward, though. He was so unsatisfying. She had entertained thoughts of going out into the streets, to be nearer, perhaps, to the type of German she admired, to meet a strong, young man and—the thought sent little tendrils of need through her. And yet such an action was impossible. She knew that she was hardly inconspicuous, with her full six feet of lithe, slim, feminine body, her Aryan blond hair. So it would have to be Karl.

"Oh, come in," she said impatiently, as the knock was repeated. She wrapped a towel around herself and went into the main room to see two impassive men standing just inside the door. They were dressed in the dark suits that

many had learned to associate with the secret police.
"Sorry," she said, "I thought you were one of my friends."

"Fräulein Margo Ostenso?" asked one of the men in a
low and threatening voice.

"Yes. May I help you?" she asked.

"You will come with us," the man said flatly.

It was a measure of Margo's love for Germany that she
felt no fear, only a surge of elation. "I will be dressed
very shortly. Please wait in the hallway."

"You may dress in the bath."

She smiled. "It is hot and stuffy in the bath. If you will
not wait in the hall you have to take your chances." And
so saying she dropped the towel casually. She noted that
the expressionless faces changed, eyes widening. One of
the men licked his lips. She did not even bother to turn her
back as she stepped into her lacy panties and quickly
covered her body with a flowing dress. She slipped her
feet into low-heeled shoes and went to the dresser to brush
her hair and pull it back into a neat bun. "I am ready,"
she announced, turning back to the men.

Otto Schellen was not a man given to speculation. He
had no preconceived idea of the Norwegian girl. When she
swept into his office, leaving the two SD operatives outside, he looked up curiously. He saw a Germanic Valkyrie,
a tall, magnificent young woman with a face that broke
into a tight-lipped smile. For a moment he wondered, in a
very unprofessional way, if she were taller than he. He
rose, gave her a curt bow with a click of his heels,
introduced himself. Yes, she was almost as tall as he.
Striking. Stunning, in fact. She would be a worthy mate
for a true Aryan.

"You are wondering why you are here," he said, as he
took her arm and escorted her to a chair.

"Not at all," she said, with a confidence that pleased
him. "Only why it has taken you so long."

"Ah," he said. "You are Margo Ostenso, a Norwegian citizen. You spent the summer of 1938 in the Horst Wessel Youth Camp near Potsdam."

"That is true." She could not keep her eyes off him. He was not in uniform, but that was the only bad mark she could give him. Otherwise, he was perfect—tall, strong, young, so very, very Aryan.

"Your record there was excellent. You expressed a desire to do certain work on behalf of the Third Reich."

"That is also true." Her smile was full now.

"It might interest you to know that I have talked with some of your instructors and some of your companions from the camp."

"I would be disappointed if you were less careful."

It was Schellen's turn to smile. "Are you sure you're not German?"

"I am Norwegian by accident of birth," she said. "If we could check it back, you and I, I think we would find a common Aryan ancestry. But shall we get to it, Herr Schellen?"

"By all means," he said. Well, she had arrogance, the tall bitch. A touch of that quality was necessary in a good operative. But for a moment he wondered how much energy it would take to punch some of that arrogance out of her—with the third fist, not the ones on the end of his arms. Perhaps he would be forced to teach her a bit of respect.

"I have in mind for you a job that I would ordinarily assign to a trained person. However, you have shown an interest and a loyalty. If there were danger I would not ask you, untrained, to undertake the job."

"I am willing at any time to undergo training," she said. "I am in Germany with this acrobatic troupe primarily because I have waited a year for a call and have not received it."

"Ah, Fräulein," he said, "we were but waiting for the proper moment. Now, a question. Would you hesitate if I asked you to perform duties that, to uniformed eyes, might seem detrimental to the interests of your own country?"

"In the world of the future," Margo said, "the interests of Norway will always be identical with the interests of the Reich."

"Ah, yes."

"Let me say that I agree thoroughly with the teaching in the camp. If my own mother were a traitor to the cause, I would denounce her."

"Fräulein Ostenso," he said. "I believe you."

"Then please call me Margo," she said. "I am unaccustomed to the use of my family name. I have performed as simply Margo for some years."

"Margo. Charming, yes. Margo, this assignment may seem, at first, to be simple and unimportant, but I assure you, for reasons that I cannot divulge, that we depend on you more than you can imagine." No harm in building her ego a bit. In fact, he was talking with her simply because she happened to be living in the Adlon. It would take time for him to plant a trained operative there. Meanwhile, he could find out about this Norwegian girl. A good administrator looked ahead. Someday good operatives would be needed in Norway, and if he could restrain the amateurish enthusiasm that was almost sure to surface, she might be of some help.

"I will do my best for you and for the Reich," she said seriously.

"Good. Here is the situation. At the Adlon, we have some indication of anti-State activity. I must admit to you that we have only a hint, not a single solid piece of information, not even a clue as to the nature of the activity. I am going to give you a list of names. I want you to learn the faces that go with these names. If, in the natural course of things, you have the chance to speak with any one on the list, do so—in your normal capacity, as a visitor to the Reich, a young girl curious about people. Do not—I repeat, do not—try to do any detective work on your own. Just observe. Make notes. I will give you a telephone number that is manned day and night. If you see anything suspicious, do not try to do anything about it yourself. Call the number immediately.''

"Am I to have a contact?"

He smiled. "Oh, yes." Then he did something very unprofessional, for she had crossed her long legs, giving him a glimpse of that creamy, long thigh. "Would you object to my being your contact?"

She quickly recognized that the question was not all business, favored him with a broad, full-lipped smile. "It would be an honor—and, I trust, a pleasure."

He noted her acceptance with a look, then returned to business. "Here is the list of names. Commit them to memory. The same with the telephone number. Then destroy the paper, by burning it or by tearing it into small bits and flushing down the toilet. Now, Fräulein Margo, my men will take you back to the Adlon. If you are asked why you were brought in, tell them that it was simply a matter of clearing a mistake in the records regarding your passport."

She sat in the back seat of an aging Mercedes sedan, not trying to converse with her two silent escorts. By the time she reached the Adlon, she had memorized the telephone number and the list of half a dozen names, among which were those of Herr Doctor Professor Johannes Welke and one Edgar Raine, an American newsman. Of the six she knew only the Professor by sight. He had spoken to her, as he spoke to all who passed him; once he had introduced himself, in a doddering, friendly way, as they waited for an elevator. She did not like old people; the very old were repulsive, full of small odors, and insulting, with their wrinkles and creaks and grunts, to the eyes and ears.

By each of the names on the list was a one- or two-sentence background summary. She noted with interest that the Professor had preached anti-Nazism. That was the ultimate sin. For a German—an educated German at that—to doubt the infallibility of the greatest German leader in history was incomprehensible. She resolved to single out the Herr Doctor Professor for immediate attention. His obvious friendliness, his desire to talk, talk, talk would make it easy.

12

THE NEWSPAPERS OF that Wednesday, August 16, continued the attack on the "aggressions" of the Polish criminals. The weather, pleasant to Ed Raine, caused Berliners to grumble. He laughed, wondering how they would fare in the American Midwest on an August dog day with the temperature up in the high nineties.

He spent the early hours of the morning in his room, waiting, expecting the knock on the connecting door, feeling mixed emotions when it did not come. Finally he couldn't stand waiting any longer and went to find John Graff Stanton at this usual place at the bar. Stanton had not been able to get any comments one way or the other about any army mobilizations or navel sailings.

Ed was about to leave the bar when he saw the one-armed colonel enter and take an empty table. He told Stanton to keep digging and made it a point to walk near von Stahlecker's table on the way out. As expected, he was hailed. He accepted the offer of a drink. Von Stahlecker examined the bruised eye—a real old-fashioned comic-book shiner—and clucked. Ed steered the talk to the world situation and, when he felt the opportunity was right, tried his gambit.

"Colonel, I won't ask you to violate State security, but I would like your reaction to a question."

"You may ask, of course," von Stahlecker said. "I may not answer, and my silence must be construed as no comment."

"I have it from reliable sources that a quarter of a million men have been mobilized and that the navy has orders to take up Atlantic stations." Ed watched the Colonel's face.

To his surprise, von Stahlecker nodded gravely. "I commend you on your sources."

"You're confirming it?"

"No. At least not for publication."

Ed chewed his lip for a moment. "If it's true, Colonel, what does it mean? Bluff? In spite of what the other newsmen write and say, I can't believe that Hitler is serious about wanting a war with England and France."

Von Stahlecker was silent for a moment. "I don't want to be overly dramatic, Herr Raine," he said, "but what I am about to say puts my life in your hands."

Ed raised an eyebrow. It did sound dramatic. "Your life is safe. I owe you that for pulling the bullies off me." he said quietly.

"You may not quote me," von Stahlecker said, "but there will be an attack on Poland."

"*Will* be? Not *may* be?"

"Will be."

"Then there'll be war," Ed said. "I don't think the English would stand for it. Hell, they've gone to war half a dozen times in the past just to keep a European power from commanding the seaports along the Channel in the

Low Countries. They won't sit still for a self-sufficient Germany sitting astride all of Central and Western Europe."

"Exactly," von Stahlecker said.

"You believe that, don't you?"

"I know it, Herr Raine. And if it happens, this time Germany may never be able to rise from the ashes."

"Colonel, would you object if I put that into writing and attributed it to a reliable source without using names?"

"It would not be wise. I would advise you, Herr Raine, to continue to hold a neutral attitude in your writings. You have developed some interesting contacts."

"You seem to be very well informed yourself," Ed said.

Von Stahlecker shrugged. "I am, after all, an intelligence officer. It's my business to know these things. And now, Herr Raine, I must be going. *Auf Wiedersehen.*"

Ed sat at the table. Highly unusual for the man to open up, to admit the troop mobilizations. He couldn't figure von Stahlecker's angle. If he had a mind to, he could get the man into a lot of trouble by quoting him on the mobilization and naval orders. It would be quite a scoop: *ABWEHR colonel confirms mobilization orders!* But he'd never violated a confidence; that wasn't the way he worked. He had a hunch that if he continued to cultivate von Stahlecker, he'd come up with a bigger story, sooner or later.

He went back to the lobby, checked his box. Still no message from Emma. He didn't really want to go back to his room again, but had no other plan, either. At the point the little Norwegian Baroness careened out of the elevator on a new tricycle and stopped in front of him.

"Ah, good morning, Mr. Raine." She spoke in English, as if to protect their conversation from eavesdroppers. "I must apologize and thank you again. I hope there was no serious damage. Your eye looks quite magnificent; is that the worst of it?''

"That's the worst, Baroness, and I forget about it until someone mentions it. And please, no more apologies; it wasn't your fault."

"I won't mention it again, then," she responded. Then, rapidly cheerful, she offered, "Would you care to come along now and see the troupe rehearse? You could start taking notes for that story."

Ed needed something to do; besides, he enjoyed the company of the strange little woman. He bowed slightly, smiling. "With pleasure, Baroness," he said.

They took an elevator down one more flight. There she pedaled down the hallway to the gymnasium, and he followed. When they were well away from the elevator bank, she stopped again, looked up at him. "I wish you wouldn't call me Baroness. We Norwegians aren't quite as stuffy about titles as the Germans are. And besides, you and I have, so to speak, done battle together." She laughed to cover her evident embarrassment. "Helga will do quite nicely, Mr. Raine."

"Ed."

"Good. Ed." She wheeled quickly ahead of him and, before he could catch up, had banged the door of the gym open, and was introducing Mr. Raine, the American newsman, to the troupe.

And so it was that Margo met the first of the men on her list. The impressions made were radically different. Margo, suspicious of Raine merely because his name was on the list, found him pushy and nosy, as all Americans were, in his questions to the troupe about their backgrounds and their feelings about being in Germany. Ed, on the other hand, was awed by six feet of female, by her grace and strength as the troupe rehearsed. He sat beside Helga, who gave him a running commentary on the acrobatic moves and occasionally called out a quick pointer to one or another of the troupe. He began to see an angle for a story—acrobatic circus in the exclusive Adlon. When Helga reminded him that Hitler would see the performance, he began to envision a long piece.

"I'd like to get some personality into it," he told her. "Talk more with some of the performers, before and after. How it feels to be performing for a man who is shaking the world, that sort of thing."

"We'll be most happy to cooperate," Helga said. "I would suggest either Karl or Margo—they're the most mature. Karl's English is, I believe, quite good, and Margo speaks German fluently."

Margo was doing a floor exercise, and as she performed balletic movements, her magnificent body was shown off in the tight acrobatic costume. She did a backbend directly in front of Ed, and he was thoroughly aware that she was displaying much more than her acrobatic skill for him. Helga did not fail to notice. When Margo finished, Helga motioned her over.

"Herr Raine is going to do a feature article on our troupe," she told Margo. "He will want to talk with you."

"A pleasure," Margo said. "Please feel free to call on me at any time, Herr Raine." She smiled. "Perhaps we can dine together?"

"I would like that," Ed said. "Tomorrow night?" He wanted to keep this evening open for Emma. Surely she'd contact him soon.

After lunch, he did some work on his long piece on the Adlon itself. He had dug up quite a bit of historical material relating to the hotel; the list of royal and famous guests who had stayed there was impressive. The Kaiser had been there with his family at the opening, along with the most distinguished scholars, artists, financiers. The

Adlon was one of the great hotels of the world, and a list of its guests since 1907 read like a *Who's Who* of the world.

Its wide entrance arch led the modern visitor into a time machine, evoking Imperial Berlin, a time of luxury and pride and beauty. In his mind, Ed could see the hobble-skirted women, the top-hatted men. Once the social life of the Second Empire centered around the great hotel. Any guests of the ruling Hohenzollerns who, for one reason or the other, did not stay at the palace were housed in the hotel's soundproofed rooms, thus building the prestige of Number One Unter den Linden. It became a must for visiting prima donnas, actresses, writers such as Gerhart Hauptmann or Hugo von Hofmannsthal. Snobs who could not afford a room or a dinner at the Adlon's prices would visit the wood-paneled Regency Salon, make off with hotel stationery, from its carved wooden writing desks, and proudly display the Adlon crest on their letters.

Ed roughed out a first paragraph:

When Kaiser Wilhelm saw the opulence of the Adlon, the sweeping staircases, the spacious lobbies, the comfortable parlors, the rare and beautiful Oriental carpeting, he openly expressed a feeling of envy, stating that it made the Imperial Palace seem shabby. And he had good reason to be jealous, for the palace had no bath; when he wished to bathe, six footmen went to the nearby Hotel de Rome to fetch a bathtub to the palace.

Like so many of the economic achievements of the Edwardian period, the Adlon was the result of individual initiative. Lorenz Adlon, a German of vast energy and ambition, noted that Berlin could boast no hotel to match, for example, the Savoy of London or the Crillon of Paris.

To build such a hotel, the first requirement was a choice location. He had in mind a specific one, namely One Unter den Linden. There was one problem. The site was occupied, and not by any ordinary building. The great builder Schinkel had designed and constructed for Count Redern a small palace that, like Schinkel buildings, was considered an architectural treasure.

Adlon was not deterred by the outraged protest of those who worshiped the past. He went to the Kaiser himself and enlisted his help. The venture was aided, unwittingly, by the Kaiser's cousin, King Edward of England. The then Count Redern liked to gamble, but was apparently rather inept, losing his entire fortune in one night to the skilled Bertie. Thus, when Adlon offered a good price for the palace at One Unter den Linden, the impious destruction of a Schinkel structure was only days away. Twenty million solid German marks later, the Adlon—with marble everywhere, thick carpets ordered from Constantinople, two hundred bathrooms, and ducal suites on the second floor—took its place with the luxury hotels of the world.

Now Ed needed current information. The manager of the hotel, a dapper man in his fifties, apologized for being too busy to help him, but said that the assistant manager, one Frau Kopf, would be able to.

The frau was, he decided immediately after being ushered into her plush office, a formidable person. He estimated her to be in her early forties. She was a handsome woman, with hair pulled back into a tight bun, piercing brown eyes, and the voice of a drill sergeant. Her fair, unblemished skin seemed to be drawn taut over her high cheekbones; her figure was full, but she seemed fit enough, as she offered her hand, to crush his knuckles in her strong grip. He noted that her one piece of jewelry was a silver swastika on a heavy silver chain. It seemed to be a grudging concession to femininity; the simple suit jacket and white blouse she wore over her well-developed bust were clearly designed to be worn with a necktie.

He stated his business briskly, inspired by her no-nonsense manner. She nodded. "I understand," she said. "The Adlon will be delighted to help you. I have read your dispatches—"

"You, too?" Ed's eyebrows shot up in surprise.

"And," she said, ignoring his question, "find them to be sensible and quite fair, which is more than I can say for some others."

"I'd like to show that the Adlon is still one of the more exclusive hotels in Europe," he said. "Perhaps you can tip me off to some of the VIPs who are staying here."

She looked at him musingly. "There is, of course, the well-known Swedish businessman, Ingo Selmer. He has access to high government figures and, indeed, has been instrumental in negotiations between Germany and the British."

"Yes, I already have him on my list. I've tried to contact him, but he's a busy man. Another angle I'd like to work has to do with speaking with long-time residents of the hotel. I've been told by the bellhops that one Herr Doctor Professor Johannes Welke has been here as long as anyone."

Frau Kopf frowned. "I don't think Welke would be of help to you," she said. "The old man's mind isn't what it used to be."

"I see," he said.

"There is a Norwegian baroness here. I understand that your American readers are rather fascinated by royalty and titles."

"I've met Baroness Gies," he said.

She gave him some more names, suggested that a widow of a general who lived permanently in the Adlon might supply reminiscences about the hotel's past.

"Thank you," he said. "I'll look her up. And I think I'll try the Professor, too, even if he is a bit senile. Sometimes old men can remember fifty years ago better than yesterday."

"That would, Herr Raine, not be advisable."

13

ED HAD RESISTED the temptation to tell Frau Kopf that who he talked to was his own business. Instead, he shook her firm hand once more and thanked her for her gracious help.

Naturally, the first thing he did after that was to get Herr Doctor Professor Welke's room number. The second thing he did was to knock on Welke's door on the top floor.

The old man wore house slippers and a gray cardigan over an old-fashioned, high-collared shirt. His thin hair was brushed neatly back, and he cradled a venerable long-stemmed meerschaum in his hand. His gray eyes looked at Ed over the top of his rimless glasses with friendly inquiry.

"Come in, come in," he said, when Ed introduced himself. "Always glad for company." He insisted on giving Ed the chair in front of the window, which overlooked the central courtyard and the garden restaurant. Even the less-desirable rooms at the Adlon were large and comfortable; the Professor had filled the walls of his sitting room with bookcases and shelves of small, probably valuable, mementoes. "I don't know if I can be of help with your story," he said, "but we old ones seize any opportunity to talk."

If this man is senile, Ed was thinking, looking into those bright, gray eyes, he must have been truly awesome when he had his full mental powers. Soon he decided that the Professor was definitely not senile. The old man's eyes twinkled as he spoke of the past. He had been a guest of the Kaiser at the opening ceremonies, had been staying at the Adlon off and on for twenty-seven years, had seen the famous and the mighty come and go. He was, Ed found, a font of information and a delightful conversationalist. He had known all of them—von Hindenburg, Müller, the last Kaiser. During the Weimar Republic he had been an adviser to the Government. As he spoke of the republic, his eyes seem to fade.

"We let it die," he said. "There were too many good intentions and too few results. There can never be too much freedom, my boy, but we came close. In our protection of individual freedom we allowed the deep, underlying sickness of Germany to go untreated, lest we step on the toes of one citizen, deny the rights of one man. And then Hitler came along. He knew what was bothering our people—immorality in public places, high prices—but most of all he knew that the German was still smoldering in shame over the defeat of 1918. He played on all the old Germanic pride, the basic love of country that is in the heart of every German. He fought the Communists. And the German people flocked to his red-and-black banner, giving up one freedom after the other in the name of the Fatherland."

"Professor," Ed said, "I don't intend to write down what you just said."

"Yes, yes, that is wise. I have spoken out in the past.

My voice is only one faint echo among the cheers for the marching Blackshirts. Yes, I am an old man now. I have learned, or I thought I had, to keep my mouth shut.'' He laughed. ''Were you not warned about me?''

''As a matter of fact, yes,'' Ed said.

''Ah, so I thought. I am the dissident, although I have not spoken in public for . . . several years. All I want now, my boy, is to be allowed to live out my few remaining years in peace and comfort.'' He dug at the bowl of the pipe with a cleaning tool. ''Yes, it's come to that. Once I would have fought on, thinking, perhaps, that by voicing my opinions I would gain a small footnote in history. I would have said for posterity that this madman, this Hitler, is leading Germany down a road that ends in fire and ashes.''

''Professor, since you're speaking so frankly, I'd like to ask you a hypothetical question. Suppose there was a group that felt so strongly that Hitler was leading Germany into war that they planned to overthrow him. Would they have any chance of success?''

Welke's hands went still, the cleaning tool seemingly frozen to the pipe bowl. ''Herr Raine,'' he said at last, ''if you are baiting me, if you are one of Himmler's men, you are doing a wonderful job of fooling me.'' He shrugged. ''If you are Gestapo, then I am yours, for I am foolish enough to accept you at face value. You are the first foreign newsman to speak with me in years. Perhaps I still harbor the desire for that little footnote in history. Yes, Herr Raine, there was such a group.''

''Was?''

''In 1938. Some very influential men, as a matter of fact. They came to me. They wanted me to lend my prestige—'' He laughed. ''Some prestige: a has-been teacher. But they came to me. I told them then that if they acted decisively they might succeed, for there are many who remember the Great War. I told them, however, that I was far too old to be of any use to them. Obviously, since Hitler now tries once more to lead us to war, the plot failed.''

"And were the conspirators discovered?''

"No, fortunately. However, many of them are now quite impressed by Hitler's easy success in Czechoslovakia. They now believe that Hitler, tomorrow, will give them the world. I know that one or two dedicated men are capable of seeing what is happening and might, just might, be trying to enlist the aid needed.'' He shook his head. "But it would require a vast amount of troops, top generals, precise organization. The German people would perhaps accept an overthrow—if the new government were headed by a strong leader.'' He chuckled, but there was a sound of sadness in it. "We Germans must have a leader, you know. There would be blood. The young, the fanatical, the SS, all would fight to the death for Hitler. However, I cannot help but feel that there are enough Germans living who remember 1918 and the 1920s, who know the result of war, so that a new government could expect support. Enough support? Who knows?''

"Professor Welke, I have to confess that it makes me nervous just talking about it.''

"And I,'' Welke said. "I was never a man of great courage. I fear pain. I should be used to it, for when one is old there is always a pain, an ache. And then, too, there is enough German in me to be appalled by the very thought of resisting constituted authority. I think you Americans have a saying, 'Our country, right or wrong.' Intensify that a thousand times and you have a German. I sincerely doubt there are many men who could overcome this ingrained loyalty to the point of openly opposing any leader, much less one so firmly entrenched as Herr Hitler.''

The old man finished cleaning out his pipe and stood up. "Now, to show you that I am not the only antique around here, may I offer you a dram of a fine old brandy?"

Ed stayed for an hour, the Professor once again speaking of the past, seemingly relieved to be off the discomforting subjects of the day. Ed couldn't remember when he'd enjoyed an interview so much. Herr Doctor Professor Johannes Welke was, he decided, a fine old man.

However, he lost some of the mellow glow when, checking his box, he found another message from Emma: She would see him the next day, on Thursday. Disappointed, he found refuge in anger, and his reaction was to pick up the telephone and ask for Margo Ostenso's room. In a sultry voice that hinted of hidden wonders, she said she'd be delighted to dine with him that night, instead of waiting until Thursday.

She came out of her room dressed in a long, shimmering gown of silver lamé. The silver seemed to enhance her hair into a golden glory. The gown was cut low, showing the firm breasts to full advantage, and when she took his arm he could feel the warmth of her body. He was not a super-egotist, but he had to admit that it gave him a glow of pleasure to see heads turn as they walked through the lobby and into the dining room.

She had a way of leaning over the table, putting her head close to his, that accentuated the cleavage of breasts, a way of reaching out to touch his hand when she made a point. She showed great interest in him, asking questions about his work, his home in America, what he'd done since coming to Germany. He found himself, primed by the brandy and wine, talking, talking, somewhat wittily, he had to admit wryly, feeling rather like a lad on his first date trying to impress the girl. Her total attention, as he seemed to hang on every word, was flattering. And she was gorgeously vital. He could almost feel her body heat across the table.

When she led the conversation to current affairs, he found himself saying that he did not think, in spite of everything, that there would be war.

"I think the Germans deserve to have their own returned," Margo said. "Don't you?"

"Within reason," Ed said. "Germany is a great nation. And once a German, always a German. Until the Germans in what is now Poland are once again a part of the Fatherland, there can be no peace."

"Exactly," Margo said. "Do you write that in your dispatches?"

"I try to be fair," Ed said. "I don't think there's any great right or wrong. Perhaps Hitler has been a little repressive, but the country was in such a mess when he took over that something had to be done. Roosevelt took some pretty drastic actions when he became president of a country on the verge of ruin, with some thinking that armed revolution was the only answer. Democracy had had a longer time to become established in the U.S., and I think that's what saved it from going one way or the other—to the left, like Huey Long wanted—he's the one who wanted to redistribute the wealth—"

"That's called Communism," Margo said.

"—or to the right," Ed said. "As it is we've gone a lot further to the left than a lot of people like."

"No one is hungry in Germany," Margo said. "Those who are able to work have work."

"Yes," Ed said. "Of course, there's been a price to pay."

"In what way?" she asked.

"A certain loss of freedom. Concentration of power in the hands of a few."

"But the Nazi party *is* Germany," Margo said. "It contains the leaders, the dedicated, the people who are worthwhile."

"Well," Ed said, "I haven't seen anyone being mistreated. "And at least Hitler's made the trains run on time."

She laughed. "No, that was Mussolini."

"I gather that you approve of what Hitler has done for Germany."

"I do," she said. "In this world one must be strong, firm, brave. To the east there are millions of Bolsheviks. The Jews control France. It is up to the Aryan nations to fight the reactionaries, to prevent the total domination of the Jewish moneychangers."

"Aryan?" He frowned. "That's a theory that's based on some pretty flimsy evidence."

"But you are half German," she said, with a look of puzzlement. "How can you doubt the superiority of the Aryan races?"

He was feeling a light buzz. The food had not dispelled it. He was in the company of a beautiful young woman and he hadn't thought of Emma for at least fifteen minutes. He was tired of heavy talk. "Well, I feel like half a superman." He laughed. "Want me to do some pushups for you?"

She joined him in his laughter. "You have no mat," she said.

"I do best with a living mat," he said, thinking, my God, here I go again, Ed Raine, the great lover.

"Ah," she said, showing him her white teeth. She was not yet sure about him. Some of the things he said showed great sympathy for Germany. Others? Well, she was just not sure. But he was good-looking, in a raw way, and his black eye gave him an air of brutality that she rather liked.

She leaned closer. "You know that I am a gymnast, an acrobat."

"And the most beautiful one I've ever seen," he said sincerely.

She was in her teens, not long past childhood. And yet she was a woman, doing an important job. At last she had been allowed to serve, to help in the all-important work of making the world a decent place for men. And she wasn't sure. How best to get to know a man? In bed. "I have been trained to have fantastic muscle control," she whispered.

It was his turn to say, "Ah."

"And I am bored by all these people around us."

He started to say, "My room or yours?" Then he remembered. What if Emma changed her mind and knocked?

"I have a thought," he said. "I am writing a piece on the Adlon. And yet I've seen only my own room."

"In the spirit of international cooperation, I will be glad to show you mine," she said, rising.

She was slightly taller than he. It was a sort of little-boy feeling to stand, with her hard, firm breasts pressed to his chest, lifting his head to take those young and luscious lips into his. She came into his arms the minute the door was closed. There was a swiftness that left him dizzy, had both of them naked before he was ready—for, although he was only twenty-nine, he had passed the stage of instant readiness, especially when he had been drinking. No matter. There were ways to overcome the reluctance of a certain member of the anatomy. Simple, blood-stirring ways involving the placement of lips on hot, damp, slick, secret places. She demonstrated her agility by bending into a fetal position, putting the top of his head next to her mouth, her lips pressing against his head, hands soothing his neck, his hair.

She encouraged him, telling him how wonderful it was, in a hoarse, low voice. Then, "Here are your orders, Herr Raine."

"Yes, ma'am," he said, his voice slightly muffled.

"You will give me two hundred pushups."

"But I have no mat."

She pushed his face away, stretched her golden limbs, reached her arms out for him. "Here is your mat."

"One, two, three," he counted. Deep, deep, lush and hot and glorious, and then he forget to count.

Completion delayed by the brandy, the wine, he found himself fighting, punishing her body, and she took all he could deliver, urging him on with that throaty, whispering voice. Telling him, "Hard, oh, do it hard." Her fingernails sent sensations up and down his spine, left white and often red marks; her legs were long, strong, lithe to an unbelievable degree. Endless. Pure lust in a bed that was soon overheated, damp with perspiration.

"Ah, ah, ah," she moaned, her hips taking up a fantastic rhythm, legs pointing ceilingward.

Then, of all things, she wanted to talk politics. He lay beside her, exhausted. She seemed as fresh as she had at the beginning, hands, mouth, words, all teasing, begging, mixing in the talk of politics. He told her what she wanted to hear; she was evidently a great fan of the Third Reich. Then he took her again, this time long, slow, the hours melting away with pure lust and pauses for the champagne he'd ordered during the first interval. And in the hours after midnight her tone changed. Completed time after time, her body was sated, tired, longing for relaxation, and yet, in his alcohol-induced lust, he kept on. "Please, please," she begged, and he, thinking she wanted more, punished her, amazed at his own hunger, his own insatiable appetite for that long, golden body. He had no idea what she meant when, finished, gasping, lying atop her, he heard her say sleepily, "A man who can do that to me must be all Aryan, not merely half." Margo Ostenso, newly appointed spy, had given him a clean bill of health. "And now, Herr Raine, you must leave me. Athletes must sleep."

He made it back to his room, but just barely. Too tired to bathe, he fell across his bed, looked once at the closed door to Emma's room, felt a childish desire to laugh. He'd shown her.

And then the image of her on Goebbels's arm froze his laughter, deflated his pride.

"Damn it," he said, pulling a pillow over his head to shut out the dawn light already coming through the window. "Damn, damn, damn."

14

ON THE SURFACE, mid-August was calm. The paucity of noteworthy events sent the foreign newsmen in the Adlon's cellar bar into the doldrums. The more enterprising ones pumped their contacts, and each other, searching desperately for material. The world had become accustomed to hard news, wars and rumors of wars—Japanese action in China, civil war in Spain, the Italians in Abyssinia, the Germans in Czechoslovakia— and Berlin, for some time, had been the hottest beat in the world.

Only those in the inner circles around Hitler knew that the calm surface hid a seething cauldron. Admiral Canaris, as chief of the Abwehr, did not know the full details, but he had a faint scent of moves that, when announced a few days later, would change the world. His feeling of desperation was a constant, nagging presence. He had called his most trusted associate on Wednesday night, and he and the one-armed Luftwaffe colonel had sat up, drinking wine slowly, until the hour grew late, talking, talking, talking. He had been assured that things were going well. A positive move toward an important goal would be made on Thursday.

The day showed signs of becoming sultry, enough to make even a Midwesterner like Ed feel the discomfort. He finished his article on the Adlon and its importance to the society and diplomatic and business life of Berlin, and sent it safely on its way across the Atlantic by cable. He felt he'd done some good work since arriving in the city—four long dispatches, including an interview with Goebbels.

In the continued absence of Emma, he decided on Thursday to make definite plans to visit a Youth Camp. Accordingly, after lunch he was picking up the telephone to call his Frau Sittenrichter at the Ministry of Propaganda when his heart leaped at the sound of a firm knock on the connecting door.

She was dressed for comfort, a silken blouse tucked inside white, wide-legged shorts that showed her wonderful legs. For a long moment he stood looking at her, feeling a variety of emotions. He remembered how she'd looked right through him in the lobby, how he'd waited, waited, for her to get in touch with him. He thought of her with the small, limping, rat-faced man and felt a revulsion that, for brief seconds, hardened his features. Then she smiled.

"Witch," he said, seizing her.

Strangely, there was no feeling of sexuality in the long, unhurried kiss. It was as if soothing breezes had begun to blow, soft music to play. He felt an utter serenity.

She beat him to it. "Oh, how I've missed you," she said.

He told her with his arms, his lips, that he felt the same. But the need for her, that hunger he'd felt all the time she was away, was not immediately evident. He had to explain his black eye to her, then he was content just to hold her, to look at her, to hear her voice as she told him of her trip to Dresden.

"Yes," he said. "But you've been back for a couple of days."

"Please," she said, looking pained and turning away. "Not now, Ed. Please, not now."

No, it was no time for unpleasantness.

She turned to him with a radiant smile. "I have a wonderful idea," she said. "Listen."

"I have an idea, too," he said, looking at her legs. The nice thing about the shorts women were wearing was that they made the delicious contents so accessible. Big, loose legs seemed built to accommodate a male hand.

She understood and smiled. "I will admit that isn't an altogether bad idea, but listen to mine, first. I have a few days before I must go back to work." She came to him, put her arms around his waist, leaned back to look up into his face. "An indecent proposition. Mein Herr, would you come away with me?"

"To Pago Pago, if that's what you want," he said.

"Just to the mountains," she said. "It will be so cool, so lovely there. Away from the heat. Away from people. Just you and I."

"I'd love it, Emma, but—"

"Your work, yes. But can you not work by seeing the Germany beyond Berlin?"

He grinned his assent. "You'll have to promise to leave off making love to me for—oh, at least fifteen minutes a day, so I can work."

"A terrible burden, but I shall be strong."

Well, German trains ran on time, too, and they were fast and efficient and the service was good and the sleeping

cars lovely, and two could get into one bed, as it was
proven, in an utterly nice way, as the train puffed south-
ward through Nuremberg. Munich was old and impressive
in the early-morning light, and the Germans he talked with
on the train and in the stations were polite, well dressed,
curious about America. They wanted to know how the
ordinary American felt about the Reich and Hitler. They
were good people, he felt, sensible people. But there were
uniforms everywhere, a jarring note. And Emma's actions
were not the actions of a girl supposedly in love in normal
times. He had time to talk with Germans on the train
because she would not leave her compartment.

"We would have no privacy if I were recognized," she
told him. Moreover, she'd secured separate accommoda-
tions for them, warned him to be sure he was not seen
coming into her compartment. He kept waiting for her to
mention the subject of a plot against Hitler, but she was
silent. His doubts troubled him, when he was alone, when
his body was sated and he was not with her.

Friday, with the Alps as a backdrop, they sat in an
open-air café in a small mountain village. He didn't need
the drink that sat on the table before him, for he was
intoxicated by the air, the clean blue skies, by Emma. A
white-haired waiter called them "my children," and smiled
fondly as Emma reached for Ed's hand. Apparently, he
thought, she wasn't worried about being seen in that re-
mote place with an American, not concerned with being
recognized.

The surroundings, the knowledge of being in a new,
beautiful place, that smug feeling of being a world traveler,
of going places within the reach of only the very rich, the
constant wonder of Emma's beauty, all combined to make
him forget that the world was threatened with a violent explosion, that he had a boss back in New York. The brief days
and glorious nights slipped away as if they were the leaves

of a calendar being blown by a gale. They would have to travel most of Sunday night to get back to Berlin, and he wanted to stay there in the mountains forever.

Churchbells echoed off the hills on a lovely Sunday morning. They had breakfast on a sunny terrace. She wore a pale yellow dress that glowed in the sunshine, lighting her face. Her eyes lingered on his; the bruise was gone. When she broke the comfortable silence her voice was full of regret.

"I'll be going on tour," she said.

"For how long?"

"A week, perhaps a bit more."

"I'll quit my job and go with you."

She laughed. "I'd love it."

"Can you afford to support me?"

"Oh, yes. I would consider it money well spent. You would, however, have to allow me at least two hours a night for my work."

"A terrible burden," he said. He looked away and down a peaceful valley. Nothing could upset the peace here, the quiet, the echoing churchbells. Bavaria was largely a Catholic area, and the people he'd talked with were stolid, thrifty. Only one had voiced a concern with the world at large, wondering why the Pope had not spoken out more strongly against Herr Hitler's threats of war against another Catholic country. War . . . And so the present reality began to intrude on Ed's thought, spoiling the lovely day.

"What have you to do with Joseph Goebbels?" he asked, taking the plunge.

Her face changed. "Have you ever had to do something you did not want to do?"

"Yes."

She sighed. "It's been so lovely. I wish it could go on

forever." She was suddenly businesslike. "I am afraid, my dear Ed, that I have let my personal feelings intrude on necessity. But we must not talk here."

He looked around. The terrace was only sparsely occupied—respectable-looking Germans and a few somnolent tourists. They had been speaking English, which certainly gave them a measure of protection. But he rose with her and did not speak until they were in their room. She sat in a chair with her back to a window; he could see the mountains over her shoulder, but the strong light behind her obscured her face.

"I don't know where to start."

"Start by telling me about Goebbels."

Her laugh was bitter. "I suppose I am an authority on the good doctor. As you may know, he is a frustrated writer."

"I got that impression when I talked with him," Ed said. He didn't really want to know about Emma's relationship with Goebbels, feared to hear that she had been intimate with him, and yet he had to know. Not only his personal feelings were involved, there was the matter of his mother's association with a dangerous conspiracy.

"After he received his PhD from Heidelberg University he wrote a novel. It was not published until he had risen to a high position in Nazi circles."

It was obvious that she was avoiding the intent of his question, but he did not push.

"I came to know him through the theater," she said. "He had also written two plays, both in verse, both rather bad. As Propaganda Minister, he pushed a production of one of them, and thus fancies himself to be the great playwright. The play had only a short run."

"And you know him only through the theater?" he asked.

"He wants to sponsor a remake of *The Blue Angel*," she said. She was not looking at him.

"Emma, are you telling me that you associate with Goebbels merely to further your career?"

He could see tears in her eyes when she did look at him briefly. "Don't worry, he has little use for women. As a small and ugly man with a bad leg he had little success with women, was badly hurt by one. He has only one use for any of us."

He was silent. And then it boiled up in him. "Goddamn it, you're not the kind to prostitute yourself just to get a movie role."

"Thank you," she said. She wiped one cheek with the back of her hand. "What kind of woman am I, then?"

"Perhaps I should ask my mother," he said.

"Ah, then we come to it."

"To what, Emma?"

"I saw your mother when I was in Dresden, after she came to you in the Adlon."

"And she told you, I hope, that I think she's crazy."

"Then so are we all, many of us," Emma said. "But I must voice my one great fear, Ed. Please, please never think that I . . . prostituted myself with you in order to enlist you in our effort. In fact, I have been deliberately avoiding any mention of things serious." She paused. "I once read a book about Mexico. Some revolution, some leader. Such leaders come and go so quickly. The federal troops, having captured a group of rebels, forced them to dig their own graves. Then, shortly before being shot to fall into the freshly dug graves, the rebels were allowed one slow, leisurely cigarette. These few days I've been smoking my last, leisurely cigarette." She stood up and walked to the other side of the room, turned to face him. Her expression was determined, businesslike, her voice calm, flat. "Now it is gone, smoked to a butt that is burning my fingers."

"Emma, you have no business being mixed up in this. You and my mother—"

"Oh, but it *is* our business. It is the business of all thinking Germans. Did your mother talk with you about the empty shops in Dresden, the confiscated holdings, the disappearances in the dead of night?"

"No."

"That is only one symptom of the sickness of the Nazi movement. The great danger is war. Germany will lose a large war. But what happens during the war will be more terrible than anything the world has ever seen. You are a newcomer in Germany. You do not know the things that some of us know. What Hitler's party has done to the Jews of Germany—"

"Emma, do you have solid information about Jewish persecution?"

"Anyone with eyes has solid information," she said. "And that is only the beginning. Believe me, Ed, when I say that Hitler will invade Poland. I have reason to know that the plans are drawn. I also know that Himmler and Heydrich have been assigned to carry out an operation with the code name *Ausserordentliche Befriedigungsaktion*."

"Extraordinary Pacification Action," Ed translated. "What does it mean?"

"It means simply that hundreds of thousands of Polish Jews will be slaughtered," she said.

Stay away from the Jewish problem, his boss had told him, unless you run into something too hot to ignore.

"Am I to believe that?" he asked.

"You have only to say the word and you will be allowed to speak with a man whose word, whose sources, you cannot doubt," she said.

"What word am I to say?"

"That you will be our go-between," she said. "That is all we want of you."

"Damn it, I'm just a newsman, and a minor one at that. Why not use someone like Ingo Selmer?"

"He is a good man, a sincere man, but he has been captivated by Hitler's lies," she said. "No, it must be someone who has no ax to grind, whose neutrality cannot be questioned. Your favorable articles about Germany have endeared you to Goebbels. You would not be suspected. The nature of your job would make travel between Berlin and London seem logical. Your press connections and your American nationality would get you access to the man in England we want to reach."

"Churchill?"

"Yes."

"You're depending on a lot of ifs," he said. "What if Chamberlain takes England into the war? Then Churchill will not be in a position of power."

"Don't you remember the Rhineland, Czechoslovakia, Munich?"

"Look, don't condemn Chamberlain. He's only trying to do what any thinking man would do, avoid war."

"But by believing Hitler he has instead assured war," she said.

"All right, Emma, you know that you are perfectly safe in talking with me. Whether or not I decide to go along with you, what you say will be between us. Maybe I've even a little flattered to be considered so important." He paused. "I don't like to think of my girl sleeping with a man just to get information out of him."

"Please, don't," she said.

"But I'll listen."

"We must have assurances that if Hitler is overthrown, the French and the English will immediately recognize our government, that they will not seize a moment of confusion to make a preemptive strike against the Western Wall.''

''What I don't understand is why you want to bypass the present English Government.''

''In 1938 we made contact with the British Government. Several contacts have been made since. We could get no guarantees, no assurances. We have no reason to think that it would be different this time.''

''Perhaps they didn't think you were all that serious, or that you could bring it off.''

''Oh, but we could have. We were much stronger in 1938 than we are now, for then we had two top generals, in command of all the troops we would need. But Chamberlain, by giving Hitler all he wanted in Czechoslovakia, doomed the effort of 1938. There is one other aspect. Although Winston Churchill is a firebrand and had advocated war, he has a good mind. He would not choose war over a respectable peace. And if he could assure that peace by coming to terms with our movement, then when Hitler is captured and put on trial he will easily move into the Government, simply by claiming that it was he who assisted in overthrowing the Nazis. You see how simple it is.''

''As simple as going to the moon,'' he said.

''It *will* work,'' she said. ''And if it doesn't, what have you to lose? When the attempt is made you will be safely out of the country. You will never face any danger.''

''And you?''

She shrugged. ''Not if we are all careful.''

''Emma, let me make a counter proposition. I'll tell my office I want to leave Germany. You will go with me. To the United States. You can pursue your career there. Hell, you can be another Dietrich. And you can forget all of this.''

''Until Hitler bombs New York,'' she said.

"Oh, shit."

"Ed, Ed, you must believe me."

"I'd rather love you, have you all to myself."

"I wish it could be so."

"Why can't it?"

"Because I am German. Because I could not live with my shame if I abandoned my responsibilities now."

"Look, we have only a few hours. Then we go back to Berlin. I don't want to talk about it any more right now. Let's forget the whole screwed-up world. I'll think about what you've said, and I'll give you my decision when I have made it."

"There is little time."

"By the time you come back from your tour, then."

"No. We can't wait that long."

"All right, damn it, before you leave."

"Then you must decide before we reach Berlin, by tomorrow, at the latest."

"Tomorrow, then. Now just shut up and come here."

"My, I do like masterful men," she said, with a sly smile.

They slept most of the way back to Berlin. She insisted that they enter the hotel, in the early-morning hours, separately, but she was back in his arms within minutes, opening the doorway between their rooms. And then it was morning.

He had a cable from his office: ARE YOU RETIRED OR DEAD?

He didn't understand. He'd just sent in two dispatches, the think-piece prompted by his encounter with the Waffen SS and the background story of the Adlon. He cabled: SS AND ADLON PIECES NOT RECEIVED? The answer read: NOTHING IN FIVE DAYS.

Emma was packing. He went to the telephone and called

his contact in the Ministry of Propaganda. "Look, I've sent two dispatches that have not been received in my home office. What's going on?"

"Herr-Raine," Frau Sittenrichter said, "as a matter of fact we've been trying to contact you."

"I've been on a tour of the provinces," he said.

"Unfortunately, both of your dispatches were misplaced. I am so sorry."

She didn't sound sorry at all. He hung up. "The bastards are censoring me," he told Emma. "I thought I was their fair-haired boy. Hell, they weren't that critical of Germany."

"So now you see," she said. "Are you convinced?"

"Emma, I just don't know," he said. "Damn it, I'd like for you and my mother both to forget the whole thing."

"I can't speak for her, but I'm sure she feels as I do," Emma said. "I must leave in an hour."

"All right, all right. I've got to cable the office, tell them what happened."

This time he had to face the assistant manager of the Adlon, Frau Kopf. He went to her office and handed her the brief message and told her he'd like it sent out via the hotel's cable connections immediately.

"You will not object, I trust, if I change a word or two," she said, with a frigid smile.

"I would object strongly," he said. "I want it to say exactly what it says, two previous dispatches censored in Berlin."

"It would be wiser to say, *lost* in Berlin," she said.

"Frau Kopf, by what authority do you tell me I can't wire my office anything I want?" he asked angrily.

"If you insist on sending this defamatory message I will have to consult the authorities," she said sternly.

"Consult them, then," he said. "Contact Dr. Goebbels,

if you have to. Look, that's my job. They think I've been
loafing over here. They haven't received anything from me
for five days.''

"I will be happy to add a comment, an official comment, testifying to the fact that mechanical problems pre-
vented the sending of your two dispatches," Frau Kopf
said. "At no charge, of course."

"All right," he said. "You do that." He'd include a bit
in his story on touring Germany about the difficulty of
communications, and preface the section with the code
phrases he'd agreed upon to inform his editor that the
following passage was false.

"You are a reasonable man," she said, with her cold
smile. "And now there is a message for you."

He took it. It was from the Ministry of Propaganda. A
tour of a model Youth Camp had been arranged for him.
He started to wad it up and throw it into the wastebasket,
changed his mind. He went out into the lobby with his
anger still seething. It was a busy time of day, the lobby
moderately full of people who fell into a sudden silence as
an elevator door opened and Professor Johannes Welke
was led out, being supported on both sides by men in dark
suits. Silently, people gave way. Welke was obviously
weak, unable to walk by himself. As he was half-dragged
nearer, Ed saw that there was blood in the corner of his
mouth.

Ed stepped forward. "Professor Welke," he said. "What
is this?"

"Out of the way, you," said one of the men.

Welke had trouble focusing on Ed's face, then his lips
curled in contempt. "You are very good at your job, Herr
Raine," he said.

Ed moved to follow. He felt a hand on his arm and
turned to see Frau Kopf's stern face. "It is not your
business," she said.

"Where are they taking him?" Ed asked. "What's going on? He's a harmless old man."

The woman smiled. "All these years," she said, "he has been successfully hiding behind the facade of a teacher."

"What do you mean?" Ed asked.

"*Jude,*" she said, with a sneer. "And a pig of the worst kind, pretending to be an honest German, ashamed of his Jewishness."

"They're taking him simply because someone thinks he's of Jewish decent?" Ed asked.

"Because the Jewish swine openly advocates resistance to the legal government," Frau Kopf said.

"Who said?"

"Ah, one never knows, for certain does one?"

He felt desperation and anger, and he almost laughed, because the serious Frau Kopf, so bloodthirstily gloating over the apprehension of a Jewish traitor, had used, in all earnestness, a phrase made famous by happy-go-lucky Fats Waller.

Yes, Fats, he thought, as he went to his room to knock on Emma's door, one never knows, do one? He would have to get to Welke some way, to tell him that it had not been Ed Raine who had denounced him. Hell, he'd had no idea the old man might be Jewish; the matter was almost immaterial to him. Who had done it? Welke had been quite open with him, so given the chance, he might have been equally open with someone else.

"Who could it have been?" he asked Emma.

"Anyone," she said. "A member of the staff, a guest. In such cases the truth does not matter. Doctor Welke has a history of objection to Nazism. A simple denunciation from a 'good' German would be sufficient."

"And what will they do to him?"

"He will be interrogated by the Gestapo and either

killed or put into a prison camp,'' she said matter-of-factly.

"What the hell happened to due process?" he asked heatedly. "What happened to the tenet that a man is innocent until proven guilty?"

"My dear Ed," she said. "Hasn't it sunk in yet that you are in Nazi Germany?"

"This could happen to you? To my mother?"

"Of course."

"To me?"

"It would be more difficult for them with you, since you're an American citizen. Of course, foreign citizens have simply disappeared."

He thought about it for only a moment. "Before you go, tell your man that I will listen to him."

"Thank you," she said.

There was time for only one kiss. He was not allowed to escort her to a taxi in front of the hotel, but saw her last as she went out the door of her room. He went into his own room, locking the connecting door behind him.

He could not forget the look of contempt and hatred the old man had given him. Who had denounced a harmless old man with only a couple of years to live?

She had found it to be laughably easy. The old man, flattered to be singled out by a beautiful young girl, had talked his guts out. She had merely to prime him by pretending to be in doubt about the intentions of Hitler's Germany and he opened like a rotten melon. And later, over wine in his room, she flattered him more by asking about his personal history. She spent two hours with him. She was bored by his silly memories, but as he began to talk about ancient history, the history of his proud and rich family, of which he was the last, she found something quite interesting.

"The funny thing about it is," the Professor said, mellowed by the wine and his attractive listener, "that the family fortune was founded by a non-German—a Russian, as a matter of fact. Came to Germany in the early eighteen hundreds after a pogrom in Russia." That was all she needed. Otto Schellen's staff took only hours to trace the history of Herr Doctor Professor Johannes Welke's family, the founder of the line had changed his name to Welke. Originally, the name had been Welkenstein.

"You have done well," Otto Schellen told her, over a sumptuous dinner in his private apartment.

"They should all be exterminated, the Jewish pigs," she said, around a bite of tender filet of sole.

"I think you deserve a reward for such success on your first assignment," Schellen said. "Have you any suggestions?"

"I dare not be so forward," she said, looking at him with sultry meaning.

"Ah," he said.

He was blond, Aryan, strong—but, she had to admit, as she was delivered back to the Adlon just after midnight in a chauffered car, Ed Raine, the half-American, was more man.

She had her instructions. Actually, Schellen knew, Johannes Welke had not been active for years. Keep a low profile, she had been told, keep your eyes and ears open. Soon, Schellen knew, he would have to put others on the job at the Adlon. The security of the Führer would not be entirely in his hands when Hitler visited the hotel to observe the Norwegian acrobatic troup, but that would not prevent him from doing everything in his power to ferret out any dangerous types before the Führer's personal security men moved in. That was his job.

For Margo, it was a glorious night. She could not sleep for her excitement, and wished for the presence of even

Karl, of any man, and especially of Ed Raine. Once, twice, she reached for the telephone to call Raine's room, but the hour was late. Besides, she had her thoughts.

"You will not go directly home to Norway after the tour," Schellen had told her. "You will be detained by my men on a pretext, which I shall plan. This will quiet your family, and put off the Norwegian Government. After you are released to go back to Norway, you will have undergone some rather intensive training, to be better able to do your work."

"Oh, yes," she'd said. "Oh, thank you. Yes, it is exactly what I want."

15

ED SPENT THE morning of August 21, a Monday, in his room, putting the finishing touches on what had come to seem an unimportant story. As he wrote about the seemingly happy and simple Germans of Bavaria, he felt he was writing an inane fairy tale.

It was not until he put that aside and began an account of the arrest of a gentle old professor of philosophy that he aroused any interest in writing. He typed three pages; writing them was a catharsis. He knew, however, that he probably would be unable to get the story out of the country intact.

He tore the story into shreds and put it into the wastebasket; then, with sudden inspiration, he began writing again. He was angry—angry for the Professor, angry because it was necessary for two women he loved to risk their lives, angry because he had been drawn into it, angry because his dispatches had been held. He wrote an account of the arrest of a dangerous enemy of the Reich, the sinister and highly experience rabble-rouser, Herr Doctor Professor Johannes Welke, throwing in phrases such as ''the Gestapo, heroic guardians of the Reich against its notorious internal enemies.'' And he put in the code phrase that would tell his editor that the whole thing was pure bullshit. Confidently, he took it to the cable office.

He had to grin when he received a call from Frau Sittenrichter at the Propaganda Ministry, congratulating him on the ''fine account of a necessary police action.'' They'd swallowed it. If they could read his asinine and cynical prose and call it good propaganda for the Reich, they were stupider than he'd have believed. He was not the first to be aware of certain blindnesses in the Nazi thought pattern, not the first to underestimate them.

He was nervous, expectant. Emma had stressed the necessity for quick action, and the day went by without anyone contacting him.

In the early evening he found himself wandering into the cellar bar. The foreign correspondents were still restless, but somehow more expectant. Things had been too quiet. Something was impending, but there were no leads. They talked among themselves, drowned their frustrations with brandy, good white beer.

Ed had coaxed John Graff Stanton away from his spot at the bar to a table. Others came and went. Ed was drinking lightly, his mind whirling with thoughts of Emma, of the agreement he'd made with her, wondering why something didn't come to him. Now that he'd agreed to enter into the conspiracy, he was anxious to begin. He looked up with interest, however, when Stanton introduced him to Dr. Karl Silex, once a foreign correspondent and now rubber-stamp editor of a Nazi mouthpiece newspaper, *Deutsche Allgemeine Zeitung*.

''Herr Silex,'' Stanton said soberly to Ed, ''thinks that the greatest danger to the world is Bolshevism coming from Soviet Russia.''

"Ah, gentlemen," Silex said, taking the offered seat and ordering beer, "it's too pleasant a night to talk politics."

"Is there anything else to talk about?" Stanton asked.

The German state radio provided a muscial background, waltzes, gay beer-garden tunes. Stanton tried to steer the German editor into talking about the chances of war, but Silex, with a pleasant smile, refused to be drawn out. When the music was halted in mid-phrase, he turned his head, with the others, to listen. A calm, cultured German voice announced that Germany and Russia had signed a nonaggression pact. The news hit the occupants of the bar like a mortar shell, leaving stunned silence as the music once again wafted out from the speakers.

"My God," Stanton said, "did you know about this, Silex?"

The editor's face was pale. "Of course," he said.

"Silex, you're lying," Stanton said roughly. "You had no idea. Hell, nobody had any idea." He killed his drink while the German tried to regain his composure. "Well, the old boy's done it now," Stanton went on. "He's fallen right into old Joe Stalin's hands. Now Russia can sit back, hope that Hitler is stupid enough to go to war with England and France, and step in and take over what's left after we beat each other to death and bleed the whole Western world into anemia."

"On the contrary," Silex said. "It is, after all, a natural partnership."

"You have *got* to be shitting me," Stanton said. "For years you've preached hatred for all things Communist. Hell, you people fought the Bolsheviks in the streets of Berlin in 1918."

"Things change," Silex said weakly, and then more strongly. "Now the Western allies will have to think twice before trying to deny the Reich her *Lebensrecht*." He smiled, having had time to reason it out. "The Führer has, as you Americans might say, put Russia in his bag. With a treaty between the two most powerful countries of Europe, England and France will have to avoid war at all costs."

"Boy," Stanton said grimly, "I don't think you know how dangerous it is to bag a bear. Bears have claws and teeth. Your Führer had better watch out that the Russian bear doesn't come tearing and clawing out of that bag just when the situation is at its worst, like when Germany is bogged down fighting the French and the English on a Western Front."

"But, don't you see?" Silex leaned forward to emphasize his point. "There can be no war now."

"No," Ed said. "Until this moment I'd have agreed with you, but now I'm damned sure that there will be a war." Unless, he was thinking, the conspiracy worked.

The terms of the Russo-German pact were made public in the early hours of the morning. No one had tried to sleep. Cable offices were busy. The radio correspondents were fighting for available facilities to send the news back to England, to the United States, all over the world. Speculation was rife. Some thought that Stalin's siding with Hitler would kill the Communist movement outside of Russia. French Communists, for example, had been fed a constant diet of hatred for Nazism. Some thought Stalin had made the best deal. Stanton pointed out that Hitler had never kept an international agreement when it became convenient or desirable to break it. Had he not signed such a treaty with Poland in 1934?

The Germans in the Adlon bar were in high spirits, saying that Britain wouldn't dare fight now. The morning papers, reacting swiftly, praised the treaty, led by Goebbels's *Angriff*, which had been the most rabid Red-hater of all the newspapers.

Ed walked the avenue, rode the subway, the streetcars.

Everyone was reading the papers and their comments were almost universally favorable. One of their greatest fears had been put to rest. No longer did they face the threat of a war such as the war of 1914, with Germany surrounded on all fronts.

As he returned toward the Adlon, his eyes red from lack of sleep, he heard them coming, a V formation of Stuka bombers, flying so low that he could see the sharkish grin of the air intake under the prop, the eaglelike look of the nonretractable landing gear, aerodynamically designed fenders coming down over the wheels like the feathers on the leg of a bird of prey. He halted, shaded his eyes with his hand, watched the dive bombers fade away to the east.

He had not heard, over the growl of the fading engines, the approach of Colonel Wolf von Stahlecker. When he looked down from the sky the Colonel was there, beside him, also watching the planes.

"East, toward Poland," Ed said grimly. Von Stahlecker nodded. "Tonight?" Ed asked.

"No, not yet," von Stahlecker said. "He is not quite ready." He nodded toward the I. G. Farben building across the street from the Adlon. Uniformed men were installing a long-barreled antiaircraft gun. "Will you walk with me, Herr Raine?"

They strolled side by side, von Stahlecker swinging his walking stick. "It is a pleasant day for traveling," he said.

"Colonel," Ed said, "a lot of people are thinking about traveling."

"And I understand the weather is nice in England."

Ed looked at him quickly.

"Just smile and nod as if we were discussing the weather," von Stahlecker said. "You will see Churchill at his country home. You will tell him that we are in readiness, that we have the support of two army corps and of many high officers, plus enough civilian support to assure a more or less peaceful transfer of power.''

"May I say, Colonel, that I was a bit doubtful about all this? I feel better, knowing that a man of your caliber is in it.''

"I am merely one of many, a small and relatively unimportant cog,'' von Stahlecker said. "You will have no trouble getting on the afternoon flight. In fact, your bookings have been made and your tickets purchased. They will be delivered to you at noon in the Adlon bar. Now listen carefully.

"Here are names that will be familiar to Churchill. First, our new government will be headed by Admiral Canaris, chief of the Abwehr of OKW. He will be supported militarily by General Erwin von Witzleben, who has all of the troops in the Wehrkreis III in his command. We will immediately control Berlin and all surrounding areas. Fortunately, most of the fanatics, the SS units, for example, are deployed along the Polish frontier. We will have time to prepare, should they fight. We anticipate, however, that there will be only limited fighting among German units. We will strike hard and fast. Among those who will be killed will be Himmler, Goebbels, Göring. We will seize the Reichsministry and other agencies dominated by Nazis in the first blow. The communications facilities will be in our hands, and we will immediately inform the German people that, to avoid war, we have seized Hitler and are holding him for trial.''

"Colonel, you make it sound quite easy,'' Ed said.

"A well-planned operation always looks easy,'' von Stahlecker said. "It is not. Here are more names. Although he is not yet decided, we expect General von Brauchitsch to join us immediately after the first blows are struck. Fabian von Schlabrendorff is, of course, with us. His name will give Mr. Churchill some confidence in us, for he was active in the abortive plot of 1938, and the fact that he is the great-grandson of the man who was the personal physician of Queen Victoria gives him sentimental English ties. We have the backing of the Catholics in Germany. In fact, Josef Müller has been in touch with the Vatican. He has assured us that the Pope will come out immediately in favor of our new government.''

"Colonel, it sounds good," Ed said.

"Please emphasize the fact that we have adequate military power," von Stahlecker said. "In addition to the troops of the Third Army Corps in the Berlin area, we have a panzer division ready to move and a crack infantry division in Potsdam. Your job is to assure Mr. Churchill that this time we will not fail. This time we will do the job."

They had walked past the Adlon toward the Brandenburg Gate. Von Stahlecker paused. "You are going to England to find the reaction of the British to the Russo-German pact," he said. "Your recent dispatches have put you back in the good graces of the Ministry of Propaganda. You will have no difficulty. We will expect you back on the morning flight."

"How do you know Churchill will see me?" Ed asked.

"I will leave that assurance to others," von Stahlecker said. "Now, my friend, we must part."

"One more question, Colonel," Ed said. "When is it to be?"

"It is most unfortunate that you will miss the performance—a special command performance, by the way—of the Norwegian acrobatic troup."

"Friday night, then," Ed said.

"The morning of Saturday, the twenty-sixth of August, will see a new and different Germany." Von Stahlecker turned and walked away, slowly swinging his walking stick as if there were nothing more important on his mind than a morning constitutional walk along the bustling avenue.

Ed returned to the hotel and sneaked in a couple of hours' sleep, leaving a call for eleven A.M. When he awoke he felt as if some small and furry animal had hibernated in his mouth. He missed his Listerine. The supply he'd brought with him was gone, and the German pharmacy could supply only a German brand that tasted vaguely of gasoline and manure heaps. He had a sandwich in the bar. His journalistic colleagues would be busy, he thought, as he should be, for the bar was not its usual, bustling place. Or else they were all asleep still, after a night of work. There were a few Germans, and at one table a group from the British Embassy. He sat alone, wondering who would come to him to deliver his airline tickets. It seemed to be an unnecessary risk, for he was fully capable of making his own bookings and buying his own tickets. He could figure only that the messenger might have more information for him. He didn't judge Colonel von Stahlecker to be a careless man.

Although he had not formally met the man who dominated the conversation at the table where the embassy people sat, he knew him to be Sir George Ogilvie Forbes, number-two man among the British delegation to Berlin, With him were what seemed to be minor functionaries and a cute little blonde in a pillbox hat who caught his eye and smiled. He nodded and lowered his eyes. He looked up again when the British group stood, their chairs scraping on the hardwood floor. Sir George nodded. He nodded back. The group went out the door with fine protocol, falling into place behind the bossman. The blonde remained at the table, and when, after the group of men had gone, Ed looked her way, there was that inviting smile again. Before he could look away she lifted her glass and made an invitation that could not be misconstrued. She was asking him to come to her table and have a drink with her. He looked around. The Germans there seemed unlikely candidates for his contact, but he didn't want to get tied up with some British blonde and make contact more difficult. He smiled at the blonde and she lifted her glass again.

The spy business, he thought wryly, was getting complicated. He didn't want to be with the blonde when his contact came in, but others in the bar had seen the invitation, and he wondered what they would think if he didn't take the girl up on it. So he stood, walked over to the table.

"It seems I've been deserted," she said. "Have the afternoon off, you know. Time for a bit of the good old hands-across-the-sea, don't you think? Friendship between English-speaking peoples."

"Who could resist such a lovely hand?" he asked. He started to sit across the table from her.

"No, no, that won't do," she said. "Hate talking all the way across a table." She patted the chair next to her. He smiled and took the chair. Her hand made a quick movement as he sat, and the chair, which had been empty, now contained, as his rear connected with it, a flat packet.

"Just smile and tell me how beautiful I am and put it into your trousers pocket later," she said, leaning toward him with a charming sway of her shoulder-length blond hair.

"Well, I'll be damned," he said, grinning.

"I know you, but you're at a disadvantage," she said. "I am, believe it or not, Bea Goodpasture."

"Oh, I believe it," he said.

"And any remarks with bovine references," she said, looking down at her ample bust, "will be considered in very poor taste, and will not, I assure you, be original. I've heard them all. I'd like to graze upon that pasture, all that rot."

"To risk displeasure, it was well put," he said, still grinning.

"Cheeky Yank," she said.

She had almond-shaped eyes the color of milk chocolate, a pert little nose, and all-English creamy skin, a trace of sun-red on her cheekbones and the tip of her nose.

A waiter came and cleared the debris from the table and while Bea was ordering another drink, Ed used the moment to slip the packet into his rear pocket along with his handkerchief. When he stood his suitcoat would cover it. He ordered gin and tonic.

"Cheers," she said, lifting her glass. "Templehof, flight two-nine-five, four-thirty P.M.: ETO London, seven-forty-five. You'll be met."

"Two-nine-five," he said.

"Lucky sod," she said. "You may be taking one of the last flights between Berlin and London that is not carrying bombs."

"Miss Goodpasture, what's your part in this?" he asked.

"I just take orders," she said. "My middle name is Ernestina, not Mata Hari. I'm the all-round girl Friday at the embassy."

"Then you know nothing?"

"Look, old fellow, we spies don't compare notes, after all." She smirked at him, her lower lip protruding attractively. "I'm curious as all Billy Hell, I'll have to admit."

"Who told you to contact me?"

"The Sir, himself. You saw him leave."

There was a reason for his questions. Everywhere he turned he found more and more people who were aware of the plot against Hitler. He wondered, if the British Embassy knew of it, why there was a need for a nondiplomatic messenger.

Bea seemed to answer his unspoken questions. "Ours not to reason why, and all that jive," she said. "I love that American slang."

"Reet," he said.

"And Benny Goodman, oh, Lord. Do you cut a mean rug?"

"If I have scissors," he said.

"Crikey, I thought all Americans jitterbugged." She moved her shoulders to an imaginary beat. The effect, at that area extending from her little chest, was spectacular. "I was hoping when you get back that you'd teach me some new steps. Nero fiddled; why can't we dance while the whole world burns?"

"You're very cynical," he said.

"When was the last time you were in love?" she asked, with a suddenness that made him laugh.

"Oh, this morning, I suppose," he said, thinking of Emma.

"Good for you. I love romantic men, especially rich American ones."

"Miss Bea," he said, "I think I already see that you're too much for me, too smart, too articulate."

"And I hate smart-mouthed Americans," she said. She patted her hair, fluffed it over one ear. "Well, I think we've made it obvious that we've become acquainted. My room or yours?"

He felt a flash of interest, and then a repulsion. He'd fallen into two beds in the past few days. He thought, rather cynically, that if things continued as they were going he'd lose his faith in womanhood. Besides, there was only one bed he was interested in falling into, and the occupant was away, on a tour of Germany.

"Coming?" she asked, standing.

"Not this time, Miss Bea," he said.

She flushed. "Oh, I say, you weren't told?" She sat back down. "We're to make it look as if we made, ah, a romantic contact, and then disappear into a room for a bit of the old slap and tickle. You didn't really think?"

"No, of course not," he said, rising, telling himself that he'd made an ass of himself.

"Actually," she said, "it will have to be your room, for we lowly embassy employees can't afford the grandeur of the Adlon."

She inspected the room, walking with a tiny, slim grace on heels that made her tall enough to come to his Adam's apple. Without them, he estimated, she would have been able merely to lean and place her cheek on his chest.

"Not bad," she said, "but I'd expected something much grander."

"This is one of the working-class rooms. Side exposure," he said.

He took the airline tickets from his pocket. He was booked for an early-morning return flight. He sighed, envisioning a night with very little sleep. Any man who could sleep on an aircraft was a better man than he. He wanted to be awake, in case the thing decided to do a belly flop in the middle of the Channel, so that he could see the shark that would eat him.

"We should stay, oh, about a half-hour, I suppose," she said. "Then I'll go out with my hair and lipstick slightly awry."

"You might as well have a seat," he said. She took the large chair and he sat in front of the window. "Tell me about Bea Goodpasture," he said.

"What's to tell?" She gave him that radiant little smile. "Suffolk. Father army, lived through the 1918 war, one of the lucky ones. Panting to be called up again to fight the bloody Huns, to give them a proper lesson this time. Two brothers. One RAF, the other in the ministry."

"Where is Suffolk? Is it a large city?"

"It's a shire—a county, you dolt," she said without malice. "We live in a small coastal village called Lowestoft.

Fishing and shipping, you know. Bloody great target for the bombers when it starts.''

"You're so sure it's going to start?''

"Old Winnie, bless him, will use that golden voice of his to call the British Empire to attention and launch them into the guns with a stiff upper lip, firing salvos of oratory all the while.''

"Do you know Churchill?''

"Lord, no,'' she said. "But I fear that I'm as bloody-minded as he. For years he's been sounding off, warning of a coming war, the conscience of England, and all the while we've been minding our gardens and supplying bloody Chamberlain with new bumbershoots to protect his delicate head from the German bombs when they start falling.'' She sighed. "Good show my pop can't hear me. Ladies don't say bloody, you know.''

"What is it with that word? I never did understand why it was so bloody vulgar.''

"Conditioning,'' she said. " 'Fuck' used to be an acceptable word. Good, solid, common Anglo-Saxon word.''

"The only word I can't really accept from a woman is also a fairly mild one,'' he said.

"Which is that?''

He grinned. "Shit. I know, it's not all that bad. But coming from the lips of a woman, well, it just sounds bad, that's all.''

"And what is your favorite word for a woman's lips?'' she teased.

"Yes,'' he said.

"It's a nice word.'' She frowned. "I don't use it much, you know. Never have. Thought about it a lot, but never have.''

"Are you always so frank?'' he asked with a little laugh.

"Oh, frankness is the best policy," she said. "Serious-ly. Now take yourself. I know you. You're a gentleman. If you thought I might, ah, say yes, you'd probably ask me to say it. But when I tell you, quite frankly and openly, that I'm a virgin, there's this ingrained honor in you that immediately cools off any ideas you may have. It's a somewhat of a paradox, isn't it? Men want virgins, or so I've been led to believe, but they will fall all over them-selves to keep a girl virgin. I love to—how do you Ameri-can's say it? To smooch. And I've got a bloody short fuse. But I just let my fella know in advance that I'm an innocent little virgin, and then I can let myself go, get all randy and panty, and he protects the honor of both of us."

His laugh was genuine. "One day you'll make a mistake and get all randy with a real cad."

"Then his punishment will be that I'll not only bleed all over him, I'll go all weepy and then he'll have to marry me." She looked thoughtful. "I've given it much consid-eration. I don't think I should like being married to a true gentleman. A bit of the cad in a man makes him more interesting, don't you think?"

"Bea, are you just making all this up to pass a half-hour?"

"To be perfectly frank—see, there I go again. I'm wondering how much of the cad there is in you."

"When was the last time you were in love?" he asked.

"Oh, just now," she said.

"You are weird. I had a friend who pronounced it we-erd. That's what you are, we-erd, we-erd, we-erd."

"I would prefer to be called eccentric. Typical British quality, you know."

"I'm not sure I know how to spell it."

"Ah, well, then, back to business." She checked her watch. "Fifteen minutes left in which to muss my hair and disturb my lipstick." She walked toward the bath.

"I have some experience in the field of mussing hair and disturbing lipstick. Be glad to help."

"Thanks, but I can manage it."

She came out, running her fingers through her hair.

"Does it have to be exactly thirty minutes?" he asked.

"Well, no. Have you any wine, by the way?"

He produced wine. She sat, crossing her legs demurely, sipped.

"Bea, what will happen with you if there's a war?" he asked.

"Oh, being diplomatic staff, I'll have a free ride home. I'll be placed in some stuffy office, I suppose. Dreadful thought. I'd rather be skiing, or swimming, or traveling."

"What exactly did they tell you when you were chosen to deliver the tickets to me?"

"Just what I've said. That's all."

"I don't understand why it was necessary to make such a big deal of it. Why couldn't I have arranged the tickets?"

"Well, there are a lot of people trying to get out of Berlin just now. Getting bookings on a flight is, at best, dicey. I suppose this trip of yours must be rather important. And then, too, the embassy people rarely get to play at being spies."

When it was time, exactly thirty minutes, she finished her wine. "Well, good luck, American." She paused at the doorway. "I've been wondering if I should ask you to call me when you get back."

He had decided that she was a compulsive flirt. "Should I?" he asked.

"Good question," she said. She mused down at the pointed toes of her pumps. "Perhaps you shouldn't."

"Whatever you say."

"On the other hand, if you don't, we'd never know, would we?"

16

ED RAINE CARRIED only a small case with one change of clothing, writing materials in with the clothing, and his portable typewriter. With plenty of time to spare, he went to the lobby, informed the desk that he would be away overnight. Wolf von Stahlecker came in through the front entrance as he started toward it.

"Ah, good day, Herr Raine," von Stahlecker said in a loud voice. "Surely you are not leaving us."

"Only temporarily, Colonel," he said. "The boss wants me to jump over to England and get the British reaction to the treaty with Russia."

"Ah, I see. I trust you'll have a pleasant journey. I hope you find our British friends not too upset."

There was, he felt, something on von Stahlecker's mind. The Colonel confirmed it. "If you have time before your plane, may I have the pleasure of buying you a *bon voyage* drink?"

Ed checked his watched, saw the meaningful look from

von Stahlecker. "A quick one would be welcome, Colonel."

They found a table in the bar, waited for service in silence. When the drinks were delivered von Stahlecker made a toast, leaning across the table toward Ed. When he'd finished the toast he spoke quickly and quietly. "I will drop two envelopes on the floor. Pick them up for me, but give only one back. Keep the brown one."

Ed felt a pang of disquiet. The mission, if it could be dignified with such a name, had been quite simple. As an American, he had freedom of travel. And, since all the information for Churchill was in his memory, even a search would find nothing. Now they were bringing in something unexpected. Nevertheless, he obeyed orders and when von Stahlecker knocked the two envelopes off the table with a natural-looking motion of his arm in the act of lifting his glass, Ed bent, spotted the brown envelope, stuck it under him in his chair, and returned the other to the Colonel.

"It was not my idea," von Stahlecker said, with a smile. "Others with more rank than I thought that our man might not be convinced by the mere word of an American newsman."

"Damn it, I've made no provisions for this," Ed said.

"There is little danger. Chances are a thousand to one against your being searched."

"And if I lose the thousand-to-one chance?"

"You are carrying your portable typewriter?" Ed nodded. "Is it not customary to wind a sheet of paper around the platen, to reduce the impact of the keys on the rubber?"

"I do it, as a matter of fact. But I still don't like it."

"Please, it is deemed necessary." He glanced at his watch. "You still have time. Perhaps you forgot something in your room?"

He left von Stahlecker sitting at the table, rushed to the desk and asked for his key, saying he'd left his shaving kit behind. In the room he carefully opened the envelope, read the contents. He flushed. There was enough in that letter to hang a dozen people—and Ed Raine was one of them. He beat down a great temptation to tear up the letter and flush it down the toilet and forget the whole thing. Oh, well. He placed the letter atop a sheet of clean white paper and fed both into the typewriter, the letter underneath. The typing on the letter did not show through, and he was as ready as he'd ever be.

Fortunately, there was still time. The afternoon was sultry and still. The taxi had all its windows down, and he sweated out a long wait as a panzer unit rumbled across an intersection, tank tracks clanking and digging up the pavement, half-tracks, weapons carriers, light tanks, and men in coal-scuttle helmets sitting erect and still as death on the troop carriers.

He was not sure whether it was the heat or his own fear that made him sweat as he checked out through passport and customs. Amazingly, he answered questions in a calm voice, telling the bored officials that his stay in London would be brief, possibly only overnight. A rubber stamp began to bang down on his papers as the official rattled off a list of contraband items; to each item he answered, "*Nein, nein.*" He waited for the search, his stomach in knots—and then he was handed his papers and it was all over.

It seemed a very short time before he saw the lights of London from the window of the sleek German airliner. And it was unbelievable to think that soon other German planes equally sleek but vastly more deadly might be flying the same route toward a blacked-out city.

The customs and immigration people at Heathrow were different in looks, in dress, but almost equal in attitude to the German officials. He went through the nothing-to-declare line, carrying the incriminating typewriter in one hand, his light bag in the other, hoping that he would not be stopped now. Not now. He knew that he didn't face a prison in England for carrying the letter, but he could imagine the mess, the explaining, the possible loss of secrecy, and the resulting danger to a lot of people across the Channel, across France.

"Mr. Raine, is it?" he was asked by a tight lipped, officious Englishman in civilian clothing as he entered the main terminal. He nodded. "Come with me, sir." He went. A quick walk through the terminal, into the peaceful night, sounds of planes taking off or landing, of automobiles with the distinctive little British horns, no words, no questions from the Englishman as he held the door of an aging Rolls and then joined Ed in the back seat.

"Are things arranged?" Ed asked, when they got underway, the driver closed off from them by the glass partition.

"Yes."

"Where are we going, then?"

"The man you're to see is not in London."

Ed was silent for a moment. The man did not volunteer information, and Ed, feeling a little bit melodramatic, would not lower himself to ask. He could be as tight-lipped as the most tight-assed Limey, if need be.

It was a rather long drive. It ended in the early hours of morning at a country estate, the Rolls turning into a tree-lined drive, roaring up a long lane, coming to a halt in front of an impressive manor house. The silent man who had not even volunteered his name escorted him in, past a butler straight out of an old movie.

"Has he been up all night?" Ed asked, as he was led down a hallway.

"I wouldn't know, sir," the man said.

The man knocked on a door. A voice called out, "You may entah." And he was inside a study of rather generous proportions, a book-lined, dark-paneled man's room, and Churchill was rising to meet him. He didn't look as if he'd been up all night, nor was there any puffy evidence of having newly been aroused from sleep. He just looked like the pictures Ed had seen—a short man, somewhat portly, with that bulldog face. Even at that hour there was a cigar in his mouth, a glass of what looked like brandy in his hand.

"Welcome to Chartwell," Churchill said, giving Ed his hand in a firm grip.

"Thank you for seeing me, sir," he said. "It means a lot to a lot of people."

"Yes, yes. Well, let's have at it, if you don't mind," Churchill said, turning his back to pour Ed a glass of brandy. The snifter looked to be Waterford, heavy, expensive, beautifully cut. Churchill sat down in a big chair, motioned for Ed to do the same.

The cocky cigar puffed dark smoke and Churchill removed it from his mouth with a typical, jerky gesture. "It is my understanding, Mr. Raine, that you have still another message from the German Fantasy Corps."

He didn't have an answer to that, only a sinking feeling. If that was Churchill's attitude, then his trip had been for nothing, and the desperate people in Germany who were fighting against all odds to stop a war had planned for nothing.

"Mind you, if there is something new, something of value, I will listen." He took a sip of brandy. "As a matter of fact, since I have been up all night and am rather desperately in need of sleep, I will listen with both ears to get this over as quickly as possible."

"Sir," Ed said, "I'll try to make it as brief as possible." He leaned toward the typewriter case, which he'd carried in with him, wondering at the time at the trust of the household to let him enter, a stranger, carrying two bags of unknown contents. He rolled the letter from the platen, separated it from the blank sheet, handed it to Churchill, and sat back down, pulling on his own brandy as Churchill glanced at it.

"Von Stahlecker, eh?" Churchill asked, looking up. "And Canaris. Other than that, the same old list of dreamers."

"Sir, I think it's different, this time," Ed said. "I know a few of those people. I know they're dedicated and quite serious. They are well organized. As they tell you in the letter, they have the means and the will to accomplish their purpose."

"I daresay," Churchill said. "Just as they did in 1938."

"Sir, they're putting antiaircraft guns atop Berlin buildings," Ed said.

Churchill snorted, stood to the straight height of his short body. "I don't know you, Mr. Raine, but I have to be, perhaps, a bit cruel. I confess that I see you as just another well-intentioned amateur with a cause, to save the peace." He paused, chuckled. "And that description covers Neville fairly well. There's Ingo Selmer. He's been scampering back and forth for weeks."

"Mr. Churchill, unlike Ingo Selmer, I am not talking with Hitler and Göring in Germany. I'm talking with men and women who are ready to risk their lives, take up weapons."

He was talking to Churchill's back. He talked earnestly, quickly, spelling it out, telling about his talks with von Stahlecker, trying to make it sound convincing, and in the end he realized how flimsy it sounded. He was just a newsman, and when it came right down to it he had only von Stahlecker's word about the plan. He ended by telling Churchill that all the plotters asked was an assurance from him that in the event of a successful overthrow of Hitler England would not march on the Western Wall while the new government was trying to get settled in.

"But this I don't quite understand," Churchill said. "I am not one to underestimate my own importance, but I am not, after all, Prime Minister—yet. Perhaps you should take your letter to Neville."

"Those who are involved feel that you're the only man in England who is not blinded by Hitler's rhetoric, by his promises. What the principals of the plan fear most is that Chamberlain and the French will stage another Munich. They feel that even though you are not Prime Minister . . . yet"—he paused—"you nevertheless are the only man who can understand the situation. These people are sure that Hitler intends to go into Poland, and they're equally sure that the British and French will fight and that, in the end, it will mean a greater defeat for Germany than in 1918."

"With that last, I agree," Churchill said. "Perhaps I'm a victim of my own prejudices. The Hun is either at one's feet or at one's throat. I've said you are an amateur, Mr. Raine, and no hard feelings, I hope. Suppose, just suppose, that you are being used, that this entire fantasy is merely a carefully devised effort to buy time, to throw us further off our guards—not, God knows, that many of us have our guards up as yet."

"I can't believe that. My own mother is a member of the group."

"Ah, and is your mother so wise that she, too, could not be deluded?" He poured more brandy, offered the fine decanter to Ed, who shook his head. "We are sitting here on this tight little island living in a fool's paradise. There is not *one* man in ten who understands the nature of modern warfare as practiced by the Germans. We have our watery moat, the English Channel. And although many of us have flown to the Continent in a matter of mere minutes, we have not absorbed the lesson involved.''

"Isn't that another reason why we should do all we can to stop a war?'' Ed asked.

"I think you Yanks have a saying, young man, something about not trying to teach an old dog how to suck eggs.'' He managed to smile at his own joke and still look stern at the same time.

"Sorry, sir. It's just—''

"It's just that you think everything is so confounded simple. I write you a letter. Your German heroes overthrow Hitler and there is peace in the world. Have you thought about the Russians? Why on God's earth do you imagine that Joe Stalin signed a formal treaty with an avowed enemy? He's buying time. Everyone seems intent on buying time. My dear young man, any student of history can see what is happening. The German nation—not just Hitler and his Nazis, but the German nation—has once again reverted to character and is setting forth on a conquest, and it is my unconfirmed belief that Uncle Joe signed the treaty in the hope of sharing the spoils. If Hitler does go into Poland, do you think the Russians would sit calmly, treaty or no treaty, and let Hitler put panzer division on their borders? It will not be the first time that great powers have made a clandestine agreement to partition poor Poland. It happened in the days of the German kings and the Russian emperors. Moreover, the terms of the treaty as we understand it give Joe Stalin a free hand in the eastern Baltic and recognize Russia's interests in Bessarabia. Herr Hitler won't be able to live with that. He'll break that treaty as surely as I'm standing here, as soon as it is convenient, and I'm not sure all this isn't a part of a plot to neutralize France and Great Britain.

"No, hear me out. I know the man. He's devious, not intelligent, but devious, like a rabid fox. He hates both

English and French, but he hates the Slavic peoples more. He at least considers us British as human. Perhaps he's even well-read enough to know that in many cases we're cousins. Hell's bells, man, the old queen provided wives and husbands for most of the royal families in Europe, and that didn't stop her grandson, Wilhelm, from starting the Great War.

"Most certainly, I believe that Hitler does not want war, at this time, with England. Well, perhaps now is the best time. It won't be easy, but we can deal with him now. We can handle Germany now, even as unprepared as we are, much better than later, when he's absorbed the oil and coal countries in the Balkans, when he's gone against the Russians, whom he considers to be subhuman."

"Sir, you can't mean that." The feeling of hopelessness grew.

Churchill stopped pacing, stopped the grand, oratorical gestures. "No, no," he said. "I don't, actually, *want* war. I am tempted, at times, to silence, to waiting, to see if I am right and Hitler, with peace on the Western Front, would attack Russia and thus bleed the German nation as white as the snows that conquered Napoleon in 1807." He sighed. "You are right in one respect. I suspect that I will become Prime Minister soon, a war Prime Minister. Let me say this. You may take my assurances to your people. Tell them that we do not, of course, want war. Assure them that we are determined, however, to march if Hitler goes into Poland. Tell them that if they do succeed in over-throwing Herr Hitler we will immediately recognize them, that we will enter immediately into peace talks based on the restitution of seized territories, the Rhineland, Czechoslovakia."

"Sir, if I may speak. There are military men involved. Those last conditions—well, must they be put up front? Couldn't such things wait until afterward? I'm sure you'd find the new government willing to discuss a fair way to settle all questions.''

''It is a basic tenet of justice that a criminal must not profit from his crime,'' Churchill said firmly. ''You came to me. I gave you my conditions. If you want more than that, go to Neville. Tell him to think of German planes over the Tower, over the Halls of Parliament. He'll probably agree with you that avoiding war is worthwhile, even at the expense of the Czechs. Tell your military men what I have said, and assure them that I am in a position to back up my words. Tell them that I, too, think of the Luftwaffe over London, but remind them of the toll our lads will take during each raid. We will knock out one-fifth of the bomber forces on each raid, and soon there'll be no more raids. Tell them that within two weeks their airmen will find daylight too deadly in English skies, and then we will have only random and uneffective night bombings with which to contend.

''Meanwhile, remind them that the Royal Navy still exists, and can bottle up the German fleet, such as it is, and destroy it piecemeal. Remind them that no war could be won without a successful invasion of England, and that was accomplished for the last time in 1066, if they read history. And in 1066 there was no Royal Navy to blast any invasion force from the water, no Royal Air Force to cleanse the skies of German planes. Remind them that it is the nation with a navy that has the advantage and the means to move an invading army. They could, at best, put a few hundred parachute troops onto British soil, and that's supposing that they can move across France and the Low Countries without losing a good part of their forces. We can take care of parachutists by hitting them over the head with beer bottles.''

Ed started to open his mouth, was silenced with a fierce glare.

"I am not finished," Churchill said. "We are determined to protect the sovereignty of Poland. We will march if Hitler violates Poland. We will make amends for his aggressions against other peoples. We will gladly avoid war, but they, your brave, determined Germans, must want peace as much as we, and it must apply to all. Am I understood?"

"I understand," Ed said.

"Then I must retire."

"Will you send a letter?" Ed asked.

Churchill mused, chewing on his cigar. "I think not. I don't think it would be wise. My word is enough."

"A letter would be helpful, sir."

"Yes, all right, then. You will write it down." He got paper and pen for Ed, paced. He dictated the terms as outlined to Ed, then continued. "For the benefit of any who might doubt the will of England to fight, here are some of the things currently being done in preparation for just such an event. As of tomorrow, the Admiralty is given authority to requisition twenty-five merchantmen for conversion to armed merchant cruisers and to equip trawlers with antisubmarine gear. We are calling up thousands of reservists for the overseas garrisons. We have approved funds for antiaircraft defenses of our radar stations. To meet the threat of air attack, we are calling up the Air Force and auxiliary reservists and canceling all leaves in the regular forces. We have issued warnings to merchant shipping to be ready to face underwater attack at any moment."

He signed Ed's copy with a flourish, and then he was gone, not waiting for Ed to put his typewriter away, to pick up his bag.

The silent man who had escorted him to Chartwell was just as silent on the way back to Heathrow. Sleeplessness was beginning to catch up with Ed, but even though he put his head back while in the car and closed his eyes he could not sleep. As he boarded his flight to Berlin, he seemed to slosh with the coffee he'd drunk. He dozed on the plane and then awoke as his ears popped in the descent to Templehof.

Another attack of nervous hit him. Once again, wound around the platen of his typewriter, he was carrying a potentially deadly communication. Once again, however, he cleared the officials quickly, without incident.

The Adlon was gleamingly clean and attractive in the morning light, but it took only the appearance of a jack-booted SS officer coming out the door to remind him that he was back in a country whose leader was a threat to the peace of the world.

He felt safe for the first time in hours when he reached his room, saw the freshly made bed, the clean towels in the bath. He soaped away the smells and soils of the flight, and the bed was an intense pleasure. There had been no arrangements made for him to deliver Churchill's reply. He would let other people worry about that. Sooner or later someone would come for it.

He thought he would fall asleep immediately, but his eyes kept popping open. He could see Churchill in his study at Chartwell, looking quite fresh after a long and sleepless night, chewing on the cigar, unable to control the temptations of oratory, even with an audience of one.

He was convinced the man had meant what he said, and he was just as certain that the conditions attached to Churchill's agreement would cause wrinkled brows among men like Canaris and the generals whose names had been mentioned. What was the just answer? The Sudetenland was German, peopled with German-speaking men and women who had celebrated wildly when the Nazis marched in. The Rhineland was German. Would the world continue to make the same old mistakes, continue to try to dictate

the loyalty of people who were loyal to their own nationality, their own country?

He had done what they had asked him to do, however,
and his part in it was over. It was up to the planners to
decide if Churchill's terms were acceptable, if it would be
wise to go ahead with the plot. All he wanted was to sleep
and when he awakened to begin to arrange his life, to see
Emma.

She smiled out at him from his half-sleep, her lips
parted, and as he dozed the face changed into a gleaming
death's mask. He awoke with a start, turned over, banished
everything from his mind, and slept.

17

EMMA FELSER-GRIEBE'S latest film was opening simultaneously in five major cities. Her tour of those cities had been orchestrated by Goebbels himself, for the film was the work of the Nazi writer, Hans Wilhelm Dorf, and had been made with the blessing of Goebbels's Ministry of Propaganda. That she made herself believable in the film was a great testimony to Emma's acting ability, for she played the part of a girl of the New Germany, a product of the Youth Camps. The good guys in the film made heroic sacrifices for the Fatherland while heaping contempt and final justice on the fuzzy heads of the bad guys, the leader of whom could have been taken as a caricature of Dickens's Fagin or Shakespeare's Shylock. In Leipzig, when the hated *Jude* came onto the screen, the audience, sprinkled liberally with men in uniform, hooted and whistled and cheered lustily as the Jew got his just deserts.

It was obvious to all who knew anything at all about the

power structure of the country that Emma Felser-Griebe was very much in favor. She traveled in Goebbels's own private railway car. She had at her disposal one of his servants, a matronly woman of some fifty years who clucked and fussed over her, and chuckled fondly as Emma, feigning a blush, showed her Goebbels's going-away gift, real silk panties embroidered with a gold-and-black swastika. The servant, who spoke of Herr Goebbels as if she secretly lusted for his small body, would have been shocked to know that Emma, after retiring for the night, rose in disgust from the huge bed—even in pristine linens it still stank of Goebbels—and slept curled up on a smaller cot in the servants' space until, with the light of dawn, she dressed and lay back down on the coverlet of the big bed.

And there were other strange circumstances to Emma's tour. Goebbels would have been more than shocked—had he known that the tour was being used for a business that if it succeeded, would cause, as one relatively minor result, his own death.

Now and then, as the train rolled eastward from Leipzig and Emma lay sleepless on the small bed, she thought of that result. She could not, although she was far from bloodthirsty, think it anything but desirable. To allow the lips of Paul Joseph Goebbels to touch her had been the hardest thing she'd ever done in her life. Only two people alive knew of the reasons she had to hate and fear men like Goebbels.

She slept at last, and awoke with the train at a standstill in the Dresden yards. With the day before her in her hometown, she had good excuse to leave the movie people aboard the train; she wanted to see her family, she told them, and just wander about and relive her childhood.

Returning to the city of her birth was always an emotional experience, and she was a bit selfish about it, wanting to experience it alone, to be able to walk for a while, to think, to savor it all. She had not had enough free time on her recent trip. Nowhere else, she felt, was there so beautiful a city. Not Paris, not Rome, definitely not Berlin. Somehow, even in the troubled days since the rise of Hitler, Dresden always seemed to remain aloof from the troubles. Somehow the Elbe seemed bluer and cleaner than the rivers that ran through other cities, the people more friendly, more refined, constantly aware of the city's proud cultural heritage. Dresden spoke to the world through its famous porcelains, presented a fair and gentle face in the form of parks and museums that contained the works of Correggio, Titian, Paolo Veronese, Andrea del Sarto, Rubens, Van Dyck, and Rembrandt. In the music houses of the city, Wagner himself had conducted; and Richard Strauss's operas had seen their first audiences. Emma crossed the central bridge to the area called Neustadt—New Town— although it was actually the older part of the city.

She was in familiar territory, walking unnoticed, dressed in a pleasant little summer suit, face partially hidden by a wide-brimmed, floppy hat. It seemed cooler than it had in Berlin; Dresden always seemed cooler in summer and warmer in winter—the effect of its sheltering hills, which became, to the south, the foothills of the Erzgebirge.

She was not far from home. There she had attended school. There, in that theater, she had performed in her first amateur play and had been bitten so hard by the stage-bug. Along these streets she had walked with her young beaux, had been kissed, for the first time, there under that large linden tree. And there, on that small street of shops topped by ancient living quarters, she had seen the black-shirted Nazis drag people who had been her friends and neighbors down the stairwells of their homes, had seen the windows shatter and spew shards of sparkling glass into the gutters, had seen those same gutters red with blood.

"Fool," she told herself.

It was nothing but torture to think of it. It had happened and was past, and those who were not dead were the same as dead to those who knew them, although there were terrible whispers. And there were still storefronts, even after five years, that were boarded.

She stood there at the head of the old, narrow street and her fingers came up to feel the hard, jeweled outline of the swastika she wore at her throat—the gift of one those who had cheered on not only the Dresden criminals but haters like them all over Germany. It seemed to burn her skin through her blouse and slip, she held it away from her breasts for a long moment as she remembered.

In 1934 she was eighteen. She could not remember the terrible years of the Great War, but she had memories of the days of inflation and fighting that followed. And she knew the stories told by her parents and their friends. In her school a stern woman spoke glowingly of Adolf Hitler, thanked God that a leader had, at long last, been sent to deliver the German people from the times of trouble.

"But, Father," she remembered herself saying, when she was eighteen, "Frau Hiseldorf says that it is the Jews who are responsible. I have heard you speak of the days when money was worthless, and was it not the Jews, with their talons gripping all the banks, all the large businesses, who profited from the inflation?"

Martin Felser-Griebe was a mild man, a silent man. "Have our Jewish neighbors on this very street profited more than I?" he asked.

It was a street of small family shops. Her father's shop was a heady place, a mixture of the lovely smells of tobacco, the sweet chocolates of the country and of Switzerland, fresh fruits, coffee, spices.

And it was true. The Jewish family shops seemed no more or less prosperous as times became better, as the republic struggled in its death throes, and it became fashionable for young men of her age to dress in the black Nazi shirts and wear the swastika on their arms. Boys she had known, boys she had danced with, were in uniform, guarding Jews who scrubbed the gutters, working on their hands and knees, hundreds of them, taking the jeers of the crowds with quiet tears, seeing their worldly possessions being carried away by looters.

And in her church the priest spoke of the Jewish persecutions, justifying them, speaking of the Christ-killers. "It is commendable," he said, "that the Government has given orders not to burn the synagogues, but regrettable."

For the truth was that in an old town like Dresden it was impossible to burn the synagogues without endangering the nearby property of good Germans.

"Frau Hiseldorf," she said to her teacher, one day during a political discussion, "I don't understand why it is necessary to mistreat the Germans who are Jewish."

There were hisses and whistles of disapproval from classmates. Frau Hiseldorf smiled calmly. "If you were not Catholic, Emma, you would understand better. If you were a better student of history you would understand."

Doubly rebuked, Emma sank down in her seat, but Frau Hiseldorf was not finished. "The great man, Martin Luther, who founded the only true church, recognized the evil that is Judaism over four hundred years ago. Think of the meaning of the word *protestant*. Luther formed the Protestant Church in protest against both the Pope and the Jews. Martin Luther did not rebel against the political authority of the day, but against false religions." She picked up a book. "Here, I shall quote to you, for it is a passage that has great relevance today. Martin Luther said, 'Rid the country of the Jews, send them away, deprive them of all their cash and jewels and silver and gold, set fire to their schools and synagogues, break up their houses and destroy them and put them in a stable, like gypsies, in misery and captivity so that they can incessantly lament to their God about us.' ''. The teacher smiled tightly. ''We have merely been tardy in recognizing the wisdom of Martin Luther.''

She was not in Dresden when the SS troopers became more outrageous, when Jews were seized, their homes and shops gutted. She was in Berlin and had already become famous, had discovered that she was not altogether alone in her questioning. In the theater, in the world of music, there were still some people—although all Jewish elements had long since been driven out, those who could afford it having left the country—who agreed with her when she said she did not understand.

She had met Clara Raine in the early 1930s, when the American-German woman returned to Dresden; Frau Raine of course spoke of her son, a newspaper man, and of America. And it was in Clara Raine's shop she first heard, about 1936, of the underground resistance to the Hitler regime. There were hints at first; later, as she grew older and began to be well known around the country, and the concentration camps about which people only whispered began to be filled with Jews, there was a guarded reference to the good that a person in her position could do.

''A woman in your position,'' Clara Raine said, ''with total freedom of movement, meeting Nazi leaders such as Goebbels''—he had seen her in a play and come to the dressing room afterward—''could be of great service to those who oppose Hitler and his thinking.''

On a later trip home to Dresden, she heard tales of the atrocities of the Blackshirts—the wanton beatings, the looting, the unpunished murders. Her parents, cautious, told her little. As soon as she could, she went next door to visit Clara Raine, for she knew that the conversation there would not be restricted, that she could get news of people she had known.

Clara told her that an elderly lady who once had spoiled her with candies and cakes had been kicked in the stomach by an SS trooper and left to die on the sidewalk; she had been denounced for "anti-state activity."

"Oh, God," she said. "I wish I could kill those animals! I wish I could contact everyone who opposed this madness and gather them together—"

"Well, there are not many of us," Clara Raine said calmly.

"You?" she asked.

"In my small way."

"But what do you do? What can you do?"

"There were four who have escaped," Clara Raine said. "A pitifully small number, but we hid them—"

"We?"

"No names, child. They were hidden and were later sent across the border into Switzerland."

"But if they knew—"

"Yes. I would be in big trouble. I could be in big trouble merely by talking with you so frankly."

"No, never."

Clara looked at her closely. She was ready. "You could be of help."

"All right, then," she said. "Tell me how."

"For now, meet the leaders. Make yourself as familiar with them as you can. Goebbels admires you. He is a notorious womanizer. When men are with women, their tongues often become loose."

"I couldn't," she said, repelled at the thought. She was no innocent—she'd given her virginity to a young man in her acting company, had loved him wholeheartedly until he left the company to enlist in the Luftwaffe, had thought that she would die without him, but had in fact lived to gradually lose touch with him. But to go to bed with a man merely to try to pry information from him, information

that might or might not be useful, that, even if useful,
might be wasted—what could a female shopkeeper do to
halt a man enthusiastically supported by most of Germany?
No, she could not coldly do such a thing.

"One does what one must do at the time," Clara said.
"We are, at the moment, few. But the number is growing,
and important men are seeing things differently."

"What important men?"

"No names, not yet."

And later, when it became apparent that Hitler would
risk war by attacking Czechoslovakia, Clara Raine sought
her out in Berlin. "Do you remember the talk we had in
my shop?"

"I think of it often." She could not resist adding, "I
must say I've seen no results."

"The time is now," Clara said. "If you are willing to
risk your life in the hope of stopping Hitler, of preventing
war, of returning the country to sanity, now is the time to
act."

And thus Emma was introduced, as a messenger, a
go-between, to the plot of 1938, the plot that ended so
ingloriously when Chamberlain gave Hitler everything he
wanted without war. And it was during this period that,
justifying her actions by telling herself that she could wash
the traces of him from her body, she allowed Goebbels to
fulfill his long-time ambition to bed a rising star of stage
and screen.

And now she was, once again, carrying the messages of
defiance and hope. In Leipzig she had dined, after the
film, with a panzer general who was wavering, assuring
him that this time the plot would not fail. She knew that
each time she spoke with someone she risked her life, but
the risk had to be taken. A year in the bed of Joseph
Goebbels had, somehow, caused her to value her life less.

Mixed emotions. She stood at the head of her small, narrow street, could see her father's shop just down the way, next to Clara Raine's shop. Later there would be a small gathering in the Raine shop—a military man, the mayor of the city, Clara. They would listen and look at her hopefully and drink in her every word as she told them the things that were passed to her by von Stahlecker.

But first she would see her parents, and this time things would be quite different. For over a year there had been a coldness between her and her father, and she knew, although he never spoke of it, the reason. It had been the most painful period of her life, while gossip circulated about the actress and the Minister of Propaganda, while her father spoke to her politely and coldly during her visits and her mother would weep silently. And to make the coldness worse, the gossip had reached them about the time of the Week of Broken Glass, when the last of their Jewish neighbors had been humiliated, robbed, murdered, when the Nazi regime had shed its last vestige of humanity.

He was sitting on a stool behind the counter. For a moment his face lit up, then clouded, like the face of a child hoping for a candy when he is told that it is all gone.

"Ah, Emma," he said.

"Hello, Father." She went around the counter and kissed him. He did not return the embrace. "You knew I was coming."

"It is in the paper," he said. His eyes were glued on the jeweled swastika at her breast.

And at last, at long last, she could do it. With a smile she pulled the ornament over her head, held it in her hand, spat on it, threw it onto the ancient hardwood floor, and ground it under her heel. She saw his eyes widen.

"Is mother upstairs?" she asked.

"She is," he said, still with a puzzled look on his face.

"Please lock the front door, Father. Put up your little

sign that says you will be back in twenty minutes.''

"The business—''

"Will wait. Please. I must speak with you, with both of you.''

He shuffled to the door, locked it, hung the little sign in the window. In the past few years he had aged terribly; he had to hang on to the banister on the way up the stairs. Her mother ran to her, hugged her.

"Sit down, both of you,'' she said, unwilling to wait another minute. This time the plot would succeed and it would all be over or it would fail and perhaps all of them would die. She had no intention of causing her parents more suffering.

"What it is, Emma?'' her mother asked, dutifully taking a chair. Emma still stood, unable to contain her energy. "Is it about your film? I understand that many important people will attend the opening of it.''

"It is about this Saturday, August twenty-sixth,'' she said. "Listen carefully. You will not open the shop Saturday morning, Father. When you close the shop on Friday evening you will take mother and go to the country, to Uncle Fritz's place. And you will stay there until you are sure that it is safe to return.''

"I don't understand,'' her mother said. Her father was merely looking at her in silence.

"I know that you will speak to no one about what I tell you,'' she said. "For I know that you love me, and even if you feel that you should warn friends you will consider that one loose word might send me to the Gestapo prison in Berlin.''

"Emma!'' her mother gasped.

"One of two things will happen in the early-morning hours of Saturday,'' she said. "You will either hear that the panzer units are moving into Poland or you will hear a broadcast from a new government.''

A curious glow seemed to enter her father's eyes. "Emma, forgive me," he said. "God forgive me for thinking what I have thought of you."

"There is nothing to forgive," she said.

"All this time," he said, rising, reaching for her, pulling her to his once-powerful body. "All this time I've thought—"

"That I was Goebbels's whore?" she asked. "I know, Father. And it's been as painful for me as it has been for you. I am proud to say that I have had some small part in making it just possible to avoid the war that Hitler seems bent on bringing. I am only a messenger. But I know of the powerful and determined men who are trying to stop the Nazi madness. I assure you that it is a serious undertaking, and that it has a good chance of succeeding."

"Mother," Martin Felser-Griebe said excitedly, "get Emma a coffee and one of those cakes she likes. Sit down, girl, sit down, tell me, tell me."

She told him. She saw tears of joy in her father's eyes. And when her mother, awkwardly, shyly, said, "I am proud of you, Emma, but I wish that you had not had to—"

She couldn't finish, but Emma laughed. "So do I," she said. "And now I must go. I have to see some people."

"There are people here in Dresden who will fight?" her father asked. "Take me to them. I will fight with them."

"It is the soldiers who will fight, Father," she said, "if fighting is necessary. We hope it won't be. But in any event you must promise me that you'll go stay with Uncle Fritz on Friday."

"The shop—" he said.

"For my sake, for Mother's sake," she said.

"Yes, I promise." He wiped his eyes. "I should have known. I thought I knew you, my Emma. I saw your pain in the time of the Jewish troubles. I should have known."

He looked at his wife. "Gerda," he said. "She is, after all, her father's daughter."

"Of course I am," Emma said, but she was puzzled by a stricken look on her mother's face.

"Yes, Gerda," Martin said. "We must."

"Must what?" Emma asked.

"I don't know," her mother said. "Martin, I don't know."

"What are you talking about?" she demanded.

It was as if she were not there when Martin looked at her mother and spoke in a low voice. "She has taken us into her confidence. She is fighting. I would have fought. I never understood why the Jews did not fight, why they merely submitted. If they had fought, I would have fought and others would have fought—"

"Don't blame yourself," Emma said. "No one really understood what was happening until it was too late."

"But you understood," he said. "Perhaps because it is in your blood, because—"

"Martin, please," her mother said.

"Yes," he said. "Now. It is time. Gerda, it is time."

"Then I will tell her," her mother said. "It is for me to tell."

"Will you please tell me what?" Emma asked.

"Yes," Gerda Felser-Griebe said, nodding her head, tears beginning to form. "It is for me to tell. Emma, my darling daughter, my little love—"

"Mother," she teased, "what deep, dark secret is this?"

"I saw you first, my darling daughter, when you were more than a year old," her mother said.

She did not understand at first.

"You are the daughter of my heart, not of my loins," Gerda said.

Emma leaped from her chair and knelt before her mother, throwing her arms around it. "It makes no difference," she said, "for you are the mother of my heart. Am I, then, an adopted child?" Her mother nodded, reached out a hand to touch Emma's tightly curled hair. "It doesn't matter in the slightest."

"Emma," Martin said, "there is more. Please sit and listen."

She sat, hands folded. Poor dears, she was thinking, keeping the secret from me for so long, as if it would have changed my love for them.

"You'd better hold onto yourself, too, Gerda," Martin said. He seemed to be unable to continue.

"Well, speak up, Martin," Gerda said.

Instead, he rose, went to the old wind-up talking machine that had been sitting in the upstairs parlor for years, dug into a stack of records still carefully kept in their paper covers, cranked the machine with swift movement and placed the record on the turntable. Emma recognized the sound immediately. She had played the record often.

Martin turned to face her. "Do you know the music?"

"Of course," she said. "It's by Ernst Gronberg."

"And it is no longer played by any orchestra in Germany," Martin said.

"I know," Emma said. "I know. He was your friend. He was in your platoon in the Great War. You've told me about him many times."

"Now I will tell you again," he said. "I saw him last in a village in Belgium. I don't even remember its name. No matter. We were ordered to destroy it. We were ordered to kill anyone who resisted."

"What has this to do with Emma?" Gerda demanded.

"Hush," Martin said. "Listen. Ernst was with me. We were mere privates. We knew we had to obey orders, so we burned. We destroyed. And then we found the family —"

"Father, I've heard it before," Emma said quietly,

wondering if her revelations had been too shocking for him, if he had suddenly gone senile.

"We were going to let them live," Martin said. "But then the officer came and forced us to kill them. When we had leave, Ernst would not return to the front, staying to protest, to try to get someone to listen."

"And he was killed," Emma said, "executed for desertion. And now his music is banned by the Nazis because he was a Jew."

"He was a braver and finer man than I," Martin went on, as if he had not heard. "I loved him. He was not only my friend, but he was my brother-in-law."

"Martin," Gerda gasped.

"Yes. I have not told you, Gerda, not even you. For I was ashamed, yes, ashamed, to have my beloved sister marry a Jew. I was young; how could I know? It was not until I saw the courage that Ernst showed, standing up to them, protesting the useless killing of civilians, that I saw my shame was bad, that Ernst was good. But even then I—would not admit it, not even to you."

"Your sister?" Emma asked. "What became of her?"

"When he saw that it was useless, that no one would listen, he ran away, deserted. He took my sister into the mountains. She was seven-months' pregnant. It was winter, and the cottage had to be heated with an open fire in the fireplace. It escaped during the night, the fire, and they barely escaped with their lives. As you were born early, your mother died. Of course Ernst was captured as a deserter. Ernst told me about it all while he was in prison, waiting to be executed. The child was with his family. He asked me to take the child, take my sister Emma's child—"

"Oh, my dear God," Gerda said.

"Yes, my dear," Martin said. "I told you the child was mine when I met you and married you. And you took her as your own." He looked at Emma, who had gone suddenly cold, was sitting, hands folded in her lap, in stunned silence. "She took you as her own. I told her I had been married, that my wife had died of childbirth fever, and she loved you as the child she could never have."

The record had come to its end. The needle clicked and scratched in the last groove. Emma rose, put the needle back to the beginning. "He was my father?" she asked in a small voice. "Ernst Gronberg?"

"He was a good man," Martin said. "A kind and gentle man, a man who had the courage to stand up for what he believed."

And she was suddenly laughing. "Oh, Emma," Gerda said, running to put her arms around her, but the laughing would not stop. Nor could she tell them why she was laughing. Actually she was imagining the look on the face of her Nazi lover when she told him, just before he was killed, that he had been sleeping with a Jewess for over a year.

The train sped westward toward Frankfurt. The conference with the conspirators in Dresden was behind her, another opening and another meeting were ahead, then the quick trip back to Berlin in time for the big day also, thank God, nearing.

So, she mused, there is such a thing as a racial memory. When I felt sorry for the Jews it was more than a feeling of "There but for the grace of God go I"—for that *was* me. All those women, men, children *were* me.

But she did not feel any different. She did not wail and beseech God and pound her chest and suffer. She had never admired that in Jews. Her scanty knowledge of history told her that they had been much persecuted. But, by God, the last time they had fought was when the Romans destroyed the temple. How could they allow themselves to be routed out of their beds, out of their homes?

How could they allow their women to be reviled by ignorant black-shirted hoodlums without fighting? Now that she was a part of them, at least half a part of them, she could hate that quality in them, could condemn them for going peacefully to the concentration camps. Someday, when the Nazis were a bad memory, she would stand up and say to them, those who survived, "If it ever happens again, you will fight. You will fight to the last man, woman, or child before you allow anyone to persecute you again." And if the plot did not succeed she would find another way to fight the Nazis.

One thing was sure. She would never again allow one of them to touch her. If the plot failed, perhaps the best service she could perform would be to crawl for the last time into the bed of Joseph Goebbels, with a long, sharp knife under her pillow. She could take at least one of them with her.

18

WORD OF BRITAIN'S resolve to protect the independence of Poland was delivered to different Germans in two different ways on Wednesday, August 23. Over coffee in the bar at midmorning Ed Raine talked quietly to the one-armed Luftwaffe colonel, telling him of Churchill's revelations of reserve call-ups and other actions. Meanwhile, the British ambassador flew to Berchtesgaden. He told Hitler that Britain would honor its pledge to fight if Germany attacked Poland.

Hitler's reactions would not be known to history for some time, but von Stahlecker's actions were immediate. He spent the day contacting, in various ways, all the members of the plot. In Dresden, the civilian mayor began making his plans to announce his support of the new government immediately, and set up contingency plans to protect the city in the event of fighting. When word filtered down to Clara Raine that Churchill had promised to recognize the new government, she sighed. Events were underway and nothing would stop them. She was proud of her small part, and proud, although slightly worried, about her son's part in the operation. It was a great comfort to her to know that Ed would be out of the country before any violence began.

Admiral Canaris, slated to be the head of state, at least temporarily, met with von Stahlecker and a man who was vital to the plot, General Erwin von Witzleben, who would supply the troops to seize the Nazi ministries and to protect the Berlin area from counterattack by pro-Nazi forces.

Von Witzleben smiled grimly when he was told that things were in order.

"There is only one possible stumbling block," von Stahlecker said. "According to Churchill, the English will insist upon the return of Czech sovereignty."

Von Witzleben's face went suddenly red. He sputtered for a moment before any words became intelligible. "The arrogance of the man. We offer him a way, an honorable way, to avoid a war, to save England from being bombed back to the age of wooden plows, and he dictates conditions."

"It can be worked out," von Stahlecker said. "I'm sure there can be a compromise. The Sudetenland is German, has always been German. I'm sure no thinking man would try to deny the right of Germans to live in their own country."

"We must contact him again, and insist upon that condition," von Witzleben said.

"No, the Sudetenland question can be taken up when we are sure we will not have to fight the French and English again, and possibly the Americans," Canaris said. "There is no time now. Our Führer, in spite of sitting down quietly with Henderson to talk peace this very day, had already had the orders written. The invasion of Poland will begin in the dawn hours of August twenty-sixth. The timing is crucial, for the panzers must be given a chance to move before the autumn rainy season.''

"I know, I know, my dear Admiral,'' von Witzleben said. "I have my orders, too. If Britain and France open hostilities I am to conserve my forces as much as possible. That will be easy. They have nothing to put against us. A few paltry and poorly trained French divisions. The British have no forces on the Continent worthy of the name.''

"Gentlemen,'' von Stahlecker said, "we have only to ask ourselves two questions. Is there any doubt that Hitler intends to attack Poland? If he attacks, is there any doubt that Britain will force France to join her in war?''

"There is no doubt on either count,'' Canaris said. "If only the fool had waited. He promised us that he would not risk war in the West until 1944 at the earliest.''

"Sir, if he had waited, would you have agreed to the war?'' von Stahlecker asked with a little smile.

Canaris was a bit disconcerted. "That is a question that, due to circumstances, need not be answered,'' he said. "General von Witzleben, the others are agreed. We have an entire panzer division in Potsdam, an infantry division closer to Berlin. Can you deliver us the Berlin area?''

"My troops will follow orders,'' von Witzleben said stiffly. "But they are German. They will not take kindly to a British ultimatum regarding German citizens in the Sudetenland.''

"Yes, yes,'' Canaris said. "All right. Beginning today, we will infiltrate men in civilian clothing into the Hotel Adlon. As you know, arms are already in place there. We are all quite familiar with Hitler's security precautions. We are to be thankful that he is basically a cunning man, for it is obvious that he plans a public appearance on the eve of the Polish invasion as a ruse. Who would think that he would be watching acrobats do tricks while his generals are preparing for a dawn attack? We have his schedule. He will return from Berchtesgaden on the twenty-fourth. On the night of the twenty-fifth he will arrive at the Hotel Adlon at five minutes of eight, and the performance will begin at eight sharp. The audience will be small. We have given express orders to our men to be very cautious, for diplomats from several countries will be there, Italy among them. We must not give the Italians a cause for alarm. That there will be shooting is certain. Our men have been carefully selected for their coolness of head, for their marksmanship. Hitler's bodyguard will be taken out without warning. If we are lucky and very, very careful, they will not have a chance to fire their weapons. At the time of the attack at the Adlon, our forces, under General von Witzleben, will be occupying the various points of importance in the city. Special teams will be assigned to kill Hitler's top supporters. By nine P.M. we should be broadcasting the news on Radio Berlin.''

Canaris lit a cigarette, and von Stahlecker noted that his hand was trembling. ''Do either of you have anything to add?''

''The attack team has been told, I trust, that above all, Hitler must not be harmed?'' von Stahlecker said. ''God knows, we don't need him as a martyr to inspire the fanatics to a civil war.''

''Yes, of course,'' Canaris said. ''Now I'm sure that you gentlemen have as much to do as I.'' He rose, dismissing them.

None of them knew that another element had been introduced. Hitler's procedures were well known. He operated on the basis of German thoroughness and with a nonvariance that was close enough to habit to allow von Stahlecker and the rest to assume, with all logic, that only his regular security forces would be guarding him during his appearance at the Adlon. They would have been astounded to know that an SD man, normally concerned only with foreign espionage, was at that moment in the hotel.

Otto Schellen was having a drink in the bar. He sat alone, a handsome blond man in a nicely tailored suit, looking more like a successful musician or playwright than a rising star in his country's secret service. He listened to the various voices, understanding most of the Italian, all of the English and German, some of the Swedish. He noted with wry amusement that the foreign press corps was there in strength, having their morning brandy, discussing the various events of the eventful days, speculating on the results of the British ambassador's visit to Hitler.

After some time he rose and went into the lobby. He sought the assistant manager, was not surprised to find a woman. Women were, more and more, being called upon to fill positions normally held by men, freeing the men for more important service in the armed forces. He introduced himself and received a lusty "*Heil Hitler*" from the imposing Frau Kopf. He explained that his mission was to take an advance look to be better able to assure the Führer's safety.

"I assure you that nothing untoward will happen," Frau Kopf said. "Not in the Adlon."

Nevertheless, he had his look. Hitler would enter via the front entrance, cross the luxurious lobby, descend a short flight of stairs. The way was short and easily protected. The street outside would be guarded by Hitler's regular security forces and honor guard. A few men stationed in the lobby would be enough.

The gymnasium was also easily covered. Being below street level, it had only high, half windows. With men outside in the alley to cover the window, a few men stationed at the entrance and exits, there would be no problem.

And yet, he weighed the possibilities. He knew that it was quite difficult to stop a determined man who had no fear of losing his life in order to accomplish his objective. There were those in Germany who opposed the Führer. In general, they were inactive and impotent, for Gestapo jails and certain camps not devoted to pleasure had long since processed the serious threats. However, the New Germany was a nation of nearly eighty million people, and among them were, no doubt, the discontents, undetected Jews, foreign laborers, various visitors. If he were involved in a plot to kill Hitler he would plant a man in a position where he would be least suspected; for example, as a newsman. He could never understand Herr Goebbels's continued attempts to influence foreign opinion, for everyone knew that the world was against Hitler and his Germany, that any foreign newsman who came to Germany would immediately seek out the most unfavorable aspects of the Third Reich and expound upon them endlessly. If he had his way he would expel all of them. Let the world think what it would.

There was a faint smell of perspiration in the gymnasium, and it made him think of the Norwegian acrobat, the tall, lithe Margo. He turned to Frau Kopf, who had accompanied him. "I have seen enough," he said. "I thank you for your cooperation."

"If there is anything else I can do." She looked as if she would like to salute and click her heels.

"No, no, thank you. You've been a great help." He followed her back to the lobby, took his leave, watched her go into her office. Then, after checking carefully to be sure he wasn't noticed, he ducked into an empty elevator.

He knew the room number, and his knock was answered. For a brief but pleasant interlude he gave no more thought to the problem of determining whether or not the anonymous tip about activity against the state, and presumably, the Führer, had basis.

19

ON ANOTHER FLOOR of the Adlon, the most immediate problem faced by an American newsman was a brief cable from his home office: RAINE RELIEVED BERLIN DUTY. REPORT ANO LONDON. Then there was the always touch-and-go attempt to complete a transatlantic telephone call.

The cable could not have come at a worse time. At his conference with von Stahlecker that morning he had been assigned one final duty, to fly to London as soon as the plot had succeeded, to inform Churchill and to urge him to stand by his pledge. Moreover, although he knew that he should, in such a crisis, divorce himself from personal affairs, he knew that Emma was due back in Berlin on Friday. If he obeyed his boss and reported to London, not only would he be effectively taken out of his assigned part in preserving peace, he would not see Emma.

And if anything went wrong—he didn't like to think about that—he might never see her again.

So he spent an hour exerting the utmost will power to prevent an explosion of frustrated vituperation against the operators of the Berlin telephone system, and against all those who tied up the few available long-distance telephone wires. At last he coaxed and begged until he was given an approximate time to expect his call to go through, "Provided, sir, that priority calls do not interfere." An hour and a half. It seemed like an eternity. He went to the bar to drown his frustrations in beer.

"You look like you've lost your best friend, boy," John Graff Stanton said. "Hell, it's only a job, after all."

Ed looked at him blankly, wondering about the meaning of the remark. Stanton had no way of knowing he'd been relieved of the Berlin assignment.

Ah, but he did. "I want you to know, Raine, that I had nothing to do with it. I didn't ask for it. They called me and said you were out and I said I didn't want to take a man's job. But since they'd already made the decision—"

"They didn't, by any chance, give you reason?" Ed asked.

"As a matter of fact, they did," he said. "Seemed they tried to find you while you were running around the world."

"I see."

"That's the trouble with you young fellows," Stanton mused. "Chasing bimbos. Don't worry, though. We'll all be out soon. Hear the British are on stand-by. Embassy's told all British correspondents to be ready to shag ass on a moment's notice."

"Look, Stanton, there's no way I can leave Berlin now. I've got to call in to the home office. No hard feelings, but don't go to work for ANO just yet. After I talk with them they just might change their minds."

"I doubt it. The man said he was a little tired of getting nothing but Nazi propaganda from you. But have at it, boy. You got reasons why you want to stay in Berlin?"

"I have," Ed said.

"Reason wear a skirt?"

"Not when I'm with her," Ed said.

He killed his beer and went back to his room, reached the overseas operator, changed the number he was calling. There were other ways he could stay in Berlin. He had to have accreditation as a correspondent, and he thought he knew where he could get it. He wouldn't have been a bit surprised to hear a knock on his door, open it to find a presumably grim-faced man from the Immigration Service, asking him his plans, now that he no longer had a job. His bet was a hundred to one that the authorities knew of the cable telling him to pack it in and go to London.

In the gymnasium, Margo Ostenso was not in the slightest fatigued by her unexpected bonus of an hour earlier; on the contrary, she was stimulated. She had never performed better, and there was much praise for the entire troupe from the diminutive Baroness.

"Tomorrow," Helga announced, "we will have one final dress rehearsal. Friday, we will rest. Costumes will be washed by hand on Friday. I need not remind you that this performance is not merely another exhibition, but is, in fact, sort of a semiofficial and friendly message to the leader of the German people."

The cheerful gymnasts went to their rooms, leaving Helga alone. She felt a bit despondent. She had the rest of the day ahead of her with nothing to do. After the frightening experience with the SS bullies on the street, she had not set foot outside the hotel.

By day's end, Ed's call had not yet come through, but, on the other hand, there had been no visit from the Immigration people. He had decided to stick it out. If he could not complete his plan he would apply for a brief tourist visa, explaining that he wanted to visit his mother in Dresden before leaving the country.

Thursday brought much talk, in the Adlon cellar bar, of war. The rainy season was nearing. It had to be soon or not at all, and all the indicators said that it would be with the dawn, or within the next couple of days. Ed chafed, knowing that he was the only man in the correspondent corps who knew the exact hour, the exact date. Dawn of August 26. Unless von Stahlecker's group succeded in stopping Hitler totally.

He was ready to leave the bar Thursday afternoon when he heard his name paged. The call had finally come through. He came out of the phone booth grinning. He was now the very poorly paid but properly accredited correspondent for the Des Moines *Morning Call*. He'd called in an old favor and, without too much explanation on his part, his request had been granted. Credentials were on the way, and his friend the editor would cable to give advance notice that Ed Raine had become the *Call*'s man in Berlin. One problem solved.

He ordered a drink in celebration. He was sitting with two British newsmen when Bea Goodpasture came into the room. She smiled when she saw Ed at the table, but it was to the British that she spoke. "Sorry, chums," she said, "but it's hit the fan. You leave tonight for the Danish border. Orders straight from the top. All British subjects not connected with the embassy. Help me pass the word?"

"Bloody hell," said one of the Britishers, but he was on his feet. "I say, Raine, could you use a nice little car? The price is right."

"Miss Goodpasture," Ed said, "why the rush?"

"Unofficially, the ultimatums are flying thick and fast," she said. "The Sir thinks Hitler has already given the invasion orders."

The bar seemed empty without the British, but there was

the efficient Miss Goodpasture, her job finished. "It'll be your turn next," she said, sitting down with a deep sigh. "The American Embassy is preparing notices to all Americans who do not have vital business to leave the country."

"It happens, my dear Miss Goodpasture, that I have vital business." He chuckled, remembering what his old friend had told him on the crackling, fading long-distance line.

"I've seen your shit in the ANO releases, old buddy," he had said. "Don't bother me with it. I'm getting the hard news from the AP. I can't guarantee I'll publish it, but since you're so hell-bent on staying in Berlin, why don't you give me a feature on Berlin nightlife on the eve of war?"

"My vital business," he said to Bea, "is to write a thing about the people fiddling while the world burns. Want to help me research it?"

"Well," she said doubtfully, "I'm finished for the night."

"All the best hot spots," he said. "Dancing and wine and all that."

"You talked me into it," she said.

So he started researching the story. He was still spending ANO money. Fortunately, he'd been careful, and had most of his first month's cash-in-advance expense money left. It served the bastards right that he was using it to cut a wide swath through nighttime Berlin with a cuddly little blonde on his arm. She turned out to be a fine dancer. He was a little stiff, but he knew the steps and he kept up with her, especially after sampling the products of about a half-dozen bars. He found the customers generally unconcerned, still not believing that war was imminent. There were friendly ones and grumpy ones and a handsome German army captain who took a fancy to Bea and cut in repeatedly, until Bea suggested that they find a less friendly place.

And, in the small hours of the morning, both of them a bit pissed, as the more profane British liked to call it, they were in the back seat of a taxi on the way to the British Embassy.

"Driver," Bea said, "please take the long way home, if you don't mind."

"Hey, it's late," Ed said. "Tomorrow I've got work to do."

"You have work to do tonight, too," she said, moving to press a hot little breast against him. "Curl my toes, sir."

A honey-and-wine mouth on his, a small, well-formed body pushing, trying to be atop him, his hands making free, the cab going slowly, slowly, the driver smiling as he tried to see the action in the rear seat in his mirror as the cab passed under street lamps.

"Sorry," the driver said, after a long, slow ride, "but we have arrived."

Ed hadn't even noticed that the cab had stopped. He came up for air. "You are absolutely we-erd," he told her, pushing her away.

"Damn," she said. "Just as you were working your way past my piggies to the second toe. Tell you what, if you promise to stop when I start trying to rape you, I'll slip you into my room."

"Bee-ea," he moaned.

"I know a way. Security is loose."

"Bea, I have no intention of being hauled up in front of the British ambassador and being accused of taking advantage of a we-erd British virgin. Get the hell out of here."

"All right for you," she said. "It will merely be worse for you next time. I promise you that."

"I can hardly wait."

Friday. A day of warm breezes and high, towering white clouds. The morning news told of a formal treaty between England and Poland guaranteeing British aid if Poland was attacked. The BBC announced that Winston Churchill was making a tour of the Rhine front and would end the day in Paris. The last day of peace. Ed wanted to talk with someone, to be assured that the plan was underway, but he dared not try to contact von Stahlecker. To kill time, he had coffee with the Baroness in her room. He wondered what would happen to the small woman during the take-over. He had an urge to warn her, but he could not. He could not say, "Helga, they're going to seize Hitler while he watches your boys and girls perform tonight. There'll be precautions to prevent harming civilians, but I'd feel better if you'd make yourself scarce when Hitler enters the gymnasium." He thought, that moment, that he might know a little bit of what an officer feels when he sends men out to battle.

Instead of warning her, he asked, "What happens after tonight, Helga?"

"Oh, we take the show into a theater for the general public," she said excitedly. "When it is reported that the Führer has made a special effort to see us, we'll be playing to standing room only."

I hope you're right, he thought. He had taken a liking to the little woman, had ceased to be embarrassed in her presence, found himself able to look into her face and talk without staring at her deformed limbs and body.

But the day became far more delightful when, after returning to his room, he saw that the connecting door was open. He had left it unlocked on his side. He felt a surge of elation and ran to the door. The most beautiful woman he'd ever known was wearing a lacy black peignoir.

"I thought you'd never come," she said, as she met him halfway, standing on tiptoe to place her lips on his.

How much I have changed, she thought, as she let her body melt to his, felt his strong arms around her. But this had not changed. This was real, vital, a dream come true, for she had thought of him so many times these past days, this American, this man who had moved her as no man had ever moved her before. He could feel in her a need—a need that seemed as strong as his own, an almost fearful, somewhat terrible urgency. She made no protest, but matched his haste, threw herself into his arms on the big bed in her room, came to him swiftly, clinging as closely as she could, whispering his name as their urgencies merged into something that ended as swiftly as it had begun, in an almost painful explosion of nearness, leaving him breathless, wondering, awed by her violence and the power of her contractions.

"My God," he said, looking into her wide, startled eyes.

"Oh, I do love you," she whispered.

"And I, I love you. God, how I do love you."

And even as he spoke he could not explain his emotions. Could it be that there was a warning in the violence of their lovemaking? The thought of her being dead came to him again, and it was so painful that he closed his eyes for a moment and clung to her as the only reality.

"You're going with me tonight," he said.

"No, that would be impossible."

"You won't be needed here. It's in the hands of the fighters now, the soldiers."

"Ed, Ed, it can't be. Not tonight. Later, when it's over. We'll be together then, my love."

"Always," he said. "Forever, damn it. And you'll go

where I go. No insubordination. No talk of career, although you can do what you want with your acting, just so you do it in America, where I am.''

"Yes, that would be wonderful.'' She did not think that she would be able to face Germany, not even a free Germany, knowing what they had done to those who were, after all, her own people. Yes, she could go with this American, start a new life in a country that would not remind her of the blood, of the suffering. "I will go with you. I promise. But now we must talk.''

"Not now.''

"Yes. I have been with von Stahlecker. It's all in readiness. It goes well. There will be a car for you parked at the side entrance. You will be near it, ready to be driven to the airport when it is clear that the mission is successful. There will be a JU-90 with naval markings there, the Admiral's own plane.''

"Come with me. It's a big plane. There'll be plenty of room.'' He knew the Junkers plane, four needle-nosed engines on broad, long wings, twin stabilizers extending on either side of the tail.

"I will be here when you return,'' she said. She made an attempt to rise. He held her, kissed her: "Please,'' she said. "I don't want to go, but I must.''

"When this is over, don't try that,'' he said, releasing her. "I'll going to take you to bed and keep you there for a week.''

"With plenty of wine and food at the bedside.'' She smiled.

"Hell, we won't need it,'' he said, watching that lovely body disappear inside silk hose, panties, bra, slip, dress. He noted with a trace of lust that she had not bothered to clean herself, that a part of him was still there, inside her.

"My God, Emma,'' he said. "We'll have beautiful children if they look like you.''

Her smile warmed his heart. "Do you think I haven't thought of that?" She bent to kiss him. "Now get your hairy American body out of my suite before you seduce me from my duties."

"Where are you going?" he asked.

"You needn't know."

"I want to know," he said, heaving himself up.

"Well, I suppose it doesn't matter. I'm going to the Polish frontier."

"No, by God!"

"It is necessary."

"You've done enough."

"There is one more duty, an important one. I must see General Halder."

"I know he was in on the 1938 plot," Ed said. "But I thought he was as keen as Hitler about this Polish thing."

"Perhaps," she said. "He will listen to reason. I think he can be convinced to lend his support to a *fait accompli*. As commander of the invasion forces, he could prevent any retaliation from Hitler's supporters."

"And if he turns you in?"

"Oh, I won't speak until news comes from Berlin that Hitler is under guard and that Berlin is in our hands. I'll be with him on the guise of building the morale of the officer corps. It was arranged by Herr Goebbels." The name brought a frown to his face. She pinched his cheek. "Now, now, none of that. You have no idea how completely a thing of the past that is."

"I'll be back tomorrow," he said. "Emma, be damned careful."

"Don't worry. For the first time I have something to live for."

"Me?" He grinned.

"Now whatever gave you such a silly idea?"

And she was gone.

* * *

Evening. Security forces already in and around the Adlon. A feeling of expectancy, for various reasons. Otto Schellen began placing his plainclothes men. The Norwegians, a bit nervous about their awesome audience, were beginning to dress. Ed Raine was walking through the lobby, on the way to the bar. He saw many strange faces, saw efficient-looking men giving him the once-over. He felt the hairs prickle at the nape of his neck. He had no way of knowing who was who, had been able to spot any of the men who would capture Hitler or die in the attempt. He could not resist checking outside the side entrance. There was no car there, but it was early.

He had a quick drink, which soured on his agitated stomach. An antacid tablet did little to help. He checked again. This time, as people began arriving, having their invitations checked at the front entrance, he saw the dark car at the side entrance, saw the glow of a cigarette in the driver's hand.

They were mostly in uniform, the men of the audience, and their ladies were resplendent in silks and satins. They talked gaily, exchanged greetings, filed toward the staircase down to the gymnasium. Ed drifted toward the front to see Hitler arrive. He checked his watch. Five minutes of eight. He listened for the sound of a motorcade, heard only the low hum of evening traffic on Unter den Linden. Eight o'clock. No need for concern. Hitler could afford to be late. The performance would not begin without him.

At twenty minutes past he noted that the stern men who guarded the lobby were getting restless, checking their own watches. And then his heart leaped as a car drew up directly in front of the hotel—but it was only an SS staff officer, who came walking leisurely up the sidewalk. He entered the lobby, looked around disdainfully. A man in civilian clothing approached him and Ed could hear their words plainly.

"You may send your men home," the officer said. "The Führer has canceled his appearance."

"*Jawohl*." The man in the dark suit backed away, called out to a man across the lobby.

It came like a body blow to Ed. Where did that leave them? And what about Emma? She was flying to the Polish frontier. Don't talk to anyone, Emma, he almost prayed. Keep your mouth shut. Entertain the troops and come back, and we'll get the hell out of here before it's too late.

For he, like the best-informed conspirators, knew that the invasion force was already on the move, making preparations for a predawn blitz.

Then he thought of the others. He raced for a telephone booth. He had trouble finding the number of von Stahlecker's office, and when he was finally put through he heard the Colonel's calm voice—calm beyond belief in view of what had happened. He hoped only that the plan had not gone into operation elsewhere around the city.

"The show has been canceled," he said urgently.

"Yes," von Stahlecker said. "I thank you for calling me, Herr Raine, but I had decided not to come anyhow. I'm sure I would have enjoyed the performance, but perhaps we can see it together at a later date."

He could not find words. Were they talking about the same thing? Had the whole "show" been canceled as well?

"I would like to buy you a drink as a reward for looking after me," the Colonel said, "for saving me a seat at the performance. Tomorrow, say ten o'clock, in the bar?"

And it was only after a sleepless night spent listening to German radio for any announcements, that he discovered that Hitler owed much to his friend and ally, Mussolini. Von Stahlecker, when he joined Ed in the bar, was calm, smiling. They took an isolated table, von Stahlecker's favorite.

"The news is unexciting," Ed said, when they had been served.

"It took a lot of doing to keep the news dull," von Stahlecker said. "General Petzel's One Corps was moving and motorized columns of General von Kleist's corps were nearing the border."

"He called off the invasion?"

"For the moment. It is our opinion that he will reschedule it."

"What happened? Did he have second thoughts about the British intentions?"

"Perhaps that entered into it. But our informant in the Reichsministry tells us that the main reason for the cancellation was Mussolini. It seems that our Italian friend got cold feet and told Hitler that he would be unable to take Italy into war if the French and English lived up to their word to Poland."

"Then that's the end of it. He won't try to go it alone."

"He still has Russia on the sidelines as neutral, even as a partner in dividing up Poland. No, that is not the end of it."

"I'm afraid it's the end for me," Ed said. "I'm not cut out for it. And I'm going to take one of your troops when I leave."

Von Stahlecker smiled. "It would be Germany's loss. But I think you underestimate the determination of a certain young lady."

"We'll see."

"In fact, Herr Raine," von Stahlecker said seriously, "we are counting on you more heavily than ever."

"Colonel, I don't want to hear it. I've had it. I'm a nervous wreck."

"Waiting is always hard. Just listen. You have the ear

of the Ministry of Propaganda. The next few days are going to be tense ones for Germany and the world. If I know Herr Goebbels, he will be more interested than ever in getting some favorable foreign press. You can give that to him, can't you?''

"I have a limited voice now, Colonel. I'm just a single-paper correspondent.''

"No matter. You can write things that present Germany in a favorable light. You have told me that Goebbels has promised you an exclusive interview with Hitler. If you impress Goebbels enough, he could bring this about. Hitler knows the value of favorable press in the United States. And he likes doing the unexpected. He had planned to visit the Adlon and he doesn't like to have his plans upset. He might be favorable to a suggestion on your part that an interview with the Führer in a hotel, a Berlin landmark, would emphasize his peaceful intentions.''

"Colonel, you're clutching at straws.''

"And a secret meeting between a newsman and the Führer would not be as heavily guarded.''

"It won't work.''

"Herr Raine, men risked their lives last night. Women, too, if I need to remind you. Will you desert them now?''

Ed put out a cigarette, savagely grinding it into the ashtray. "I won't promise you that I'll stick it out,'' he said, "but until we see which way things are going, I'll start on it. I'll write better propaganda than Goebbels himself could write.''

"Good, good. I can ask no more. I'm sure you'll see the necessity when the time comes.''

"When will Emma come back?''

"Soon. It seems that the movement of certain troop units is being explained by saying that they were merely being taken to a central location for a personal appearance by one of Germany's leading actresses. She will do one or two shows, then she'll be back with you." He frowned. "I know that I don't have to warn Emma, but are you fully aware of the necessity of keeping your relationship with her absolutely secret?"

"I think I am," he said. "But I'd like to hear it from you, Colonel, just to make sure I'm right."

"If you suspect and it makes no difference, I will not put it into words."

"I want you to. It's Goebbels, isn't it?"

"Her relationship with Goebbels has been very useful to us." He raised an eyebrow. "I'm a bit surprised, I must admit. I thought you Americans were so romantic. It's commendable of you to understand the necessity of her actions."

Ed did not speak. So it was true. He thought of her in the arms of that rat-faced little man and a fury rose in him. He knew, at that moment, that he would stay until the bitter end, that he would do all in his power to help her.

20

AS EXPECTED, AMERICANS who did not have vital business in Germany were advised to leave. The newspapers were quite interesting that Saturday morning. There were reports of complete chaos in Poland. With good reason, Ed thought, for they could not have been unaware of the troop movements on the night of August 25. German families were reported fleeing Polish territory, and the Polish Army was said to have been pushed to the German border. In Germany, however, one could not be sure of the truth of the reports. Whether the Poles were ready or not was a moot question, but Ed knew that it had been a near thing. that the Germans had been ready to move—were moving—when the orders came to hold back.

He took time to go to the room of the Baroness to console her in her disappointment. She shrugged and said the performance had gone well, in spite of the absence of Herr Hitler. Her boys and girls were, of course, disappointed, but then that was not the only disappointment, for Hitler had also canceled a Nazi rally at Tannenberg scheduled for Saturday.

"There is nothing to do," she said, "but go on with our plans to open in the theater. But in the meantime, I think I shall become slightly drunk." She giggled. "My body is so small it takes only a minute amount of alcohol. So if you'd care to join me there will be plenty for you."

"Best offer I've had all day," he said. He poured. A fine old champagne. And it was true that she was a cheap drunk. She began to get giggly on the third glass and then refused a fourth. After a few minutes, she changed her mind and decided to have another glass; as she poured she looked up into his face with wide eyes, her breath a rapid, rasping sound.

"Did I tell you?" she asked, in her piping little voice, "that alcohol goes right straight to the seat of my pants?"

He almost swallowed his tongue in an effort not to laugh.

"Come now, my friend Ed," she said, her full lips in a teasing, nearly seductive, smile, "you will admit to being curious?"

He grinned. "Baroness, I do admit it. I am curious."

"In that area," she said, "I am fully developed."

"Helga, I like you. I know you have a heart as big as any woman. I think I can give it to you straight."

She nodded. "I have been rejected before."

"Now that's self-pity," he said, "I'm not rejecting you, I want to talk to you. Look, I'm basically a small-town boy. When I went into the big city I wore a tie that my dad bought sometime long before World War I. I was brought up in a moral household." He waved his hand. "I'm not making judgments. It's just that I was taught to believe that men who tried to seduce women were as immoral as women who walked the streets trying to seduce men.''

"So what I've heard about Americans is true," she said, with a little smile.

"I was in love with a girl," he said. "And she was killed in a bus crash. I'm not virgin, but I wouldn't call myself a Don Juan. Not until I got to Berlin, anyhow. And suddenly I'm outclassed. You outclass me. You, apparently, are a woman of the world. Hell, Helga, everywhere I turn, a woman is trying to give herself to me, and I frankly can't handle it—especially since I've fallen in love with one of them.''

"Oh, for heaven's sake, why didn't you just say so?'' she asked. "There is nothing more disgustingly moral than a man newly in love.'' She reached for the bottle and managed to pour without spilling it, although her thick little hands had trouble holding it. "So we will just have another toast and then I'll let you run along to your love.''

"Helga, are you really sexy?'' he asked, grinning.

"I was married to a man as large as you," she said. And her smile was warm. "Now I feel better about being rejected, for you *are* curious.''

"I'd feel like a child molester," he said. "But the idea does give rise to what I admit is a rather large amount of interest.''

"Well, here's to the future," she said. "Perhaps you will fall out of love, perhaps you will remember Helga and be curious.''

"Could be," he said.

"I am in the book," she said. "In Oslo. It's a pretty city in the summertime.''

"I'll remember that," he said.

He spent the rest of the day writing the most blatant propaganda, praising Hitler for bringing Germany into the modern era, writing of the universal love of the German people for their Führer, doctoring the prose to make Hitler seem to be a modern German saint.

At the cable office, he told the woman that he would be pleased to know that copies of his dispatches were sent to the Ministry of Propaganda. "I want my friends there to know that I've been thinking, and that I think Germany is getting a bad rap in the world press," he said.

There was a cold smile. "Your request is noted, but it was unnecessary."

He called Frau Sittenrichter at the Ministry and found her working on Saturday. "I think you're going to like what I've sent off today," he said. "I'd like Herr Goebbels to see it, if possible. In fact, I'd like to see him if I may."

"He's very busy," she said. "But I'll pass the word."

"Please tell him that all my doubts have been removed. I've seen Germans all over the country. So many people can't be wrong. Tell him that I'd consider it a great privilege to have that opportunity to talk with the Führer. Tell him that I'd appreciate it if he'd look into it, and if it works out, to prepare a list of questions. He'd know more about what the Führer would like to present than I."

He could detect a note of new interest in the cool, efficient voice. "Well, yes, Herr Raine, I will tell him."

So there was nothing more to do but wait. He had little hope that Goebbels and Hitler would rise to the bait. They had more important things on their minds, for on Sunday it was announced that in view of Poland's hysterical war actions it was necessary to put the Germans economy on a war footing. There would be ration cards for food, soap, shoes, textiles, coal.

The newspapers said that the whole of Poland was in a war fever, making it seem—and this was ludicrous to

THE ADLON LINK   213

those who knew the true facts—that it was the rabid Poles who were determined to wage war.

It was a sultry day. A huge Nazi rally planned for Nuremberg was canceled. Hitler was in Berlin, speaking to the members of his thoroughly emasculated legislature, the Reichstag. For the first time the German people were told that the Führer considered the Polish situation grave. On the streets people grumbled about the announced rations —700 hundred grams of meat per week, 280 grams of sugar, 110 grams of marmalade, one-eighth of a pound of coffee substitute; and 125 grams of soap per person for four weeks.

Tongue in cheek, Ed did a piece on the generosity of the German Government willing to cut down on guns to give the people little luxuries, and ironically noted:

One hundred twenty-five grams of soap per person for four weeks is a far more generous allotment than most expected, enough to allow the German people to continue the habits of personal cleanliness for which they are famous the world over. One hundred twenty-five grams is the equivalent of almost four ounces, or one small bar of Lifebuoy, enough to last the most fastidious German for a month.

He waited outside the cable office, saw the woman there reading through the feature, saw her look and nod of satisfaction. He had not misjudged the Germanic trait of taking things seriously. Any American reader would see that he was poking fun, but the German mind just did not work that way. He grinned and went whistling off, but then he regretted it—maybe Goebbels would see and resent his humor. He'd risked a lot just to allay his boredom.

He called himself an idiot, tried to drink away his guilt

and fear at the bar, missed the English, talked a bit with some of the Americans.

And when he went to his room he had more evidence of his seemingly irresistible attraction to European women. The voice on the phone was low, intimate. Margo suggested that he come to her room, saying that she was bored and lonely.

"You are such a good conversationalist," she said. "I was thinking who would I like most to spend an evening with? And the answer was Ed Raine, for he is such an interesting . . . *talker*."

And, good God, wasn't he tempted? He remembered with his entire being the tall, powerful body, the white, beautiful skin, the fire of her responses.

"Ah, Margo," he said, "you tear my heart, for I would love to spend the evening with you, but I can't. I just can't. I have these people to see—" A lie, of course, for the only person he had any interest in seeing was Emma, and he had no idea when she would return. He hung up the telephone with a sense of loss and regret, but with a smug satisfaction in having been able to resist so pretty a temptation. He tried to forget her last words. If he remembered, and thought about her, he might just weaken and call her back.

"I'm not sleepy in the slightest," she had told him. "I suppose I'll be awake until all hours, so if your meetings end before too late, I'll be here."

Twice during the next hour, as he tried to read, he started to reach for the telephone. Then it was three times, as he threw the book aside and paced the room, looking at the instrument that he would merely have to pick up to end loneliness and take his mind off the unknowns of the next few days. He had his hand on the telephone when he heard the knock on the connecting door.

She was still in her travel suit. She felt so wonderful in his arms that he stood there in the open doorway, rocking back and forth, clinging to her. She had not eaten. They ordered from room service. She bathed while they waited, and came out in a lacy thing that did wondrous damage to his blood pressure. Then came a lovely evening of talk and closeness and, of course, love, their mutual need bringing them together on the large and comfortable couch in Emma's sitting room.

He had not taken time to close the door to his own room. He had not bothered to lock the hall door to his room. It was far from his mind to be concerned about locks and open doors. He had the woman he loved in his arms, and she gave of herself with a love and an intensity that erased everything.

Margo had not been able to sleep. She decided to have a walk, returned to the hotel late, after midnight, reluctant to go to her room. She had thought long about calling the American, and was not a little angered to be rejected. She did, however, have enough ego to make it impossible to think that he had lied. No man would reject her with a lie, so he had, indeed, had meetings. As she rode up in the elevator she looked at her watch. After twelve. Surely he was finished. She got off on his floor. She stood before his door indecisively for a moment. She could see light through the keyhole, so either he was there or he'd left his lights on. She smiled. Perhaps he had left the door open. She would surprise him. She turned the knob. The door was open. She peered in and saw the empty room. Ah, he was in the bath. What a delightful surprise for him to see her standing in the doorway; then she would join him in the tub and give him a wash and a massage that would make him remember her forever.

She was halfway to the bath when she noticed the open connecting door. She halted, frowned. She started to leave, not knowing who occupied the adjoining room, but her libido had been aroused. Perhaps he was merely talking with another foreign newsman. If so, he would still be pleased to see her. She tiptoed to the open door and looked through—to see the well-known face of the German movie star, Emma Felser-Griebe, eyes closed in bliss, and Ed Raine.

Her first reaction was anger. Meetings, indeed! Never before had she been so rejected. Ah, but this was a movie star. So? Was she not prettier? Surely, judging from the bitch's half-active response, she was more accomplished. And then the true meaning of the situation came to her. Emma Felser-Griebe was an idol. Her movies—she'd seen some of them— were always patriotic, full of praise for the New Germany. She was a Nazi idol, an example for all the women of the Reich, and she was there, being lustily fucked by a foreigner, a non-Aryan.

She tiptoed away, went up to her room. She chewed her lower lip in indecision while she wrote her report. She could not very well say that she'd crept, in the dead of night, into the American's room. In the end she merely glossed over how she knew about the situation between the idol of Germany and a foreigner. But it was her duty to tell someone that Emma Felser-Griebe was not what she seemed.

Margo had not seen Otto Schellen since the night of the performance, the night of disappointment when Hitler did not come. She called the number he'd given her and was told that he was out of town. She had no way of knowing that Schellen no longer had any interest in the possible anti-State activities at the Adlon. In fact, he was in Belgium, meeting with a very good agent who delivered to him a complete set of the defense plans of that small country. Margo's contact knew little of her, only that her name was on a list, that Schellen had plans to try, sometime in the future, to make an agent of her.

"What can I do to help?" the man asked.

"I have information for Herr Schellen," she said.

"In his absence I can take it," he said. "Does the nature of the information call for a meeting?"

She thought about it. It did not seem overly urgent. "No, I suppose not," she said.

"The Berlin mail service is quite efficient, if the information in not urgent."

The letter was posted in an Adlon mail slot on Monday morning. The efficient Berlin mail service picked it up and began the swift movements. It was on the desk of Margo's contact in the last delivery of the day. He opened it carefully with a sharp, swastika-adorned letter opener. He smiled. Lucky son-of-a-bitch, he thought, to be bedding Emma Felser-Griebe. He might consider giving a couple of toes off his left foot to be allowed to do the same. The Norwegian kid was a fireball, seeing threats to the Reich in such action. Hell, this Raine bastard was the one who was Goebbels's fair-haired boy, the one who wrote for foreign consumption as if he were one of the little man's own hacks writing for Germans. He wouldn't have been surprised to know that Goebbels had sicked Emma onto Raine to make sure of his continued loyalties.

But Margo Ostenso was the boss's girl. The boss was the one who ran her, so he put the letter into a file marked *Att: Schellen*, and left it on Schellen's desk. Schellen didn't ask his permission to leave the office nor did he tell him when he'd be back. He'd see it sooner or later. No problem. But as he started to leave Schellen's office he had another thought. It wasn't a well-kept secret that Goebbels also had an interest in Emma Felser-Griebe. Somehow he couldn't picture the Minister sharing such a prize willingly, not even to get good stories in an American newspaper. He wondered if he should pass along the information to the Ministry of Propaganda. Decided quickly against it. Goebbels was a big man. He was also a bit paranoid, and one never knew about the actions of such a man. He just might have a tendency to shoot the messenger who brought bad news. Let Schellen decide. The Norwegian cookie was his girl, his operative.

21

"THE MAN IS like a cat," Admiral Canaris said. "He has nine lives. Saved by Chamberlain in 1938 and by Mussolini in 1939."

"It is my opinion," offered General Witzleben, "that the situation has solved itself. He will not dare go to war without the support of Italy. Now he will have to cease these adventures and settle down to give the German people bread and butter. He won't last two years without the external 'threats' that he has continuously manufactured to assure the unity of the people."

Dr. Hjalmar Schacht, the economist who wore the Nazi party's highest decoration for his leadership—and fiscal legerdemain—so helpful in expanding German's production for war, nodded in agreement. "I think," he said, "that we should consider ourselves well out of it. Now we will not have the blood of a single German on our conscience. The people will cook Herr Hitler's goose quickly, for the man is an economic moron, and will alienate the people quickly by his inability to run a peacetime economy.''

Von Stahlecker could not believe what he was hearing. Once again, as in 1938, the very dedicated conspirators were seizing the first opportunity to back out of their grandiose plans. ''Gentlemen, I must remind you that our information tells us that the cancellation of the invasion of the morning of the twenty-sixth is merely temporary.''

Dr. Schacht drew himself up proudly. ''I have no intention of neglecting my responsibilities,'' he said. ''In fact, I have already drafted letters to Hitler, Ribbentrop, and Göring informing them that they must have constitutional permission from the Reichstag to go to war.''

''God in heaven,'' von Stahlecker said.

''I beg your pardon?''

''He does not even have to ask,'' von Stahlecker said. ''He has only to order. The Reichstag will obey.''

Witzleben cleared his throat. ''As a field-grade officer, it is my considered opinion that even Hitler will see the folly of going it alone. The threat of war, my friends, is past. The moment is lost. In another fortnight the rains will start in Poland, making the movement of panzers impossible. No, it is over. Before favorable weather comes again, next summer, the German people will have had enough of Herr Hitler and his goons.''

''But if you are wrong,'' von Stahlecker said, ''what then?''

''Then we will simply go ahead,'' Canaris said.

''Without plans?'' von Stahlecker said. ''Will we simply storm the fortress where Hitler is currently holed up?'' He leaned forward urgently. ''There is a very good chance, gentlemen, that we can lure Hitler to the very place where we wanted him on the evening of the twenty-fifth, to the Hotel Adlon. You know of the activities of the American, Ed Raine. You know Goebbels's desire for good propaganda. You know Hitler's love of the limelight. It is my opinion that the thought of having a rave article in one American newspaper will bring him into our hands. We must not slack off. We must continue the plan as originally conceived.''

"But without the threat of war to arouse the people," General von Witzleben said, "we would be labeled as mere power-hungry adventurers, trying to overthrow the man who has made it possible for Germany to hold up its head in pride once again.''

"What will it take to make you agree?" von Stahlecker said.

"Concrete proof, proof that we can give to the public, that he intends to go ahead with the invasion of Poland," Canaris said.

Von Stahlecker's voice was urgent. "Walk with me along Unter den Linden, see the troops moving eastward. They are in moving vans, grocery trucks. The British ambassador is in the Chancellery at the moment. The Frenchman, Daladier, has been there. He told Hitler that if French and German blood is to be spilled as it was twenty-five years ago, the French will fight in all confidence of victory but that destruction and barbarism will be the real victors. I agree. Along with Stalin and the Bolsheviks. Have you not noted that Hitler has passed word to Switzerland, Luxembourg, Holland, Belgium that he will respect their neutrality? Can there be any doubt? Those are not the promises of a man who intends peace, but of a man who intends war. The words of the French are not the words of a nation that will back down again. The people now see that there is a real threat of war. Ration cards are not issued by a government that intends to preserve the peace. Don't live in a dream world, gentlemen, as we did in 1938!''

There was silence as von Stahlecker looked at them one by one.

"I will agree to this," Canaris said. "Keep the plan alive as a contingency. Have your man, Raine, push for his interview with Hitler. Perhaps Hitler will use the opportunity to announce peace, who knows? If so, we have lost nothing. If not, then we will be ready."

"Thank you," von Stahlecker said. "I will inform the others around the country that we are staying in a state of readiness."

22

"BE STILL," SHE hissed at him, knocking his hands away playfully. The radio was turned low. It was Wagner, the "Liebestod" from *Tristan and Isolde*, strings fading, harmonies resolving, unutterably sweet. "Show some respect."

"I don't have a one-track mind," he said. "I can listen and do this"—he used his hands gently—"at the same time."

"An American expressed my feelings," she said. "Thoreau. He said, Listen to music religiously as if it were the last strain you might hear."

"He was a nut," Ed said. "Hiding off around some pond. Probably playing with himself."

"Oh, you," she said, giving up, rolling to lie in his arms. She had a feeling of burned-out blackness inside her. She felt as if she should be doing something. To think of it was acid on her consciousness. Lovemaking, sleep, seemed only to be postponement. As he kissed her the music seemed to fade, to change, to become the scratch of the old record in her father's living room over the shop, to grate around dust-filled grooves in diminishing circles of endless, hypnotic space. Not even his kiss, not even her love for him could overcome her feeling—not dread, for she was not often given to fear, but—something.

Was it only the sure and certain knowledge that the madman was still intent on his Polish adventure? She had been under a strain for so long, had expected it to end, one way or the other before now. Even failure and capture seemed preferable to another endless suspense. Hitler had demanded that the Poles send a man with plenipotentiary powers to settle the questions. It was an ultimatum. He gave them only twenty-four hours, and von Stahlecker, glum, slightly drunk, had told her that he was not sure the others would act, that it was 1938 all over again.

One thing she knew: never again could she allow Goebbels to touch her. Fortunately he was busy, had left her alone, made no attempt to call her. But, as Tuesday night passed, she feared that more than anything in the world. How terrible to have to kill him and be killed in return just when things were, once again, coming to a climax, when, if God were willing it would soon be ended.

She faced the day with that feeling of darkness. The weather it was, she was sure. Heavy, threatening rain. She was not superstitious, yet she could not shake the feeling that something would happen, something terrible.

Perhaps it was only the news that came Wednesday afternoon: Poland had announced general mobilization. "That's not terribly impressive," Ed said, "since they've already mobilized everyone who has shoes."

Neither of them would mention their fears that it was too late to stop it, that both Goebbels and Hitler would be

too busy to consider the interview. He called the Ministry
of Propaganda shortly after hearing the news flash from
Poland. Goebbels, he was told, had just come back into
his office and the matter was in his hands. When he told
Emma what had been said he crossed his fingers.

The news came with a telephone call. They were dining
in Emma's sitting room when, through the open door to
his room, he heard his telephone ring. He recognized the
sharp, businesslike voice immediately.

"Herr Raine," Joseph Goebbels said, "the Reich will
always remember its true friends."

"Thank you," he said. "I hope I am included among
them."

"Yes, indeed," Goebbels said. "I have spoken with the
Führer, Ed, if I may use that familiar name with you."

"I'm honored, sir," he said.

"I have called his attention to the fact that at least one
American has not had his good sense eroded by the flood
of vicious propaganda put out against Germany. He was
pleased. He said, and I quote, 'This young man should be
rewarded.' In short, Ed, he has agreed to make time in his
busy schedule to meet with you personally. It will be
difficult, for the situation, as you well know, is rather
urgent. It's difficult for a rational man to understand the
actions of the Poles, the blindness of the English and the
French."

"Yes," Ed said, crossing his fingers. "Sir, may I make
a suggestion? As you know, I've done some material on
the Hotel Adlon as a landmark of Berlin. To a lot of
visitors, this hotel *is* Berlin, a living symbol of its past
greatness and its present prosperity. Wouldn't it be fitting
if I could meet the Führer here?"

"Ah, the mountain comes to Mohammed, eh?" Goebbels said. "But, like you, I am one who recognizes the
elements of a good story. Yes, it would add color. The

present leader of Germany dining in a spot that speaks of the Imperial glories of Germany, returning the Adlon to the spotlight it once held, a place where important events of state took place. Yes, yes. Will you be available at this number for a while?''

"I'll stay right here until I hear from you, sir," Ed said.

"Good." Goebbels hung up.

Ed returned to Emma. "They're nibbling. The bastards are going to fall for it. I know they are."

The telephone call came within a half-hour. "Herr Raine, Ed, the Führer had a good laugh at what he called your audacity. He said, 'Goebbels, I like that young man.' He is quite taken with the idea."

"That's wonderful," Ed said, nodding at Emma, who had followed him to his room and was watching, her face tight with tension.

"Let me ask you a hypothetical question, Ed," Goebbels said. "Suppose the Führer used his interview with you to make a very important policy statement. Could we expect the other American press services to pick up that story from your newspaper?"

"If it were important enough, yes," Ed said. "It would go something like this: 'In a copyrighted story in the Des Moines *Morning Call*, foreign correspondent Edgar Raine reports that Adolf Hitler'—well, you know the formula, being an old newsman yourself."

"Yes, I see," Goebbels said. "Yes, it would be as you say. Could you make yourself available in the late afternoon tomorrow?"

"Only one thing would make me unavailable, and that would be if I suddenly dropped dead," he said, giving Emma a "O" sign with his thumb and finger.

"I can't name the hour, not just yet," Goebbels said. "After four, surely, and probably before eight."

"No problem," Ed said. "I'll stay right here until I hear from you."

He was having a drink with von Stahlecker within the hour.

The cellar bar seemed even more deserted than ever, the people there more subdued. DNB, the German News Agency, had announced that they would be issuing late-breaking news throughout the night. One could almost smell the tension in the air. Von Stahlecker nodded as Ed recounted the events.

"Yes," he said, when Ed was finished. "Yes, it goes along with what we have feared. Hitler is tenacious when he has an idea. He was going to use his appearance at the acrobatic exhibition to draw attention from his preparations on the Polish front. I think he has the same thing in mind again. We know that there is furious activity toward the east. It is my bet that the panzers will move on the morning of September first, day after tomorrow. It would be my guess that he will use the interview with you to state what he's said in many ways before, that it is the blood-thirsty Poles who are provoking war, that if they would be sensible and return German citizens and their lands to the Reich he would be a man of peace. I think he feels that he can put pressure on England and France by getting good publicity in the United States."

"Sounds logical," Ed said. "But why not issue such statements through the regular channels?"

"They are vindictive people, the Nazis," von Stahlecker said. "Herr Goebbels was speaking their belief when he said that friends of Germany should be rewarded. Some-times relatively minor things take precedence over things of more note in their strange little minds. They would think it divine justice for those who have criticized, which includes most of the foreign press, to have to take the leavings from a man who has said kind things about them.''

"Then you'll move, as planned originally?'' Ed asked.

"The plan will be the same,'' von Stahlecker said. "The car will be waiting for you.'' He smiled ruefully. "There are two reasons for that. One, the word must be carried personally by a person the English can believe, and secondly, my friend Ed, in the event of failure there is no need for you to be caught in the middle. Whatever happens, you will be safely on the way to England.''

Back with Emma, he could not relax. This time there was a feeling in the air, a feeling that it would happen. Strange to think that he had a part in changing the world. Lovely to think that in a day, two days, it would be over and he could walk onto an aircraft with Emma on his arm and take her out of Germany. On the other hand, it might not be desirable to leave Germany. With the Nazis overthrown the German state would be more free. And for years there would be newsworthy events as Germany reshaped itself. With the huge scoop he could expect from this plot in which he was a part, he could name his own job with any news agency in the world. Ed Raine, the newsman who helped overthrow Hitler, who helped save the peace of the world, would have the ears of the highest officials of the new German government. They could stay in Germany as long as they wanted, and Emma could continue her career there until it was time to start a family.

Emma was moody. When he became a bit amorous she did not spurn his advances, but her distraction, her lack of interest cooled his ardor and left him merely holding her, telling her that things were going to be just great for Mr. and Mrs. Ed Raine in the future. When, after a long,

pleasant time, Emma did begin to respond, felt that she
needed the ultimate closeness which two people in love
can experience, neither of them knew that their soft words,
their signs, were less than totally private.

23

OTTO SCHELLEN RETURNED from Belgium well satisfied. Of course, the Führer had guaranteed the neutrality of Belgium, but in the event of a war on the Western Front, one never knew what the French and English would do. Schellen knew that in a big war, neutrality would be impossible for any European country. It was his job to see to it that the military men had total knowledge of Belgian military resources. What he brought home with him went a long way toward completing the job.

Although he enjoyed field work, it was always nice to be back in his office. With a total lack of drama, he removed the poison-filled cap from his tooth. It was routine, part of his job. He replaced the loaded cap with a solid one, sat down at his desk with a pleased sigh. He would take his time catching up on paperwork before going home. His work was his life. At the moment he could think of no place he'd rather be than in his fortified office with its hidden little tricks ready to blast the living hell out of anyone who threatened him. One day he'd have to test them out. Make a bloody mess, of course, shooting into the walls. How about ricochets? No, the paneling and soundproofing would absorb the bullets. Maybe borrow a Jew or two from one of Heydrich's camps. Good test, that.

Reports. Initialing each. And then he came upon the letter from his budding agent, Margo the sexy Norwegian. He chuckled in delight. Served the ratman right. He'd never liked Goebbels. Old lover boy had been shafted again. Give him something else to write bad verse plays about. But there was something else that kept nagging at him. He ceased his chuckling. There was the anonymous report that something was going on in the Adlon. According to Margo's letter, the movie star and the American shared adjoining rooms, the door always open. It didn't ring true. Emma Felser-Griebe was German, as German as Bismarck. Her pin-up pictures were on the wall of every barracks in all the services. She was the dream of every red-blooded son of the Fatherland. Didn't make sense at all for her to be shacked up with an American.

At that moment he'd have given an eyetooth to know who sent the original anonymous tip. The son-of-a-bitch had known something. But what? Too great a coincidence to overlook that Hitler himself had scheduled an appearance at the Adlon right after the tip was received.

Well, it would be fun to see the ratman's face when he found out that his lady love was putting out to a foreigner. Too good to miss. He reached for the telephone and told the switchboard operator to get him Goebbels, chase him down at the office in the Ministry or at home or wherever the hell he was. While he waited he churned it all over.

He was put through in minutes. "Herr Doctor," he said, "you are working late."

"And you, Herr Schellen," Goebbels said. "What can I do for you?"

"A moment or two of your time, sir," Schellen said.

"A confidential matter I do not care to discuss on the telephone."

"If this line isn't secure," Goebbels said, with a sharp little laugh, "may God help us."

"Nevertheless, Herr Doctor—"

"Very well. But only a minute. In case you are not aware, this is a momentous night. I am personally supervising the news bulletins that are being broadcast by DNB regarding the warlike actions of the Poles."

"I will be there in ten minutes," Schellen said.

He had to wait an additional quarter-hour before he was ushered into Goebbels's office. He did not sit down. "I want to say, first of all, Herr Doctor, that this is not a pleasant duty for me."

"What can be so bad?" Goebbels said. He was having the time of his life. Soon the panzers would roll. Soon the subhuman Poles would be German slaves. And after that, ah, after that. "You may tell your grandchildren, Herr Schellen, that you heard the news first that the Führer is, as of twelve midnight, a few hours from now, announcing the formation of a war cabinet."

"I have been expecting it," Schellen said.

"Göring, Frick, Funk, Keitel, and Lammers," Goebbels said. "Excellent choices, don't you think?"

"The Führer is always wise in his selections."

"Of course. But your bad news, Herr Schellen. I am a busy man."

Ratman, Schellen thought, it is not I who delay with gossip about a yesman war cabinet. "It concerns a well-known personality," Schellen said. "You may know her. Emma Felser-Griebe."

Goebbels's eyes jerked upward. "What about Emma?"

Silently, Schellen handed him the letter from Margo Ostenso. He watched with silent satisfaction as he saw emotions change Goebbels's face. The man would never make an actor.

"Who is this Margo Ostenso?" Goebbels flared.

Schellen told him.

"And how did she get this information?"

"She is, or has been, quite reliable," Schellen said. He began to be just a bit worried. He was a man on the way up. It suddenly dawned on him that if Margo wasn't right in her report he could have one of the more powerful men in the Reich after his ass. You'd better be right, you little Norwegian bitch, he thought. You'd better be right.

All the joy had been taken out of the evening for Goebbels. In his mind he could picture Emma in that room he knew so well, rolling in a sweaty bed of lust with another man, but his pain was soon drowned in cold anger. He calculated it quickly. He knew Otto Schellen as an efficient and rising man. He could not allow such a man to think that he had been cuckolded by his lover.

"I knew of this, of course," he said. "I am wondering why your agent is meddling in an affair that does not concern her."

"Ah," Schellen said, "I suspected as much, Herr Doctor. He chuckled. "This American writes as if he is a true friend of the Reich, and now I know why. I congratulate you, sir."

"Tell your agent to mind her own business," Goebbels said. "And now, Herr Schellen, I must ask you to excuse me. As I told you, it's a busy night."

Schellen couldn't decide whether he had made a good or a bad impression on Goebbels with his report. He left the letter with the good doctor. Damn it all, he was thinking, if I hadn't reported it and he found out later that I knew and didn't tell him, then it would have been trouble. He decided, in the end, that Goebbels could think only that he was a man doing his job. You can't fault a man for doing his job.

Goebbels sat at his desk, his hand clutching the sheet of paper. The words burned into his mind. He was thinking that they would pay, all of them. Once before he had been betrayed by a woman. She could have been the wife of the Minister of Propaganda, but she choose a tall, handsome von-something-or-other. Now she was fat and her tall, handsome von-something-or-other was on duty on the Polish front as a minor officer and he hoped he'd get his von shot off in the first exchange of fire. And now it had happened again.

Or had it? It was, after all, the word of a foreigner. He'd go to Emma, ask her to deny it.

No. The Minister of Propaganda for the Third Reich could not put himself into such a position.

He put through a call. Within a half hour two men were in his office. He gave instructions. The Minister of Propaganda was a powerful man, with almost unlimited resources at his command.

So it was that shortly after midnight when Ed and Emma lay entwined, whispering, talking of the future, two silent and efficient men were in the room on the far side of Emma's suite with some newly developed devices.

So concerned were they with their love for each other that no mention was made of the plot, nor of Hitler, nor of anything but their love and their hopes for the future. And when, an hour later, Goebbels had the wire recorder on his desk and, in privacy, heard her say, "No man ever made me feel this way," Goebbels threw an ashtray across the room to smash against the richly paneled wall.

"Oh, lovely," she moaned. Goebbels knew the sound, the passion. In that moment he hated her as he'd never hated an individual. And then he heard Raine's voice, making love talk, their increased pace, their breathing. Unmistakable.

She would pay, and pay dearly. And the American. He'd have the son-of-a-bitch flayed alive.

"God in heaven!" Goebbels was not a religious man. The American was scheduled to interview the Führer tomorrow. That posed quite a problem. He himself had sold the Führer on the idea. It wouldn't do to go to Hitler and say, "Führer, the interview is off because Ed Raine has been screwing my mistress." He'd look like a damned fool.

But, ah, there were other ways, and the interview would be over tomorrow evening—and then, ah, then.

Meantime, he could begin. To refresh his memory he called for the dossier on the American. Yes, as he remembered. He had a mother in Dresden, a woman who had lived many years in America.

The two silent men whom he had borrowed from his colleague, Himmler, stood before his desk. "The woman Clara Raine," he said. He gave the address in Dresden. "Her sympathies are not with us. I have solid reason to suspect that she regularly sends information detrimental to the security of the Reich to the Americans. Must the Ministry of Propaganda also handle internal security? Is that not the job of the Gestapo?"

"Sir," said one of the men, "for an answer to that I refer you to Reichsführer Himmler."

"My son," Goebbels said, with a disarming smile, "you give me an impression of a man who would like to see a camp—from the inside." His eyes became hard. "Don't think for one minute that I couldn't arrange it. One telephone call—"

"There is no doubt in my mind, Herr Doctor," the man said.

"Good, good." Goebbels beamed. "Take the woman Clara Raine into custody immediately."

"*Jawohl*, Herr Doctor."

"I assume you have people in Dresden who can do it?"

"If I could be allowed the use of a telephone," the man said.

"In a moment. I want her unharmed. I will interrogate her myself. Is that understood?"

"Quite well, Herr Doctor."

"If you need my authority to have her transported by military aircraft, tonight—"

"Thank you, Herr Doctor, but the Gestapo has certain resources."

Goebbels made the other arrangements. First there was a telephone call. It was answered on the second ring; she had not been sleeping.

He smiled into the mouthpiece. "Emma, my dear?"

24

"WHO WAS IT?" Ed Raine asked, noting the look of hatred on her face. He'd never seen Emma like that.

"Goebbels. I am to come to him."

"Damn," he said. "Couldn't you make some excuse? All we have to do is get through the rest of the night and one day."

"One does not make excuses with Goebbels," she said.

"What does he want?" He feared the answer. To think of her, at the last minute, having to submit to the rat-faced man made him almost physically ill.

She shook her head in wonderment. "He said he had good news for me about the remake of *The Blue Angel*."

"At one o'clock in the morning?"

She had been thinking hard. True, she had resolved to kill him, rather than give her body to him again. But, as Ed pointed out, there was only the rest of the night and the coming day, and then in the evening Hitler would come to the Adlon and Goebbels would be dead. She told herself that she had submitted to Goebbels for less reason than that in the past, in the hope of gaining information useful to the resistance, and that he had never so much as hinted at anything useful, talking, instead, of his love, reciting to her his inane poetry. Now she had a reason. The plot was near its climax, and there was Ed. Perhaps Goebbels did have news about the remake. He was a man of vast nervous energy; it would be like him to be working on a pet project in the midst of supervising the flow of anti-Polish propaganda. Perhaps she would not be faced with the choice.

"I have to go," she said. "There is no other way."

He had never felt so helpless in all of his life. Yes, he knew she had to go. To stir Goebbels's suspicions now would ruin everything.

She dressed slowly. He tried to kiss her good-bye, but she, thinking of what was to come, averted her head, was on her way out the door when the telephone rang again. She picked it up to hear the distinctive buzz of long distance. "*Ja, Ja,*" she said. "Yes, Father." And as Ed watched he saw her face go pale. In a moment she said, "I understand. Yes. Do you remember, Father, how we talked of a visit to Uncle Fritz's place for you and mother? Yes. Tomorrow would be a lovely day for it. Do you understand?"

And as she turned to Ed there were tears in her eyes. "It's your mother," she said.

"What's happened?" The sick feeling in the pit of his stomach grew worse.

"Just ten minutes ago she was taken from her home by the Gestapo," she said.

He had a vision of the gentle old Professor Johannes Welke being dragged across the lobby by two hard-faced men. He could not speak.

"My father happened to see it. He said they did not treat her roughly, but with politeness and respect."

"My God, do you suppose they know?"

"If they knew, she would not have been treated with politeness," she said. "If they knew about her they would know about others. No, we can only hope that it is merely a routine check of a woman who has lived abroad. Such things are common."

"And then this call for you," he said.

"No, there is no connection," she said, with conviction. "If they suspected, they would come for me, not give me time to escape."

"I've got to know what's happened," he said. "Do you think von Stahlecker would be in a position to find out?"

"Don't call him from this room," she said, "or from yours. Go to a booth out on the boulevard."

She turned to smile at him as she went out the door. The look of love and concern seemed to linger, like the smile of Alice's Cheshire cat, for a long moment, and then he went into his room, closed the door behind him.

A few minutes later he was talking on an outdoor phone. "No, I was not sleeping," von Stahlecker said. "But it is an unusual time for a call, Herr Raine."

Ed told him about the arrest of his mother.

"Perhaps it is nothing," von Stahlecker said. "I will make discreet inquiries tomorrow."

"This is tomorrow," Ed said.

"When the offices open," von Stahlecker said. "I will see you in the morning in the bar, Herr Raine. Perhaps I will have some news."

He finally dozed off around three, was awake before seven. In the dining room the people were talking openly of war, some complaining about being a bit in the dark about developments. Ed almost groaned when he saw the bouncing British blonde come in. He stood, held her chair.

"Hi," she said. "Notice that I've picked up some American lingo?"

"Not a hell of a lot of it," he said. He was in no mood for Bea Goodpasture, no matter how charming she was.

"My, my, aren't we cross! One would expect a more enthusiastic greeting. Especially since this may be my last day in Berlin."

"Do you know something I don't?" he asked.

"Oh, we all have our bags packed," she said. "Herr Hitler has not answered the British note of yesterday, which was rather urgent. As you colonials say, it looks as if this is it."

"Bea, my mother was arrested in Dresden by the Gestapo. Could you people do anything about finding out why for me?"

"Oh, I dare say," she said, her face turning solemn, "we could in normal times. These are hardly normal times. I'd suggest you go to the American Embassy."

"Thanks for nothing," he said.

"Ed, I'm worry I sound glib. It's no good, though. If we made any inquiries about anything at this point—about the *weather*, for Pete's sake—all we'd get is a high runaround."

"I imagine I'd get the same high old runaround." No, he'd wait for von Stahlecker. Because he had other problems. Emma had not returned. Where she'd been, what she'd been doing he didn't want to think about.

"Ed, I'd get out, too, if I were you," Bea said. "I don't know what you're involved in, but being an American citizen won't help much if you're caught."

"I plan to do just that," he said. "Look, Bea. I'm not good company this morning."

"So I've noticed." She rose. "I should be getting back to work. If I don't see you again—if you're ever in London, just ask for me at the Foreign Office."

"Sure thing." He tried to smile convincingly, but failed.

As she left, von Stahlecker entered, walked through the lobby without coming into the dining room. He was early, Ed noted. After a hurried bite or two, he signed the chit and made his way to the nearly empty bar. He nodded to von Stahlecker and accepted the invitation to join him at his table.

"To get directly to the point," von Stahlecker said, "there is a certain amount of cooperation between our organization and the Gestapo. I am told by my friends there that Clara Raine was picked up for routine questioning. It is not unusual for a person who has spent much time abroad to be interrogated. Perhaps some minor functionary in the Gestapo wanted to get her view of America. As simple as that."

"You didn't ask to have her released?" Ed asked.

"My dear Herr Raine, my contact and association with you are merely as a casual acquaintance. We happen to frequent the same bar and you, as a newsman, are always looking for information from an officer of the Abwehr."

"Colonel, you may be able to take a more detached view of this, but it's my mother who is in custody. Damn it, she loves Germany."

"But not the present German Government," von Stahlecker said. "I remind you that she, like you, is involved in trying to depose the Government. She knew the risks when she began her activities, as did we all." He raised a hand to halt Ed's angry reply. "However, there is no reason for concern. She will be questioned, then released. If she is not, we will be in a position, after tonight, to secure her release."

He thought about it. "No," he said, "that won't do, Colonel. I want her out now. I want her in Berlin. I want her to go out of the country with me tonight."

"That, my friend, would be impossible."

"I don't think so. Go to the top if you have to. Go all the way to the Admiral. Hell, he's chief of the Abwehr, a powerful man. Have him make up some story."

"Herr Raine, to jeopardize the operation now—"

"Look, I'm going to do my part. It seems to me that the success of the whole damned thing depends on me. What if I pull out right now, get on a plane, and leave Berlin this afternoon?"

"I don't think you'd do that," von Stahlecker said.

"Try me. Get my mother out, bring her to Berlin. When I know she's safe, and not before, I will do my part."

"You're a determined man," von Stahlecker said. "Well, the impossible has been accomplished before."

"And there's something else that worries me," Ed said. "Goebbels called Emma at one o'clock last night. She hasn't returned."

This brought a sharp intake of breath by von Stahlecker. "She went to Goebbels?"

Ed told all he knew about the telephone call. The Colonel seemed to relax. "She will be back."

"Doesn't it worry you that two of our members are either in custody or missing?"

"It worries me very much," von Stahlecker said. "What I am going to say may seem brutal, Herr Raine, but necessary. There is no reason to believe that your mother is suspected of anything. If she were, she knows only three or four people. Emma is one of them, but if your mother had talked, thus resulting in Emma's detention, she would also have given the name of the other members she knows. I spoke with the Mayor of Dresden by telephone only a half hour ago. Besides, she was arrested about the same time that Goebbels called Emma. So neither one caused the other. Now, let us take it a bit further. Suppose, by some unkind quirk of fate, Emma is suspected of something. The Gestapo has ways of assuring that people will talk, but a strong man or woman can hold out for a long time. I think Emma Felser-Griebe is made of stern stuff. I think she could hold out for at least twenty-four hours, which would be more than enough time.''

"Are you saying they might be torturing her?''

"No, I think not. I think she is merely keeping Herr Goebbels company.'' He looked coldly at Ed. "Would you prefer to think of her being tortured, rather than being—''

"You Prussian son-of-a-bitch,'' he said, seeing von Stahlecker stiffen under the words. He leaned forward. "I want you to find her. I want to know, and I want to know within the hour. And remember what I said about my mother. Suddenly I don't give a damn about you, about your plan, about what the hell happens to Germany. Maybe it would be best to let Hitler go into Poland, then we'll all gang up and beat the bastard to nothing. Maybe it would be best to reduce Germany, once and for all, to a nation incapable of making war, ever, because I don't think there's an ounce of compassion in eighty million fucking German hearts.''

Von Stahlecker rose stiffly. "I will be in touch, Herr Raine,'' he said. And for a moment, in his face, Ed caught a glimpse of the young man who had been willing to fight against all odds to restore pride to his Fatherland. "Be happy, Herr Raine, that you are needed and that I am not ten years younger with two good arms.''

Ed sat drinking coffee moodily. His imagination altered between images of Emma in bed with Goebbels and of Emma on some old-fashioned instrument of torture—the rack, burning splinters under the fingernails, thumbscrews.

Silly, he told himself. Things like that just didn't happen, not in a civilized world.

She had been seized in front of the Ministry of Propaganda. It came without warning, two men stepping from the shadows to take her arms, one putting a big, muffling cloth over her face. She was half-flung into an automobile and the two men sat close on either side of her. She told herself to be calm as the muffling cloth was removed from her mouth.

"You're making a mistake," she said. "I am Emma Felser-Griebe. I was on my way, by invitation, to the office of the Herr Doctor Goebbels."

"You will be silent," she was told.

She recognized the tone of the voice, dead, cold, a voice to be obeyed, the voice of a man who had absolute power and answered to no one. She was silent. Soon she would face someone in authority. Then she would be allowed to explain. She had, she felt, merely been mistaken for someone else. Or else strict security measures had been put into effect and she was being taken somewhere to be questioned about being on the streets at such a late hour.

She followed the progress of the dark car along the familiar streets of the city she had come to love. Yes, she was being taken to the dark, stern pile of stone of the Gestapo headquarters. There she was whisked into a side entrance and escorted, not too gently, down dim halls, down flights of stairs. The air was cool there in the lower reaches of the building, and the room she was thrust into was cell-like, furnished only with a hard, straight chair and a cot that stank of other bodies. There was a pail of water and a washpan, a filthy cloth hanging beside it. The room felt dank and chill, and she was not sure, as she was left in total darkness, whether she could hear the rustle of small, crawling things or it was imagination.

She sat silent in the dark as long as she could stand it, then pounded on the door. "This is a mistake, do you hear? I am Emma Felser-Griebe! I demand to speak with someone in authority!"

She did not have long to wait.

25

AS COLONEL WOLF VON STAHLECKER sat in the office of the Admiral, his pride still smarted from the tongue-lashing he'd received from Ed Raine. He quickly outlined the latest developments.

"We can do nothing about the woman Clara Raine," Canaris said.

"She is being flown to Berlin aboard a Gestapo aircraft," von Stahlecker said. "I fear, sir, that the American means what he said. And I have this suggestion. I will place a call to Gestapo headquarters and tell them that Clara Raine is one of ours, that she has been working undercover for the Abwehr from the time she lived in America."

Canaris frowned. "They will say that we are exceeding our mission, that we have no business with civilian operatives."

"I will tell them that we are unhappy to have one of our operatives in Gestapo arrest, that we will meet the aircraft in Berlin and take custody of the woman. If I use your name, sir, they will not dare protest. I consider this action to be vital to the success of our plot, for the American is irrational, and is fully capable of carrying out his threat to leave the country. Without him, the only option will be to attack Hitler on his own ground, where the odds against success will be immeasurably less."

"Damn it all," Canaris said. "Do what you think best. However, use your own authority. Do not use my name."

"Admiral, it won't matter after tonight."

"You have your orders," Canaris said coldly.

Instead of calling, von Stahlecker ordered his driver to take him to Gestapo headquarters. There he confronted a man with whom he had dealings from time to time, using every bit of his aristocratic pose, a style that automatically made the hairs stand up on the Gestapo group leader's neck. There were times when arrogance had its uses. Immediately the group leader was on the defensive. He shuffled papers, called for a file on the Raine woman, was more than puzzled when there was no written word. At last he had to summon the agents who had ordered that Clara Raine be picked up and flown to Berlin. The revelation that the order had come from Goebbels caused von Stahlecker to feel his stomach tighten, but he was in too deep to back down now.

"I think you can see, Colonel, what position this puts me in," the group leader said. "On the one side the Abwehr, with whom we maintain good working relations, on the other hand Herr Goebbels."

"It would seem to me," von Stahlecker said, "that you would welcome an opportunity to remove yourself from the middle. I will take custody of the woman. I will make a report in full to the Minister."

"You will sign for her, of course."

"Of course. There will be no problem," von Stahlecker

said. But there was a growing, gnawing worry in him. First the Raine woman and then Emma received the attention of Herr Goebbels. It seemed quite likely to von Stahlecker that the entire future of Germany was being placed in doubt because, to put it bluntly, of a piece of ass, for there was only one solution to the puzzle. Somehow Goebbels had gotten wind of the affair between Ed Raine and Emma. He would not take kindly to a betrayal. And he was in a tight spot, having arranged for the Führer to be interviewed by the man who was stealing his mistress. Yes, it was entirely like Goebbels to have the offender's mother picked up, merely to show that he had the power to make things very, very sticky.

There were still several unresolved questions. For instance, where was Emma? If she had been just an ordinary woman, he would have said a silent prayer for her and told her good-bye in his mind. But she was a symbol of the New Germany. Not even the third most powerful man in the Reich could cause Emma Felser-Griebe to disappear without having to account for it.

He signed the papers giving the Abwehr custody of one Clara Raine, of Dresden. He was at the airport when the ancient Junkers JU-52 landed. He always took pleasure in the solid looks of that plane, with its three engines, one on the front tip of the nose, one in each wing. A good, dependable plane, not as sleek as the huge new four-motored transports, but admirable for carrying troops or passengers.

He was surprised to see that Clara Raine was a youthful-looking woman, and quite handsome. He presented himself to the two Gestapo agents who had picked her up and flown with her to Berlin. Even Gestapo agents were conditioned to obey orders without question. And when he smilingly told them that he would not report the time of the exchange if they didn't, giving them a chance to spend some time in Berlin, there were smiles in return and they parted on the best of terms.

Although Clara had kept telling herself that there was no possible way that her part in the anti-Hitler conspiracy could be known, it had been a nervous time for her. She held her peace until von Stahlecker's limousine had rolled into motion, then she said, "Colonel, may I ask what I have to do with the Abwehr?"

The glass partition was in place between the passenger compartment and the driver, who rode in the open front seat. "You are among friends, Mrs. Raine." He mentioned the name of the Mayor of Dresden.

"It's kind of him to look after me," she said, knowing that one could not be too careful.

"You will join your son at the Hotel Adlon," he said. "We will then see if it is possible to get you out of Germany this afternoon."

"I am not ready to leave Germany," she said. "I don't even know why I was picked up by the Gestapo."

"Ah, *there* is the question," he said. "Since none of our friends have been arrested, we can only assume that it has nothing to do with our plans."

"Our plans?" she asked, feigning puzzlement.

"Oh, come now," he said. "We have no secret pass-words. It will happen tonight, Mrs. Raine. Your son has been granted a personal interview with the Führer. He will meet Ed at the Adlon. Are you now convinced that I am not trying to worm information from you?"

"Yes," she said.

"There have been certain complications," he said. "Emma was summoned to Goebbels last night and has not returned. I fear Goebbels has discovered the attachment that has formed between your son and Emma."

"There were absolutely no questions asked of me," she said. "I was treated quite politely. They served me sandwiches and coffee on the plane."

"There was no hint as to why you were being brought to Berlin?"

"None," she said.

"It was on the orders of Goebbels. That we know. I can only hope that he is too busy with state business to try to attend to his personal problems quickly. That interview must not be canceled."

"Perhaps it was a mistake to remove me from Gestapo hands," she said. "I could not face myself if I were in any way responsible for failure."

"An admirable attitude," he said. "Unfortunately, your son didn't feel the same way. He insisted. He threatened to leave the country, to cancel the interview, unless you were, ah, rescued." He removed his handkerchief and wearily wiped his brow. "Without doubt it does add additional risks. But then, all life is a risk."

There was only one way to enter the hotel, openly, even defiantly. He entered the lobby with Mrs. Raine on his arm, rode up with her in the elevator to Ed's room. A wide smile greeted them. Ed threw his arms around his mother and when she began to scold him for risking everything for her, he put his hand over her mouth. "Hush," he said. "There are some things not worth risking." He looked at von Stahlecker. "Is there any word of Emma?"

"Since I have been busy following your orders," von Stahlecker said, "I have no way of knowing." He clicked his heels together and made a curt bow. "Now, if I have your permission, I will go about my business."

"Look, Colonel," Ed said, "I want to apologize. I got a little carried away this morning."

"We are all under a considerable strain," von Stahlecker said. "I will see what I can find out about Fräulein Felser-

Griebe. In the meantime, I wonder if it is wise for both of you to be in the same room. We have no idea yet what Goebbels wants with you, Mrs. Raine."

"Any suggestions?" Ed asked.

"At the moment, none," he said. "However, if all this is a result of jealousy, Goebbels might be watching you. Hitler's security men could call on you to check your room and person for weapons. Where the Führer's safety is concerned, personal freedom and privacy are immaterial. If nothing else, since you seem to have access to Emma's room—"

"It's only until tonight," Ed said. "She can leave with me then."

"On that point I must be adamant," von Stahlecker said. "We will not put the personal safety of one person above the most important event of our era."

"Nor would I allow it," Clara said. "No, Ed. You must move fast and alone. There are other ways. I can merely stay in hiding until it is over."

"And if it fails?" he asked.

"We will not increase the odds for failure by burdening you with a woman who is, perhaps, being looked for at this very moment. There's risk enough in what you've forced the Colonel to do," Clara said.

"Well," he said, "there are other ways."

As soon as von Stahlecker was gone, he called the British Embassy. After holding the line for about five minutes, he heard the bright and cheerful voice of the bouncing little blonde. "Bea," he said, "meet me in the bar?"

"Love to," she said, "but only for a farewell drink. We're on our way, lover boy, in a couple of hours."

She was in the bar within a quarter-hour. "Not a very private place for a good-bye," she said. "I'm disappointed in you."

"Would it be possible for you to take someone out with you when you go?"

Her smiled faded. "It would depend."

"My mother."

"Is she involved in whatever it is you're doing that requires me to smuggle you airline tickets?"

"Bea, I can't tell you. Not yet. You'll hear about it soon."

"I'd have to take it up with the Sir," she said.

"Can you do it now?"

"By telephone?"

"No. Go there now. Call me in my room. Say just yes or no. Tell him that it's vitally important, more important than I can say, for her to be with the embassy personnel when they leave Berlin."

"Oh, I just love big, strong, mysterious men," she said, batting her eyelashes in a burlesque of coyness. Then, all serious business, she said, "He will ask me questions. Is she being actively sought by German authorities?"

"Yes and no," he said.

"I'll have to know more than that."

"Just tell him that Churchill himself might be interested in talking with my mother when she arrives in England."

"Oh, my," she said, making a mock face of awe.

"I'm damned serious, Bea. Can't you be?"

"I'll call you as soon as possible. Things are quite hectic, as you might imagine." She blew him a kiss and was gone.

The day was only half over, and already it seemed like an eternity. He went back to his room, for he hadn't yet heard from the Ministry of Propaganda about the time of Hitler's visit to the Adlon. He wanted a drink more than anything, but he dared not take one. In his state it would take only a ounce or two of booze to make him high as a kite.

Two o'clock.

"Goddamn it," he said, "why doesn't he call?"

"Profanity won't help, Edgar," his mother said primly.

He had to laugh. Here he was involved in plotting to overthrow a government and kill a lot of men and his mother was concerned about taking the Lord's name in vain.

He paced the floor. Emma. Emma. Oh, damn it, Emma, come home. Come on back here. It doesn't matter what's happened. I hope to hell Goebbels *did* want you merely to make love to you. At least, that way, you'll come back.

26

SHE HAD NOT believed that she could sleep, but she had. The blanket on the filthy cot stank, but it kept away the chill. Her jaw ached so badly she could barely move it; she must have been clenching it fiercely in her sleep. Still pitch dark. She glanced at the glowing numbers on her watch. Morning, or almost morning. Five A.M. Or maybe afternoon. No, she was still tired; she hadn't slept that long. At first she did not know what had awakened her. Then the noise repeated itself. Footsteps in the hall. A key turning in the lock. She sat up. Bright light from the hallway blinded her, and then the light in the small room made it worse. She held one hand in front of her eyes, squinting through her fingers.

When she saw who was standing there she knew instinctively what to do. "Joseph, darling," she cried, leaping to her feet. ''I know you'd come for me.''

He hit her across the face with his open hand, the force of it stopping her in her tracks, a hand flying up to the hurt, eyes going wide.

''Whore,'' Goebbels said.

''Joseph? What—''

''You could have been with me in victory,'' he said. ''With me, the Minister of Propaganda.''

''I don't know what you mean,'' she said. ''Please, tell me what's wrong.''

''And all the while you were laughing at me—''

''Oh, no, never,'' she said, beginning to learn a cold, heavy fear. She knew his personality, knew his possessive jealousy.

''I think,'' he said, with a cold smile, ''that I shall now have a laugh or two myself.''

Two men appeared, as he stepped back from the door. She was seized and half-carried out into the hallway. She looked over her shoulder. Goebbels was following, his face grim. She was taken into a larger room with a bare steel table in the center.

''Joseph!'' she cried, as one of the men ripped her blouse, exposing her underthings. And then the strong hand was tearing at her clothing. Futilely she fought until she was stripped, standing naked on the mat. ''Joseph,'' she said, weeping in hopelessness.

''Position her,'' Goebbels ordered.

The two men seized her. There were straps attached to the table. She struggled but she was soon spreadeagled on the cold steel table, legs opened wide, feeling so totally helpless that she could not even weep.

''And now, my love,'' Goebbels said. ''I will leave you. Let me say only that I hope you enjoy it.''

She did not try to speak to him again. Black hate sprang

up in her and she regretted that she had not killed him sooner. And then she was alone in the room with the two men.

"Are you comfortable, Fräulein?" asked one, standing at the foot of the table, his eyes glued to her nakedness.

"Would you at least tell me why I'm here?" she asked, her voice shaking in spite of her resolve not to give them the satisfaction of seeing her terror.

"Oh, you'll know in just a few minutes," the other man said. He let his hands run over her nude body, tweaked a breast. She cringed and he laughed. "What a waste," he said. "God in heaven, what a waste." He let his hand pass downward and a finger penetrated, whirled around, found moisture. "I have your picture in my quarters," he said, with a smile. "In a brief costume. I have to admit that many a night I have gone to sleep thinking of you."

"Please tell me what this is about," she gasped, as he used two fingers cruelly.

The man looked at his companion. "Such a waste," he repeated.

"Something could be salvaged," the other one said.

"I was thinking the same thing."

"Being braver than you," the taller of the two said, "I will be first."

"I am not one to take seconds," said the man who had thrust his fingers into her.

"Nor I, friend."

"We will toss a coin."

She watched. The taller man won. And she watched with a sick, fearful fascination as he removed his boots and lower clothing. She closed her eyes when he came to her. There was no pain, for the fingers had moistened her, and she tried to pretend that she was not there, that the poundings were something totally impersonal and not connected with her.

Each had seconds. Apparently neither was too put off by that limitation. She kept her eyes closed, tried to stop the slow flow of tears, tried to think of Ed and how sweet it would have been had their dreams come true, if they could have had the children they talked of, big-eyed little girls and sturdy little boys. And then it was over and she was not being molested. She opened her eyes. The two men were cleaning themselves.

"Hell," one said, "she's just like any other cunt."

"But a famous cunt," said the other. "I wish I could tell someone."

"Tell me, friend. No one else."

"Of course."

They were dressed. One went out of the room and came back with a ragged, bewildered-looking man. His face had been ravaged, one eye completely closed. There was blood on his tattered clothing. He was led to stand directly at the foot of the table.

"Pig," said one of the Gestapo men, "does that sight arouse you?"

The man looked at the questioner blankly with his one good eye.

"It is all for you, pig. Can you make it stand for such a piece?"

"Please," the battered man whispered. He was struck heavily in the kidney by a fist. He didn't even gasp.

"Do it or we will cut it off, and you will have not even this last chance to use it," said the tall man.

"Yes, yes," the battered man whispered.

The tall Gestapo man grabbed Emma's hair, turned her head until she was looking up into his face. "I have been instructed to tell you, Fräulein Emma Felser-your-fucking-highness-Griebe, that since you take so much pleasure in giving your German body to foreign pigs, you will be given all the opportunity in the world. You will be given subhuman Jews until you beg, plead, scream for death.''

She looked at the battered man with interest. So it had come to this. Like to like. Jewess to Jew. And with no reasons given. At least, thank God, it was not the plot. It had to be Ed.

Oh, Ed, Ed, she told herself, I would have loved you even if I had known it would come to this.

Atop her, the battered man tried desperately, to no avail. Then, slowly it happened and he was erect and using her and whispering into her ear, "Forgive me."

"With all my heart, brother," she whispered back.

Thus began an endless morning. Some of the men who were brought to her were in far worse shape than the first and could do nothing, although, in fear and torment, they tried. Those who could not were forced to use their mouths as the Gestapo men laughed and made comments about the fare being eaten by the Jewish pigs. And she was numb. There was only a dulled awareness of being used, and then a slow ache and a pain and bruised, screaming tissue.

"There is a sameness, don't you agree?" asked the taller Gestapo man.

"Quite boring," said the other.

They enlivened the game by striking a young man across the shoulders and buttock with a whip as he screamed and plunged. And then, two men later, a new experiment. One who managed, quite well, and was nearing his climax, was suddenly killed by a thin, sharp knife plunged under the base of his skull. As his entire body spasmed, the two men laughed heartily.

"Never had such a bang in his life," laughed the tall one.

"Please," she begged, "oh, God, please."

"Don't worry, Fräulein, he was not given any special favor. Each of your patrons has met the same fate."

"You've killed all of them?" she asked.

"Can't have Jews going around bragging about having had Emma Felser-Griebe, the famous Aryan movie star."

The next man, having been forced to clean away the contents of the dead man's bowels, was sickened, and was unable to perform. But there were others.

27

HE WAS IN a trap of his own making, but in the end he would be the only one laughing. As he told an underling to put through the telephone call, he pictured the betraying bitch there in the Gestapo's basement and wondered how many had punished her. And down underneath his anger there was an amusing little thought. It had always been said that there was no limit to the woman's ability to perform sex. Wouldn't it be interesting to see if a healthy young woman could be fornicated to death?

"Herr Raine," he said, not bothering to identify himself. "The time has been set. Your guest will arrive at half past five. You will be waiting in the Rose Room, alone." The Rose Room was a plush, small private dining room. In a tasteful arrangement, on one wall, were pictures of the famous who had dined there, among them two kings of England and a half dozen other ruling monarchs.

Soon, Goebbels thought, there would be no need to withhold his vengeance on the mongrel from America. At the moment he had his uses. Due to the time difference between Berlin and the United States, the American could have his copy written and cabled in time for the morning newspapers. Thus, while English and French newspapers were condemning Germany for entering Poland, the United States would be reading about Hitler's reasonableness. The Führer could be a very convincing man. With a sympathetic writer his "proposals"—which, Goebbels knew, had been designed to seem reasonable but were, in effect, an ultimatum—would seem logical to U.S. readers. Unlike some, Goebbels worried about the United States. In spite of occasional differences between Britain and the former colonies to the west, the English-speaking cousins had a way of hanging together when the going got rough.

Even with Russia in Hitler's pocket, the prospect of having to fight the three great Western democracies at one time was enough to give one pause. He was often approached by concerned military men who begged him to use his influence to urge Hitler to postpone his plans until the military might of the country would be sufficient to meey any challenge. But since 1933 he had seen wonders performed. In one year, two years, three years, Germany would have weapons that would make the world gasp in wonder and awe. German technology and German genius would change the world, and Hitler would rule it, taking along with him those who had been with him from the first trying days. So he was confident, most of the time, that Germany was capable of taking on the world, if necessary.

However, it would not hurt to continue to make efforts to keep the United States out of a war, if Britain and France lived up to their threats to fight for the subhuman Slavs in Poland. Goebbels was never remiss in his duty to supply information to those in the United States who were sympathetic to the German ambitions. Fortunately, next to those of British ancestry, more Americans were descended from Germans than any other single nationality, he told himself. There was a solid core of support in the United States; witness the strength of the German friendship organizations, the Bunds. There were hundreds of thousands of people who would see to it that Ed Raine's exclusive interview with Hitler received maximum exposure.

Then it would be time to arrange a little accident. There had been a time in the past when he would have shrugged off the incident as just another example of the perfidy of women. He'd had plenty of experience. He knew. But now he was the Minister of Propaganda. He sat in on the most important meetings of state. He was the third most powerful man in the most powerful nation in the world. Through years of hard work—and, in the beginning, of danger—he had earned the right to show the bastards of the world that Paul Joseph Goebbels was not an ordinary man, not a man who would suffer, ever again, the betrayal of a woman.

All was in order. The script for the night's broadcasts was ready. Beginning at nine P.M. German radio would broadcast Hitler's latest and last proposals. Now there was time to enjoy his power. He ordered his driver to take him to Gestapo headquarters, for just knowing of her humiliation was not enough. He had to see it for himself. It was, he had to admit, an ingenious revenge. When the subhuman Jews had finished with her she would never be able to look a man in the face again. She would live the rest of her life knowing that she was not above punishment.

Perhaps he would even allow her to continue to work, after she recovered. She was, after all, valuable. Every man in Germany was a little bit in love with her, and her films were great morale-builders. During war she would be useful to entertain troops fresh from glorious victories, a little reward for brave German youth—who would never know that Emma Felser-Griebe, the sex symbol of Germany, no longer had the slightest interest in sex.

When word came from Ed Raine that the meeting was on for half past five, Colonel Wolf von Stahlecker immediately sent word to Canaris. And the afternoon became alive with secret and guarded communications. Since there were still troops moving toward the east, it was simple for General Witzleben to shift his Wehrkreis III troops into their desired positions, ready to seize all the Nazi ministries, the controls of power, water, communications. Berlin would be in a tight sack within an hour. Under the guise of maneuvers, the panzer division and the infantry division that would secure the southern part of the country were on the alert. Josef Müller was in Rome, and he had been assured that the Pope would immediately recognize the interim government.

There were still some question marks. General Halder, commanding troops on the Polish front, had not absolutely opposed the new plot, but von Stahlecker had the feeling that the man could go either way. It would be necessary to present Halder with an accomplished fact. Halder would not turn German troops against German troops, not when he was being offered a place in the Military Government. However, it would be necessary to have someone at Halder's headquarters at the time of the overthrow. With Emma still missing, there was no good choice. He called Dr. Schacht, who, although not enthusiastic about the assignment, agreed to fly to the Polish frontier to present the picture to Halder as events unfolded.

Meanwhile, men were watching each of the high Nazis who were ticketed for assassination. Göring would be simple. He had taken lunch with his Norwegian friend, Ingo Selmer, on the grand terrace at the Hotel Esplanade.

There, no doubt, Selmer had continued his futile attempt to convince Göring that, this time, the English would fight. The affable Göring had invited Selmer and the British Embassy counselor, Sir George Ogilvie Forbes, to have tea with him at five P.M. Touchy, that. Von Stahlecker made it a point to remind General Witzleben that his men would have to be extremely careful not to harm the Norwegian or the Englishman when Göring was killed.

Himmler, of all those henchmen who were to die, would be, perhaps, the most dangerous. Von Stahlecker went over the plans to eliminate Himmler carefully with the Army colonel in charge of that affair until he was sure that the plans were as airtight as possible.

In midafternoon, a possible snag developed. The Admiral's personal plane, undergoing a check-out, developed engine trouble; another airplane was needed for the American's flight to London. If communications facilities were captured intact, Raine's trip to England would be unnecessary. However, it was vital to have the news known in London immediately, so the back-up procedure was, in von Stahlecker's mind, one of the more important aspects of the plan. He had a spot of trouble procuring another plane. He had to call on a Luftwaffe friend who owed him a favor.

"Wolf," he was told, "you're crazy. Every plane capable of flying has an assignment. Man, don't you know what's going on?"

"I have some idea," von Stahlecker said, "but this mission *must* be flown, my old friend. Surely there is some plane capable of reaching England—London, to be exact."

"Wolf, if you'll wait a week or so, we'll have a few hundred flights a day to London." The Luftwaffe man laughed.

"But not landing, sadly," von Stahlecker responded.

"This one must land. Look, I'll break security a bit; I know I can with you. This flight is our last chance to plant a very, very good agent in England, a man who will be extremely valuable to us."

"All right, Wolf, I'll take a look around and call you back."

He finally located an old Dornier DO-28, a square-bodied, wide-winged relic with nonretractable landing gear, two engines, and just enough range to make it interesting for the pilot to play a guessing game about whether or not he should prepare for a water landing. The creaky old plane was in place at Templehof by three. The crew was instructed to take one man, Ed Raine, to London without question.

Ed, meanwhile, had received another call. He met Sir George Ogilvie Forbes in the British Embassy. "Now, Mr. Raine," Forbes said, "just what is this problem that is keeping me from important business?"

Ed had decided to pull out all stops. "Sir George, you know that I flew to England and talked with Churchill. You helped arrange it. How much do you know about why I went?"

"Oh," Forbes said, with an airy wave of his hand, "I suppose it's the same old pipe dream about overthrowing the Nazis."

The man's casual attitude sent a hot flush of anger through Ed. The tensions, he decided, were getting to him. Emma. His mother. "It's more than a pipe dream," he said, letting his anger show in his voice. "It's scheduled for five-thirty."

"What I don't understand, old fellow," Forbes said, "is your part in this."

"You don't have to understand, old fellow," Ed shot back. "It is my assumption that you have orders to cooperate. If I'm wrong, tell me and I'll get the hell out of here and you can explain to your government later.''

''Now, now,'' Forbes said soothingly. ''Tell me what it is you need.''

''I want you to take my mother out with you when you evacuate the embassy.''

''That might get a bit sticky.''

''Look,'' Ed said. ''You know and I know that you have extra sets of papers available. They're not going to be checking you too closely. They're all hot for war and they'll see your leaving as just another sign that it's on the way. They'll be glad to get rid of you. My mother speaks English with a British accent, because she learned it from English teachers here in Germany as a child.''

''Why is it necessary to get her out at this moment?'' Forbes asked. ''If this plot of yours succeeds she'll be perfectly safe here.''

''I'm willing to take my chances, but my mother has already been picked up by the Gestapo once. It took the influence of the Abwehr to get her out. I'm not going to give them another chance at her.''

''Can you get her to the embassy?''

''Yes.''

''We will be sending personnel to the airport, beginning'' — he checked his watch—''in shortly over one hour.''

''Do I take it that means yes?'' Ed asked.

Forbes nodded. ''Leave a physical description with your friend, Miss Goodpasture. Bother, this, but I suppose we can find time to prepare a set of papers.''

Ed decided that openness was the only way to get his mother from the Adlon to the British Embassy. The only problem was she didn't want to go. ''I have only the clothes on my back,'' she protested.

''You can buy clothes in London.''

"I had a part to play in Dresden. I don't see why I should be forced to desert my duties."

"You're not in Dresden, Mother," he said. "And you have no purpose here. You're a danger rather than an asset. You know that."

In the end she did what she could with her rather wrinkled dress. She brushed her hair, using Ed's hairbrush —after washing it thoroughly and informing him that the oil he used on his hair was rather heavy. He called the desk and ordered a taxi to be waiting at the side entrance. Though the embassy was only a short distance down Wilhelmstrasse, Ed felt it would be wiser to approach by taxi; they'd be less likely to be detained by officious policemen. When they went into the lobby the Norwegian acrobatic team was there in a group. Helga, astride her trusty three-wheeled steed, spoke to him. He looked around. Nothing threatening in the lobby.

"I would like to thank you once again for the kind things you wrote about our troupe," Helga said. Ed was in a hurry to move on. He saw the tall, lithe Margo examining his mother with great interest.

"Glad to do it, Baroness," he said. "Are you leaving, then?"

"On orders from our embassy," Helga said, with a sigh. "And with tremendous audiences turning out to see the show."

"Well, have a nice trip," Ed said, starting to turn away.

"Aren't you going to introduce us to your friend?" Margo asked, with a wide smile.

"Excuse me," he said. "Don't know what I was thinking of. This is my mother, Clara Raine."

The smile faded from Margo's face. She had thought that the woman was a bit old for him, and was intending to cause him embarrassment.

"We're just on our way," Ed said. "Sorry."

"Well, Herr Raine," Helga said, "remember that you will have a welcome if you ever visit Norway."

"If I'm ever there I won't fail to call on you," he said.

"The tall blond one," his mother whispered to him, as they neared the side entrance. "She looked at you with hungry eyes."

"Your imagination," he said.

She laughed. "I've know you a long time, Ed Raine, and I've seen the girls look at you."

"You're totally impossible," he said.

The taxi was waiting. He felt a bit safer once he was inside, but his mood changed drastically as the vehicle neared the British Embassy. With safety only a block or so away, traffic became snarled; there was a roadblock ahead. Cars were being let through one by one.

"What's going on?" he asked the driver.

"Nothing unusual," the driver said. "A check of papers, that's all. Probably another spy scare."

"Look," Ed said, "we're in a hurry. Can you turn off before the roadblock and approach the embassy from another direction?"

"I can," the driver said.

He circled a couple of blocks and approached the embassy from the south. Again there was a roadblock. The driver, without being asked, turned off and tried once more. When another street approaching the embassy was blocked Ed said, "Look, we'll just get out here."

The driver turned to look at them. "My friend, is there some reason for you to wish to avoid the roadblocks?"

"No, no, not at all," Ed said, "just the nuisance of it, that's all."

"You will note," the driver said, "that they are checking pedestrians, too. That is, if your idea is to walk to the British Embassy."

"We'll just get out," Ed said.

"For, apparently, the idea is to prevent someone from reaching the embassy," the driver said. "Of course, I realize you have no reason to wish to avoid the road-blocks, the paper checks, other than the nuisance of it, but if I were someone who did not wish to be checked, I should leave this area of the city immediately."

"Why would they want to prevent anyone from reaching the embassy?" Ed asked, wondering if the driver were truly sympathetic or if he was merely trying to get him to make an admission.

"Oh, who knows?" The driver shrugged. "They are leaving, the British, as are the French and many others. Perhaps someone fears that the British might be taking someone out with them, someone that another someone wants to stay in Germany. Shall I turn away, sir?"

"Yes, I think so," Ed said. "Our visit to the embassy is not important. We can wait until it is less inconvenient."

"Where to, sir?"

Where to, indeed? Norway . . . The Norwegians were leaving. Norway was a neutral country. "The Adlon," he said. Now he was more determined than ever to get his mother out. When they walked through the side entrance, porters were taking the troupe's luggage out the front to a waiting van. Helga was supervising, circling the area furiously on her tricycle.

"Wait for me in the garden restaurant," he told his mother. He chased the little woman down. She smiled when she saw him.

"Ah, another chance to say good-bye." She beamed.

"Helga, can I speak with you a moment?"

"Surely."

He led the way to a deep chair in a quiet corner of the palm court and sat down. The splashing marble fountain would cover their conversation, making it impossible to eavesdrop. She parked her trike facing him, eye to eye.

"Helga, I'm going to lay a heavy burden on you. If it's too heavy, just say so, but promise me that what I say will be between us."

"Of course," she said.

"I must get my mother out of Germany. It's as simple as that. You're going. I don't have any idea how it could be accomplished, but it is important."

She looked thoughtful. "We are already cleared with German customs," she said. "Our embassy saw to that." She brightened. "If your mother would not object to a half-hour's discomfort—"

"What do you have in mind?"

"A large steamer trunk in my room. It has not yet been brought down."

"She can't stay in it," he said. "She would not have enough air."

"No, of course not. We are flying a special charter aircraft, one I hired myself. I know the pilot well. I will inform him. At the last minute, having left the steamer trunk until last, we will open it, she will pop into the plane, and we will take off."

"Helga, you could all get in trouble. I don't even know how much. I just know that the Gestapo wants my mother."

"Trouble, hah!" she said. "The world is full of trouble. The risk is only yours, and your mother's. Should we be caught they would not dare detain us. We are neutrals, and I think Herr Hitler needs all the friends he can get. I happen to have the ear of some powerful men in Norway—family connections. Should an incident occur, I'm sure that it would not be serious for me or my troupe."

"Helga, you're wonderful," he said.

"Remember that, and meet me in my room as soon as you can get there."

* * *

"I very definitely will not fold myself into a trunk like a rag doll," Clara protested, as Ed lifted her bodily into the emptied trunk. The contents, costumes and equipment, were hidden in the closet of Helga's room. "There is no way you will get me to stay in here quietly," she protested, as Ed positioned her, cushioned her head, closed the lid.

Her voice muffled came out: "I will scream and kick, and they will find me!"

"And then I will be unable to finish the job," he said, holding his mouth close to the lid.

"Damn you, you young bully," she said.

With the trunk in place in the van, he joined Helga in a taxi. At the security gate at the airport he explained that he was merely seeing his Norwegian friends off and was allowed in. In the terminal building they parted; Helga joined her troupe at the desk for passport clearance, while Ed went to a window where he could watch the loading.

Margo was not with the troupe. She had become suspicious; she had stopped to call her contact to say that something was definitely wrong, and that it involved the American reporter, Edgar Raine. In any case, she had no intention of getting on the plane, but to save explanations and argument, she had accompanied the troupe to the airport. It was all arranged with her last-minute telephone call: she would be detained at passport check. She was just a bit angry, because she'd been trying to get in touch with Schellen to make arrangements since the unexpected word came that they were to leave the country, and all the time the arrogant bastard had had things under control. Oh, well, everything would be all right. As she loped through the lobby, she took time to wave at Ed Raine, hoping that he would be in deep trouble as the result of whatever he and Helga were doing.

Schellen, having been informed of the imminent departure of the Norwegians, was waiting at passport clearance. He stood there, hands behind his back, until Margo, not daring to look at him, came abreast of the desk. The others had all been cleared, and were waiting for her.

"Name." The official demanded.

"Margo Ostenso."

"Nationality of passport?"

"Like all the rest," she said irritably. "Norwegian."

"Just answer the questions," the official said testily.

"I'll will talk with this one," Schellen said, stepping forward to take Margo's passport. "You will follow me."

"Margo, you will do no such thing," Helga said, having observed the actions from the seat of her trike. "You, sir, just what the hell is going on?"

"It is a formality," Schellen said. "There is a small discrepancy in her papers. Please, I assure you there will be no trouble. Just board your aircraft and we will bring the young lady out afterward."

"The Norwegian ambassador will hear of this," Helga said.

"Go on, Helga," Margo said. "I'll be along."

They filed out and approached the DC-3. The baggage carts were there, and the luggage was being loaded. Helga rode up to the group of three men doing the loading. "Leave the trunk to the last," she ordered.

"Fräu," protested one of the loaders, "it should go in now."

"I don't care what you have to do," she said. "I want it to be last on, so that in Oslo it will be first off."

The man shrugged. "Smuggling jewels?" he asked. He turned to his crew. "Do as the Frau says."

She wheeled the trike, looking for Margo. She could not imagine what had happened. But as the others filed aboard the aircraft she made her decision. Margo was Norwegian, and quite capable of taking care of herself. She could take a commercial flight. She would be safe.

Now the woman trapped in the trunk needed attention. All the other luggage was loaded. All but Karl were aboard; he was waiting nearby, to help her up the stairs into the plane. She had told him what would happen. The only question was what would the men who were loading the plane do when she opened the trunk?

The pilot had been alerted and was ready. When he saw that everything was loaded except the trunk, he pushed the starter for the engine on the wing away from the loading door. There was a whine, spits and coughs, and the engine caught. The man in charge of the baggage detail cursed.

"Tell him to stop the engine until we are finished," he yelled at Karl, over the sound of the revving engine.

Karl held his hand to his ear. "What's that?" he said.

"Out, get out," the foreman told his men. "We will not finish until he shuts off the engine."

The men withdrew to a distance. It was working well. Helga motioned to Karl. "Can you close the baggage door?" He nodded. He closed the door, locking it with the tool left by the workmen. He could hear a faint yell of protest from the foreman.

Helga wheeled up to the cart with the trunk. She had to stand on the seat of the tricycle to reach, and the hasps were difficult, but then they were soon open. "Now," she called, trying to lift the lid.

Clara pushed the lid up and climbed out. "Quickly," Helga yelled, as Karl seized her and she swung onto his hip. Clara was running for the boarding stairs. Helga could hear yelling as Karl leaped upward, two steps at a time. Two crew members were at the door; when the three of them were inside, the crew members kicked the ramp, hard, so that it rolled on its wheels, and slammed the door shut. Helga could hear yelling from outside, drowned out as the other engine roared into life, and the plane started moving.

"Take me to the control cabin," she told Karl. There she heard the pilot talking with the tower, getting takeoff instructions. He had told her that he would have time, before word could be sent to the tower, to get into takeoff position, after that they'd be on the way.

When they were alone, out of hearing of the men around the passport desk, Margo had said, "You took joy in keeping me in suspense, didn't you?"

"A good agent does not panic," Schellen replied with a smile.

"Have you been in contact with your office about my call?"

"No. Why did you call?"

"There is something going on," she said. "The American was at the Adlon with a woman whom he called his mother. They left and came back immediately. Then they went to the room of Helga Gies and the woman did not come out. The American came to the airport with us."

Schellen saw the possibilities immediately. "Was there an extra person in your party?"

"No."

"Any extra piece of luggage you noticed, after the appearance of the American?"

"No. Only the steamer trunk from Helga's room."

"Damn," he said, breaking into a run, bowling past the guards without explanation just in time to see the woman leap from the trunk and bolt up the boarding stairs. "Stop her," he yelled ineffectually toward the loading crew, but he was too far away to be heard over the sound of the engines. He ran back into the building, picked up a telephone, got the terminal's main switchboard, and demanded to be connected with the tower.

"That is not allowed," he was told briskly.

It took him almost a minute of serious-voiced identification and threats to convince the operator to connect him. Then he gave orders to stop the Norwegian aircraft.

They were at the end of the runway and the pilot was running up the engines, testing. He informed the tower that he was ready and requested permission to take off, received it. The engines roared and the plane lurched into motion, accelerated down the runway. He could feel the tail wanting to rise when the tower came on, excitedly, giving his designation and orders to abort the takeoff.

"Negative," he said, "negative. We have reached the point of no return." He had not. The tail came up slowly.

"You will circle one hundred eighty degrees and land on the runway you have just left," the tower ordered.

"Templehof tower, your transmission is breaking up," he said, with a grin upward at Helga, perched on Karl's hip. "Will you please repeat your transmission." As he spoke he flipped a switch off and on rapidly, giving the impression that his radio was cutting in and out intermittently. And then he cut it off entirely.

"We're on our way, Baroness," he said. "Hope you haven't done anything serious enough to make them shoot us down."

"I don't think so," she said doubtfully, not having thought of that possibility.

The two ME-109s picked them up over Rostock. They had been flying in radio silence. One of the sleek fighters took position off the port wing, waggling, the pilot making motions with his hand, pointing downward.

"They're telling us to land," the pilot told Helga.

"I don't think I want to visit Rostock," she said.

"We'll be over the Baltic in a few minutes. Then over Denmark," the pilot said. "How badly do they want us to land?"

"I honestly don't know," Helga said. "But I don't want to land."

The pilot waved cheerfully at the pilot of the ME-109, whose gestures became more frantic. And then there was water below. The Norwegian pilot was an old barnstormer, and his experience stood him in good stead as the German fighters buzzed past, sometimes dangerously close. He waved and grinned when they came close and once, when a fighter positioned itself just over his nose and gradually eased downward in an obvious effort to make him go into a dive, he held his course, although his sphincter muscles were quite tight, until the German gave up the game of chicken. As the 109 peeled off and away, he waved and grinned, then took both hands off the wheel and clapped them in front of his window so that the German could see his approval of a tricky bit of flying.

The two fighters left them with the gentle coast of the Danish islands underneath. He breathed again and opened his radio, made contact with Copenhagen control, and requested permission to cross their land space en route to Oslo.

Margo Ostenso, left behind during Schellen's frantic attempt to stop the aircraft, went into the lobby to see Ed Raine still standing before the observation window. Her first impulse was to confront him and demand an explanation. This, however, would, as the expression went, blow her cover as a German agent. Instead, she stayed out of sight, and when he left, the Norwegian plane out of sight in the sky, she followed. He took a taxi. She did likewise, telling the driver to follow Raine's cab. When he went into the Adlon she was at a loss. She could scarcely go back there. She waited. When he did not come out she found a telephone booth.

Otto Schellen joined her down the avenue from the Adlon in a half-hour. "Where the hell have you been?" he asked.

She explained that she had followed the American back to the Hotel Adlon.

"This woman he introduced to you," Schellen said. "Did you get her full name?"

"Of course. Clara Raine."

"Describe her." He made notes. It wasn't his affair, but the American was showing up too much in his life to be dismissed. He gave Margo money, told her to check into another hotel and wait for him. Alone, he took a cab to Gestapo headquarters. Within minutes, an administrator there had Clara Raine's file on the desk in front of him.

"For information concerning Clara Raine," he told Schellen, "you must contact the Abwehr."

"Oh, shit," Schellen said. "So that's all it is. Just another way to plant an agent." All that trouble, and it had been only the Abwehr up to their usual tricks, trying to usurp the territory of the foreign intelligence division. Well, he'd had enough of that.

At the Abwehr headquarters, he asked to see the Admiral. Impossible. Soon he found himself exchanging salutes with von Stahlecker.

"Colonel," Schellen said, "can't you find less dramatic ways to get your agents on aircraft?"

"I beg your pardon?" von Stahlecker said.

"The woman Clara Raine."

Von Stahlecker felt himself go cold inside, but he kept his composure. "I have already had to convince the Gestapo today that she is one of ours," he said. "And now you?"

"No, no," Schellen said, laughing. "The very clumsiness of the operation told me it was Abwehr. Stahlecker—"

"There is a *von* in front of my name," he said.

"Excuse me, Colonel. When are you people going to learn that foreign intelligence is a field for experts?"

"We try, in our small way, to learn," von Stahlecker said, with a little smile. "We are always willing to learn."

"Then enroll in classes," Schellen said. "Is the Norwegian midget an Abwehr agent as well?"

Von Stahlecker became coolly guarded. "There are some things best not discussed." The puzzled intelligence man's greatest defense—secrecy. He waited to see if that would satisfy Schellen.

"You will share, I hope, any fantastic secrets you turn up in Norway using midgets, women, and children, won't you?" He rose. "Thank you for your time."

"If at any time I am able to make a contribution to the accumulated knowledge of your service, please call on me," von Stahlecker said.

Schellen left, laughing himself out of an opportunity to insure his rise to power.

Von Stahlecker had midgets and women and children and Norwegians running around in his brain. He couldn't sort them out, but it was late. Already men were in place. Already the Führer would be making preparations for the short drive that, if things went well, would be his last as the leader of Germany.

28

IT HAD BECOME a thing almost removed from her by the time it ended. She did not realize, for a long time, that it was over, that her body was not being subjected to the helpless, heartbreakingly broken men. She could not open her eyes. The hard, cold steel of the table top had chilled her through and her hips ached with bruises and her entire body was an ache like an abscessed tooth. She knew only that she had peace, at least for the moment, and when she felt herself being lifted she moaned a protest. Her legs would not support her; hard mens' hands held her arms.

"God, she smells like a Polish whorehouse," she heard on one side of her.

"I wouldn't know." And a laugh came from the other.

Gradually strength returned to her legs and she was able to take the weight off her arms. There would be bruises on her arms where their fingers had dug in, too, but that didn't matter. Nothing mattered.

"Look at me," a voice said. She knew that voice. She felt the edges of a hatred that seemed to become a sharp knife in her. She forced herself to stand straight, opened her eyes, her weakness overcome by the terrible desire to lash out at that voice, to slash and tear at that face.

"You could have been with me in victory," he said. "With the Minister of Propaganda."

She tried to spit in his face, but she was weak and he was too far away. The spittle drooled down her chin.

"Very pretty," Goebbels said. "If you haven't had enough yet, whore, we can find some more Jews for you."

Her voice was a croak. "Each of them was a better man than you."

His eyes narrowed. She could never have imagined how she hated him. "Give her a few more Jews," Goebbels said.

"Herr Doctor," one of her tormentors said, "we should wash down the room with a firehose. It stinks."

"Let her wallow in it," Goebbels said.

She had to hurt him, to slash at his pride with the knife that grew within her. Her hatred, otherwise, would consume her.

"Joseph—" she began.

"Do not address me by that name."

"Herr Doctor Reichsminister Goebbels," she said. "I find we have one thing in common." She drew herself up. "Gentlemen," she said to the Gestapo men, looking at first one and then the other, "the distinguished Minister of Propaganda shares one thing with me—my love for Jews."

He stepped forward, gloved hand raised to hit her, then withdrew in distaste.

"Oh, it's true, Joseph, darling," she snarled. "You've been making love to a Jewess for over a year."

"She is delirious," he said.

A deadly fear washed over her. What had she done? For in striking out at his pride she had condemned her parents. "Oh, it's true," she said. "It can easily be checked. Not with my adoptive parents—" She was jerked roughly by one of the guards.

"Let her speak," Goebbels said, his face white.

"My father was a Jew. He seduced my adopted father's sister, who was too ashamed to tell. She, my real mother, did not tell anyone that I am half Jewish. My adopted parents had and still have no idea. I learned of it."

"You lie!" Goebbels's voice trembled.

"Jew-lover!" she said. "And it was good, wasn't it, darling?"

"Work with her," Goebbels said. "Get me the name of her father."

"Oh, they won't have to work with me," she said. "I will tell." She gave him her real father's name, told him where he could find the certificate of birth for a baby girl to her real mother.

He believed her. One of the Gestapo men snickered, thus signing his own death warrant. This put a different light on matters. He, Joseph Goebbels, tricked into making love to a Jewess! It was an intolerable situation, which had to be remedied.

"Keep her here," he said. He was thinking furiously. Only three men knew that Emma Felser-Griebe was in Gestapo headquarters, aside from himself. And now one more would have to know, for the unrepentant bitch had changed the situation entirely with her revelation. He had not expected defiance. "You stay with her. Do not leave this room."

Doctor Willy Hindsinger's laboratory was also in the lower level of the building. Hindsinger was a specialist. Goebbels thought he was mad, but he had his uses. His medical degrees gave him delusions of grandeur, but they were overlooked in view of his usefulness. He was a small, withered-looking man. It was rumored that he quite often experimented on himself with various drugs, but this, too, was overlooked.

"Ah, Herr Doctor Goebbels," Hindsinger said, as he perceived the identity of his visitor. "You have at last come to see the collection."

"That is not the purpose of my visit," Goebbels said.

"Ah, but you must see, now that you're here." Hindsinger led the way into a room which stank of formaldehyde. Ranks of carefully labeled jars lined the shelves. "It is the most complete and scientific collection of its kind," Hindsinger said proudly. "Soon I will begin the preparation of my paper, the definitive study of human and subhuman genital size."

Each jar contained the severed genitals of a man.

"You will note," Hindsinger said, "that the members of true Aryans are generally more delicate, and thus more sensitive than the gross, clumsy ones of the subhuman races such as Jews, Poles, Czechs, and the like."

"Yes, Herr Doctor, fascinating," Goebbels said. "But I am interested in your studies on women."

"Ah, yes," Hindsinger said.

"In fact, I am in need of your services. A matter of some . . . delicacy."

"You have an interesting subject for me?" Hindsinger asked hopefully. "I am sick of doing work on subhuman whores."

"A true Aryan type," Goebbels said. "You were doing studies on the threshold of pain and pain tolerance in the subhuman Jewesses, I believe. I thought you might welcome an opportunity to check your results on an Aryan."

The fastidious Hindsinger insisted on clean, if not sanitary, working conditions, so the room was after all hosed down, and Emma was given a cursory cold shower. She had been placed on the steel table again and her arms and legs strapped down.

She was aware that four men were now in the room. She raised her head and saw that Goebbels and another man had joined the guards.

The newcomer was in white, a kindly-looking small man with a wrinkled face and a nice smile. He spoke to her in a soft voice.

"Are you comfortable, my dear? You may be frank with me, for I am a doctor."

For a moment she felt hope. "Have you come to help me?"

"Oh, yes, yes," the man in white said. "But first you must help me, my dear, with a few little tests."

He dug into his doctor's black bag, which he had set on the table near her foot. The instrument he pulled out looked almost like a nutcracker. He came to her side. "Now my dear, you must tell me when you first begin to feel pain." He was clamping the instrument over her finger. "Not an awareness of pressure, mind you, but pain, real pain."

He began to tighten down a chrome thumbscrew, watching a small pressure gauge carefully. She determined to be silent. He was kind, and she would be strong for him. But as the doctor frowned down and tightened the screw, she let out one moan.

"Come, come, you are not cooperating," the doctor said. "Tell me when you *first* feel the pain. Let us begin anew."

Now she understood; he wanted her to feel, to admit to pain. "Now," she said, when she felt the pressure on her finger turn to pain. He repeated the process with her other fingers, making careful notes in a pad. Then he clamped the thing onto her toes, one by one. "Now," she said, each time she felt pain.

"Ah, you are an excellent subject," he said. "Now we get down to serious work." He turned to Goebbels. "She had a threshold of pain slightly lower than most subhumans; that is, she is, as one would expect, more sensitive," he said. "About average, judging from my incomplete work with Aryans. It is most interesting. And now you might want to see the instrument I have devised to test the ultimate threshold."

Emma saw Goebbels move closer to look. But she was watching the kind doctor in the white coat; he pulled out a long, blunt instrument attached to an electrical box of some kind.

"There are several ways to approach the problem." His kind voice lulled one part of her mind, but another part was alert, trying to run away. "But I have found that psychological terror, the helpless feeling of being totally violated, somehow makes the pain more unbearable." She couldn't put the kind voice together with the words it was saying; first one, then the other, came into focus, a kindly drone, then horrifying words. "In addition . . . area we treat with this instrument . . . narrowly separated from several of the internal organs . . . ovary, subjected to electrical current . . . nerves that cannot be reached with external stimulation . . . ."

Emma watched in utter horror as the kind man carefully, as if fearful of hurting her, inserted the blunt instrument deep into her vagina. She felt nothing, nothing. And then there was a tingle.

She heard a chuckle. She couldn't see anything anymore— only brightness. And she saw the tingle grow. Distantly she heard a voice, retreating further. "No need, Herr Goebbels, to ask . . . cooperate now . . . we will know

. . ." She could not stop the scream that clawed out of her belly, searing her throat.

Then blackness.

Then she saw the dim tingle again, saw it grow, saw it turn to a scream, and then blackness again.

Then light again, and the sweet loving voice: ". . . to spread the pain throughout . . . walls of the vagina . . . not rich in nerve endings, but the surrounding tissue . . . stomach . . . lower spine, richly endowed . . ."

This time she saw the tingle coming and begged for death, then came the scream and blackness.

The next time she understood it. They *knew*. They *had* to know. That was why they kept doing it, again and again, crooning with those strange words, whipping her with that pain. If she talked it would be over and they would kill her and she would not know the unbelievable pain.

"Von Stahlecker," she gasped, as the tingle began again, willing to do anything, anything to stop it; but the pain and the scream grew and stopped again.

The blackness went away, and she clung to her discovery.

"Von Stahlecker, the Adlon," she gasped. "Hitler."

"Ah, the poor woman," the kind voice crooned. "She becomes maddened. We should stop now."

"No, wait!" The other voice. She knew it, or used to know it. "What about Hitler and the Adlon?"

But the pain had stopped and she could see clearly again. She could hear her voice echoing in her ears, but could not hear what it said. She would say no more. Then the tingle began again, and things lost focus, slipped to noise and darkness.

"You see," the voice crooned, "the tolerance increases. A puzzling phenomenon."

"What about Hitler?" It was the other voice, the one

she used to know. "Tell me and we will leave you in peace."

One name rang in her mind, one means of stopping the pain. "Von Stahlecker. Capture Hitler."

"Capture Hitler?" She felt her head being shaken, felt his fingers in her hair. A different pain, one she knew; things snapped into focus again. "There is a plot against Hitler? And others?"

"All of you." She smiled, staring at him—Goebbels! That was who he was. "You will die, Jew-lover."

"Who else is involved?"

"Jew-lover! Jew-lover!"

"Give me the control!" Goebbels said. The tingle came. "Who else is involved? How do they hope to succeed?"

"Von Stahlecker."

"The American," Goebbels hissed. "Ed Raine, he is a part of this plot?"

The sound of his name was like a wind cutting through the fog in her brain. "No," she said. "Innocent dupe. My job to convince him to ask for interview."

"You lie!"

"Raine knows nothing" she said. "Thinks he's getting a big scoop."

"He's in on it!" The tingle came and grew, slowly. "Say it! He's in on it!"

"Herr Doctor," the kind voice said, "you will kill her."

It grew slowly, but larger than ever before. She would say nothing more; to keep from speaking, she screamed and screamed, and a great scream, and then was darkness.

"Joseph, you are mad," Reichsführer Himmler said.

"Don't just sit there telling me I'm mad," Goebbels said. "We must act."

"Emma Felser-Griebe?" Himmler asked. "If it gets out

you've killed her, every man in the nation will be after you."

"That is not the problem. There is a plot."

"A one-man plot to capture Hitler." Himmler laughed. "His name is Superman, like the American comic-book hero?"

"Shall I go to the Führer himself?"

Himmler looked thoughtful. "All right, Joseph. First, we must clean up this mess you've made. Even if there is a plot, we can't let the nation think that an idol like Emma Felser-Griebe, the Aryan dream girl, was a part of it. Damn you, Joseph, you've cost me two good men."

"Three," Goebbels said. "Hindsinger."

Himmler shrugged. "He is so mad he would not have recognized her."

"I won't take that chance," Goebbels said.

"I'll handle Hindsinger. His work is invaluable. His experiments in the nature of pain will be of great help." He tapped his fingers, very much the schoolmaster. "We'll have to destroy the film."

"What film?"

"Oh, these experiments are recorded by automatic cameras." He smiled a thin smile. "It would be a shame to destroy it without looking at it."

"No one must see it developed."

"Oh, we can fix that. There is one photo-lab man who isn't very good at his work anyhow." He rose. "Yes, I do want to see it. I'll arrange copies for you, if you like."

"The Adlon," Goebbels said.

"Yes, the Adlon," said Himmler, picking up the telephone.

29

THE MEN WERE in their places. They were good men, real men, men von Stahlecker knew he could trust. It was going to happen, after all. When he heard the crazy story of the Norwegian plane affair, von Stahlecker had lost his temper and yelled at the American, who yelled back. If Otto Schellen had not been so smug, so certain that the Abwehr was composed of a bunch of idiots, they would all be enjoying the attentions of the Gestapo. But now it was going to happen. Hitler's car had left the Chancellery.

Ed Raine was already in the Rose Room. Von Stahlecker, nodding to the security men who guarded the door—he had explained his presence as an additional security measure— went into the room. "The car is on the way."

"I wish it were dark," Ed said. "I'd feel better about the whole thing."

"Opportunity does not know time," von Stahlecker said. "You know what to do?"

288

"I know," Ed said.

Von Stahlecker returned to his station near the front door. He checked his watch. In trial runs it had taken only ten minutes. Each minute seemed to crawl.

Inside the Rose Room, Ed fiddled with pencils and paper for the benefit of any security man who might look inside. He, too, was checking his watch. The lobby of the hotel had been emptied of all but the security guards. Von Stahlecker's men were hidden on the stairwells, in reception rooms off the main lobby, in the gymnasium—all explained as part of his reinforcements for the benefit of the Führer's security. Some of them were now armed with automatic weapons.

"He has arrived," he heard von Stahlecker say in a loud voice. "He is getting out of the car." About fifteen seconds for Hitler to reach the entry, where he would be sheltered from stray shots. Ed moved. He burst past the startled guards at the door.

"Jesus, fellows," he said, "I've got to make a quick trip to the john."

"The excitement of meeting the Führer," one of the guards said, as Ed half-ran.

Once he was around the corner, he broke into a full run, emerged from the side entrance on Wilhelmstrasse. The limousine was there. He leaped into the rear seat. He heard the first shots behind him. The driver hit it hard, causing him to lurch back in his seat.

"All right," Ed said, the sound of gunfire fading behind them. "Slow it down. We're in the clear."

Ed had pointed out the flaw in the plan, that he would be running for the airport without knowing for sure whether the plan had succeeded. "If he comes, success is certain," von Stahlecker had replied. "Besides, I have promised you that you would be out of it one way or the other, succeed or fail. If we fail you will know."

The Dornier DO-28 was, he thought, a strange-looking old bird, sitting low on her nonretractable wheels with streamlined covers. The motors cranked up as he went aboard, found his way to a rather uncomfortable metal seat. Once they were airborne he unbuckled and made his way forward.

"Can you get Radio Berlin on any of those?" he asked, pointing to the bank of dials and knobs. The copilot, a smiling young man with a handsome face and blue, blue eyes, tuned in. There was only music.

The pilot, wanting to be friendly to this very important man who could command a plane all to himself, pointed out the route on the navigation chart. They had clearance for a straight-line shot, thank God, for the range of the aircraft was limited. The route lay roughly over Braunschweig, Münster, Rotterdam. The radio continued to play Wagner, reminding Ed of Emma. Jesus, Emma. What had happened to her? Well, now that the good guys were in control, they'd find her. By now the top Nazis were dead, Göring, Goebbels, Himmler, several others.

Come on, come on, he said silently to the radio, willing it to interrupt the music, to broadcast the glad tidings. Instead, it made a sudden fleeping sound and went all static. The copilot thumped it, fiddled with dials. "Sorry," he said. "It is, after all, rather old equipment. Even the most careful maintenance—" He shrugged.

The plane was slow. It seemed to drone its way westward at about the speed of a one-winged pigeon. Unable to get the radio going again, the copilot dozed. Ed tired of standing and took his seat. Incredibly, he dozed. He awoke with someone shaking his shoulder. There was a strange, stuttering sound, and with a blurp of his heart in his chest, he realized it was the engines.

"What the hell?" he asked.

"You'll need this, Herr Raine," the copilot said, extending a life jacket, "unless you can swim for at least twenty miles."

He looked out a window. The Channel was below, and coming up with appalling swiftness. The copilot shrugged. "It is rather old equipment, this plane. Even the most—"

"—careful maintenance," Ed finished.

One engine was dead, with the prop feathered. The other one spit and coughed valiantly, but was unable to maintain the plane's altitude. "We're going in, then?" Ed asked.

"Life raft," the copilot said, pointing. "Self-inflating. Fortunately, this plane has good flotation characteristics. Perhaps we will all get out, but you first, Herr Raine. The moment we cease forward motion you turn this, kick here. Do you understand?"

"I understand," he said.

"I will help the pilot. One straps oneself in, but one is careful to be ready to unstrap the moment we cease violent motion."

"Yes," Ed said. He was strangely calm. He'd been scared as hell back there in the Adlon, but this didn't seem to raise his blood pressure at all. "By the way, did you send out a Mayday?"

"We tried," the copilot said. "It is very old equipment."

The water was quite close, covered with small white-caps. "Brace yourself," he heard, and then came a ripping, tearing thud, and then silence as the plane bounced into the air again. The pilot managed to keep the plane from flipping over; brought it down level for more rippings and tearings and bumps that almost caused him to bite through his cheek. The plane slowed, and he unbuckled while it was still moving. In spite of the copilot's optimism, he expected the plane to go down like a rock. He turned the handle, kicked the hatch. Water sprayed his face briefly before the plane stopped. He could almost feel it settling under him. Water began to run into the hatch.

"Come on," he yelled. The copilot was struggling out of the cabin, the pilot a limp mass in his arms.

"The raft," the copilot yelled. Ed seized the raft, ripped it from its moorings, tossed it out. He was trying to decide whether to go help the copilot when the starboard wing tank went, the side of the plane seemed to dissolve in flames and the concussion kicked him right out the open hatch into the water. Flames began to spread as the plane settled and he was yelling to the copilot to hurry and then, his hair singeing, swimming away.

He could see the life raft inflating itself. He reached it and clung to it, looked back. There was only flaming gasoline atop the water. There was no sign of the pilot and copilot. He felt suddenly weak, so weak he had to wait a long time before climbing into the raft.

Twenty miles, the copilot had said, but twenty miles from where? From the Netherlands coast or the English coast? Two men dead back there. Burned or drowned. How many at the Adlon? But how many if Hitler had gone to war? For he felt sure that it was over. He could not have felt as calm, as confident, if things had gone wrong back there.

There was still a lot of daylight left. He had no doubt that he'd be picked up soon. The Channel, after all, was one of the busiest stretches of water in the world. The whole British Navy would be on alert because of the war threat, patrolling the waters around England and the European coast.

The last couple of hours of sun dried his wet clothing somewhat and the small whitecaps seemed to be abating with evening, but it could be chill, for a man who was damp and at water level, even in early September. He was restricted in his movements in the small raft and spent the early part of the night alternately slapping his arms against his sides to warm himself and looking hopefully for the running lights of a vessel.

With the dawn a single sea bird kept him company, circling above him, now and then rending the silence with a hoarse cry. The sea around him was empty. It was Friday, September first. His watch had been put out of order by the crash and seawater, and his only means of telling time was the sun. It was a lovely day.

He began to think of a drink, a tall, cool, long one, sometime during the afternoon. It seemed near when he saw, on the far horizon, a low shape that could only be a ship. He stood and waved, then he took off his jacket and waved it. The ship didn't wave back. Twice more before darkness he saw ships in the distance.

His confidence never failed him. He would be picked up, or he'd hit the coast. He knew that, even if a bit uncomfortable, a bit thirsty, a bit hungry, he could last for days, if necessary. Once or twice during the afternoon he saw planes high overhead. Small chance of anyone up there spotting the small raft in the waste of waters.

Thanks to the calmness of the sea, the raft took very little water and only a bit of spray now and then, so he was almost dry. Darkness came.

Sunday, the sky was in keeping with the peace of a sabbath day. A cool, clear dawn; the sun coming up from the water molten red, beautiful, if he'd been in a mood to appreciate it. He'd slept some, but now it was beginning to get to him, thoughts of Emma with him always, wonder about the outcome of the battle of the Hotel Adlon. But mainly Emma. Emma. God, he'd have a lot to tell her. Not every man had the adventure of ditching at sea. Ed Raine, the heroic freedom fighter, having had a part in saving the world, spent a few days in an open lifeboat, would be rescued. Bearded, thirsty, a bit thin from loss of weight, he would say, "Hey, Emma, it wasn't so bad. Gave me a lot of time to think. I've decided on three children for us, two girls and a boy. And we'll put in the order for the little boy right now."

As the sun slid behind a low bank of clouds on the western horizon, the fun seemed to go out of it. "Now look," he told the water, the empty sky, "enough is enough. I have things to do."

He didn't see the fishing boat at first. It was a low, solidly built trawler and it was coming from behind him. When he roused himself from his lethargy for one last look around before darkness closed in, he saw her. She was so near he was sure they could hear him shout, but not heading toward him. He rose, balancing himself precariously in the unsteady raft, yelling, screaming, waving his jacket, and after what seemed to be a lifetime he saw her turn, point her prow toward him.

By the name she was Danish. Strong arms reached down and lifted him bodily into the low boat, others salvaged the raft. Questions came at him in Danish. He didn't have a single word of the language. "English?" he asked. "German?" The bearded seamen, some of whom smelled rather highly, shook heads. "Water," he said, making drinking motions. It was the nectar of the gods, but one of the men shook his head, waggled a finger, and made him stop, gave him another couple of swallows a few minutes later as Ed struggled vainly to make himself understood.

"Radio," he said, making motions of things coming through the air, of hearing. "Radio?"

"Ah, radio!" said the man who was better dressed than the others. He took Ed's arm and led him to the small, enclosed pilot's cabin.

"Damn," he said, for there was no transmitter, only a shortwave receiver. He turned on the power. He had to know. He began to search the dial. The old set was in bad shape, but now and then sounds came through, in various languages not English or German. And then, faint, distant, static-ridden, fading in and out, he heard English. Jesus, in the middle of the English Channel and the first station he found was American, and some smooth-voiced announcer was introducing the news.

Outside, the wind was rising, the low bank of clouds to the west having climbed the sky to send showers over the small trawler. He could hear the whine of the wind. The skipper offered him a cigarette. He took it, lit up. He needed food, but he needed more to know what was going on in that world out there that seemed so far removed from a small boat somewhere in the Channel.

He heard through the fadings and static the familiar Midwestern voice of his favorite newscaster, Elmer Davis. And as the words came, he sank down weakly into the pilot's chair.

"Great Britain went to war against Germany today, twenty-five years and thirty days from the time she entered the war of 1914 against the same enemy. France is expected to follow suit within a few hours. The state of war—"

And he was gone, faded into the static. Ed fiddled the dials furiously. He was stunned. Success had been assured. What had happened?

And where was Emma?

30

SUNDAY, SEPTEMBER 3, was a lovely day in Berlin, the sun bright, the air that glorious September day a mix of coolness and warmth that encouraged Berliners to take to the streets, to seek out their beloved woodlands and lakes. But Hitler had struck Poland in the predawn hours of Friday, so there was, in the streets, in the beer halls, a sort of numbed astonishment. Berliners checked their ration cards, tried to hoard a few gallons of gas.

The windows of the British Embassy showed stark and empty, for most of the staff had been shipped back home during the past two days. However, there was a small group in the personal sitting room of Sir George Ogilvie Forbes. Forbes was holding forth.

"Finest dog I ever owned," he said. "A rather small Yorkshire terrier. Quite intelligent. She had a keen grasp of the language, knew more commands than any dog I've ever seen."

Bea Goodpasture nursed a drink. She did not know why

she'd been selected by Sir George to be in the last group to leave Germany. She could not understand why they were not at war. It was, after all, two days since Hitler's attack on Poland. She thought war had come on the morning of the first, for the sirens wailed and Berliners rushed to cellars clutching their gasmasks. But, although the nights had been illuminated by a strong moon, there had been no bombers. Now she wanted only to go home.

Finally, the declaration of war came at eleven A.M.—a significant hour, the hour of the armistice of 1918.

"Well," Sir George said, rising, after hearing the announcement on German radio and checking it on the BBC. "I suppose it's time for us to toddle off, chums."

They were treated with amazing politeness by the armed detail that escorted them to the airport. There they boarded what was to be the last British plane to land in Berlin for over five years.

By pounding his fists and pointing to charts, Ed managed to convince the Danish skipper of the trawler to land him on the English coast. They made landfall at Margate, where they were greeted by suspicious men carrying guns. After some agitation and several telephone calls, wearing a borrowed suit that did not fit very well, he headed for London.

Not knowing exactly where to go, but desperate for information—he'd heard plenty of talk about war and not a single shred of information about an attempted coup in Berlin—he went directly to the ANO office on Glasshouse Street just off Piccadilly Circus. Barrage balloons were being sent up over the city, but otherwise it seemed unchanged. The cab driver talked cockily of teaching Mr. Schicklgruber a lesson. "Won't get bogged down as we did in 'fourteen, old boy. Take it to him, don't you know?"

He was greeted like returning royalty at the ANO office; the European Desk supervisor wanted him to sit down immediately and write his tale about "the last plane out of Berlin."

"Okay, in a bit. First, do you have the German papers of the last couple of days?" Ed demanded.

"We have the Saturday papers," the supervisor said. "Something seems to have interfered with the delivery of the Sunday editions. Perhaps a small war?"

The story shared the front page with the news of the invasion of Poland. IDOL OF GERMANY MISSING. She was presumed to be missing as the result of an aircraft accident while flying to "bolster the morale of the proud and brave sons of the Fatherland facing the Polish menace on the Eastern Front." It took him some time to read the glowing article; his eyes kept going dim with tears. It reviewed Emma's acting career, speaking of her as if she were dead. But, he told himself, there was still hope.

He checked each paper from front to back. No mention of an attempt on Hitler.

Only one conclusion to be drawn. It had failed. Somehow. On the brink of war, with German panzers lancing into Poland, Goebbels and the Nazis wouldn't allow mention of any disloyalty, of any attempted coup.

"Now about that story," the supervisor said, as Ed rose and started to leave.

"Later," Ed said, vaguely. "Can't now."

"Ed, it's going to be a long war. I'm short-handed here. I know you got into a little trouble in Berlin, but I know you're capable of good work. Take a day's rest and report back here, okay?"

"I'll get in touch with you," he said.

It took him the rest of the day to find his mother. He finally obtained her address from the foreign office, although he was unable to get in touch with Bea. She had already found a little room in an ancient house on a pleasant green square in Paddington. She greeted him with tears and a big hug.

His first question was, "Have you heard anything?"

She shook her head. "I've been listening to German radio, watching the papers. Nothing. No mention of anything." She paused, looking at him to see his reaction. "Except about Emma."

"I saw it in the papers at ANO."

"Perhaps she's alive," Clara said.

"She is," Ed said. "I feel it. If she were dead I'd—I'd *know* it."

"You were right in forcing me to leave," Clara said.

"We have that, at least," he said. "If anything had happened to you—"

"I know," she said.

In a darkened room—the city was under blackout conditions —they listened to the news, talked in low voices. He told her that he was going back to work for ANO. "But I want you on the first boat to the States, before the subs start sinking ships."

"I just locked the door and walked away from my shop," she said. "From my home, from my native country."

"I know, I know. But, Mother, Germans aren't going to be popular here when the bombers start coming. It'll be the Great War all over again. I don't want you in England with bombs falling."

"But I have no home in America," she said. "And I must do something. I told the people in the foreign office I would be willing to work as a translator, anything to help. I think they were interested."

"Is that what you want?"

"Yes. I must make some sort of contribution."

He reached Bea the next day, met her in a borrowed small office. He brought up the subject of his mother's desire to work for the war effort.

"She'd have to be cleared, of course," Bea said.

"Bea, she was fighting Hitler and the Nazis while you British were still sitting on your butts drinking tea and thinking it would all go away."

"Ah, you have a point," she said.

Sharing the one small room was inconvenient, but London was filling to the seams as the war effort got underway, and couldn't find a place of his own. Clara started working for the foreign office, reading German newspapers and magazines, summarizing or translating anything of interest.

The Polish fortress of Graudenz fell; the panzers smashed through the Polish corridor; Cracow, Poland's second largest city, was in German hands. Not one shot had been fired on the Western Front.

And it seemed that the war had been going on for weeks. He'd been working hard and it was good copy.

She brought the news the day German troops reached Warsaw, September 8. A battered body had been identified as Emma's. She had died in a small plane with the pilot and two other passengers. The wreckage had been hidden by dense woodlands, and lay undiscovered for days. He could not even weep. As the days had passed his optimism, his hope, had faded. In a way it was kind, for he had come to accept her death gradually. Now there were two of them in his memory, two beautiful young women, both smashed, broken, dead.

Twenty-five British planes bombed Wilhelmshaven, but the Western Front was eerily silent. Newsmen coined the phrase, "The Phony War." But it went on.

He was coming out of the ANO office one evening when he heard his name, looked up to see the blond curls of Bea Goodpasture. He got into her small car. She took him to a dim, dank pub and found a secluded table.

"Since you won't come to me," she said, "I've decided to pursue you."

"Watch out," he said, "you might catch me."

Her eyes widened. "Oh, what a terrible thought." But when dark ale had been delivered she became serious. "I thought you'd like to know, Ed," she said. She pulled out a small clipping from her purse.

> Colonel Wolf von Stahlecker, front-line soldier 1915–18, holder of several war decorations, officer of the Abwehr. Born January 12, 1900, deceased August 31, 1939, in Berlin of heart attack. The burial will take place privately on home soil.

"You knew him, didn't you?" Bea asked.

"Yes. You knew something was afoot, Bea. Von Stahlecker was the organizer of a plot to capture Hitler. When I left Berlin I left to the sound of gunfire, thinking that he'd succeeded in stopping the war. Obviously, he didn't."

"I'd be flayed alive if it were known I'm telling you this," she said. "It happened only yesterday. A man came to us asking asylum. He said he'd been involved in the plot."

"His name?"

"He was only an enlisted man," Bea said. "But he seemed to know a lot. He said he was at the Adlon and saw Hitler's Mercedes pull up in front. But the man who got out of the car wasn't Hitler. Then all hell broke loose—a couple of companies, at least, of Waffen SS came in, shooting everyone in sight. He said he got out through a basement window. Now get this. He said it was his duty to call two people if the plot to seize Hitler went wrong. One of them was General Erwin von Witzleben. Does that ring a bell?''

"Von Witzleben was to use his Wehrkreis III troops to secure Berlin, the radio, the ministries." He shook his head. "And all the time the bastard was hedging his bets. He waited to move to see if von Stahlecker made it at the Adlon, and when he didn't, I'll bet my hat he put the same troops to work cleaning up elements of the other conspirators. Funny, though, someone should have moved. Nothing about any attempt to kill any Nazi leaders or take over any installations?''

"Not a word," she said.

"Did he know how von Stahlecker died?"

"He said he'd been issued a cynanide pellet himself. The obit says a heart attack. They could hardly cover up bullet wounds with that. We spies all carry poison pellets." She took his hand. "Sorry. Don't mean to be flippant. I don't feel that way. I read about your Emma, too."

"Thanks, Bea," he said.

"You loved her very much, didn't you?"

"Bea, I did."

"I won't say I wish it were me." She smiled. "It's too soon for that. But I'm sure that it won't do your ego any harm to realize that I'm going to chase you, after giving you a little time."

"It does my ego a lot of good, Bea," he said. "But give yourself a break. I seem to be bad luck for women. That's the second one I've lost."

"If, in the future, you find that you're a teeny bit interested, I'll take the chance," she said. "But in spite of the fact that I promised to chase you, I do have my pride, sir. I won't call you. Call me when you're ready."

"The Polish state," German radio said, "no longer exists,

thus making the treaties of alliance with it mere nonsense. We cannot believe that the British and French will spill useless blood against the impenetrable Western Wall of Germany.'' There were many rumors of peace offers from the Germans. Russia had joined Germany in picking the bones of helpless Poland. By the end of the month reports out of Europe spoke of Germany's desire for peace, blaming the state of war on the British, saying, "All Europe awaits the word of peace from London."

He called Bea. "Bea, just some company, huh? Pay is a good dinner and some American-style jitterbugging, if you're brave enough."

She was. London was gay, in a fever, and it was an evening during which he could forget, from time to time, and with the help of good gin he was properly numbed as he escorted her home, kissed her good night in front of her flat, and flatly said it wasn't time to come inside and curl her toes.

But there were other nights, as the phony war continued. He began to curl her toes with heated kissings and, to make her predictions come true, to be the one who, in the privacy of her flat, their bodies pressed tightly together, said, "Whoa, girl."

"Please," she said, "I'll never survive the war as a virgin. I'm too tender-hearted. I'll fall in love with some soldier and give it to him as a going-away present. I'd rather give it to you."

What did he feel for her? He didn't stop to analyze it. He liked being with her. She was witty, vivacious, pretty, lively, fun. She was one hell of a kisser and his own toes did a lot of curling. But Emma was dead and it was too soon. What was he, some kind of fickle ladykiller who could dismiss love after mere weeks and find a new one?

But now the matter came to a head. "Ed," said his supervisor. "How are you fixed for long-johns?"

"I don't like the sound of that," Ed said suspiciously.

"Scandinavia," the supervisor said. "A quick tour. What do the people think? Will the Danes, the Swedes, and the Norwegians continue to be neutral? Do they sympathize with Hitler? Deep think pieces, the kind of bullshit you can sling without any effort."

"How long?" he asked.

"Until I say enough."

He told Bea. "Oh, damn," she said. "And just as I was about to seduce you."

"We-erd." He laughed. "Are you really virgin?"

"By all that's holy," she said.

"All men want to marry virgins, right?"

"I don't know, never having had the experience."

"Would you consider marriage?"

"To whom?"

"Me, goose."

"Oh, I'd think about it," she said, cuddling closer. "It would have to be proposed in more concrete terms, such as, my lovely and charming Bea, would you do me the honor of being my wife?"

"I'll have to do some rehearsing, to be sure I get it right," he said, for he had a quick vision of Emma. He knew, however, that sooner or later he would. Or he thought he would.

That was before he received the packet. It came in without benefit of censorship or customs inspection, carried by a small-time newsman coming out of Switzerland.

It was in an eight-by-ten stoutly reinforced manila envelope, and it took some doing to get it open. He was seated at his desk. He withdrew a thick packet bound up in heavy, stiff cardboard, untied some string, saw her face first, eyes closed, face contorted.

He had noticed it before—when a beautiful woman is nearing sexual climax, the look on her face cannot be distinguished as either pain or pleasure. Seeing that look brought back vivid memories, all in a flash, of nights in the Adlon with Emma in his arms. But then his eyes traveled and he uncovered the rest of the top picture, and it chilled him. It was taken from a high angle and it showed her on a table contraption with a man astride. He thumbed quickly through the next pictures. They were all the same, but the men were different. His shock grew, so that it was some time before he realized that she was helpless, tightly strapped to the table. He felt sick. He felt like screaming out. He rushed from his desk to the bathroom, locked the door behind him, feverishly shuffled through the sameness of twenty, thirty pictures. At the last one he felt lightheaded and dizzy and had to sit on a stool.

Eyes wide, mouth opened in a silent scream. He knew the look of death.

He examined the stack of horror. Her expression became duller in the later ones, then in the very last ones it changed, became a different sort of agony. And no back of a man, only the head of a white-coated man at the edge of the shot. He couldn't look again at the last one. He checked carefully, looking at the blank backs of the prints. No clue who had sent it, but he knew.

And he knew that he himself had killed her with his love, for he had known of her affair with Goebbels. He had killed her with his love. She was dead in that last picture, not in the crash of a light plane—that was a cover-up. Just as the Nazis could not admit that there had been any attempt on Hitler, they could not admit that the idol of Germany had been tortured and killed.

Damn, damn, damn. Sheer revulsion was mixed with hate in him; he wanted to go out, to hit someone, anyone, especially a German.

Instead, he sat looking at the face of his Emma in death and let the scalding tears come.

31

HE LEFT FOR his tour of Scandinavia without calling Bea. He didn't deserve the love of a girl like Bea. He had killed his love as surely as if he'd tortured Emma himself, and he would never do that to another lovely woman. Nor could he leave himself open again to being gutted, drained by the loss of a woman. The only refuge was work.

Some Danes thought they might be next. They didn't trust Hitler. "A madman," a high government official said. "He will not be content until he has outdone the great conquerors of the past. His ambition is the world."

And some Swedes thought the same, although, in general, there was more pro-German thinking in Sweden than in Denmark.

He called the small Baroness the second day he was in Oslo. She was ecstatic when she heard his voice, insisted

306

that he come right out to her house. He wanted to see her, and he wanted to thank her in person for getting his mother out of Germany.

"It made me feel quite heroic," Helga said. "I thank you for the opportunity to do some little something against the Germans." He noted that her careful neutrality toward the Germans seemed to have changed.

Her house, one of several that had belonged to her father, had been remodeled especially for her. The furniture was scaled down to her size; in a large room carpeted luxuriously in animal skins, she sat in a chair designed and made for her. A tall blond serving-girl kept feeding Ed small crackers with a delicious cheese that made the vintage wine taste wonderful.

Helga directed the conversation, talking easily of her life, of the situation in Norway. She was an acute observer of moods and of politics, had connections throughout Scandinavia, and spoke with grace and precision. For a while, Ed took notes; whole paragraphs of what she said could be used practically without editing.

But the wine kept coming, and he put down his notepad. "Helga," he said, at last, "I'm getting drunker than a skunk."

She laughed aloud. "I've never heard that! Is it an American saying? How drunk can a skunk get?" she asked, in her cheerful, piping voice.

"About as drunk as this," he said. But he was in good company and with Helga's good talk and the wine he could, for a few moments, wipe away the look of death on Emma's face and forget his hatred for the man who had seen to it that he knew her exact fate. No kind and swift death in a plane crash for the mistress who had cuckolded Joseph Goebbels.

Helga was talking about plans to redo her ancient house all in red, to make it look like a Victorian brothel. And he was hearing her words while shaking his head and repeating it over and over, "Oh, that son-of-a-bitch."

"Who?" Helga asked.

"Sorry. Told you I was drunk. Got lost there in my head for a while."

"There is something very sad in your head," she said. "If you wish, I can be a good listener."

"You wouldn't want to hear this, Helga. Not this."

But it was happening. He was talking, starting with the love, the warmth of her, and then, sometimes becoming almost incoherent, stoking the pain with wine, he was describing to a white-faced Helga the last picture, the final picture, the picture of death on Emma's face.

The little Baroness waddled to him, patted his knee, saying, "There, there. You didn't kill her. *They* killed her, the Nazis, those people who will kill millions before this war is over. But that will mean not as much to you as the death of one person, your Emma. For that loss there is no comfort save time, my friend Ed."

He tried to stop the tears, a grown man weeping in front of a woman. "There, there," she said. He managed to control himself, looked. She was smiling at him, holding out a glass of wine filled well past the point of politeness. "There is only one temporary comfort," she said. He drank.

He awoke in a strange bed, head pounding. A manservant was raising blinds.

"You are awaited for breakfast," the servant said.

"You put me in this bed?" Ed asked.

"Yes, sir."

"Thanks."

"It is nothing."

Helga wore a bright yellow outfit, some sort of coveralls. "Now you feel worse but you feel better."

"I feel worse." He sat up. The coffee he drank turned to acid. "Sorry about last night, Helga."

"I have seen drunk and weeping men before."

"I'm sorry I told you about what they did to Emma. No decent woman should even—"

"Shush," she said. "You had to tell someone. Sooner or later you would have exploded if you hadn't."

"You're a good listener," he said. "Thank you." He found he had enough courage to tackle a hunk of good bread and soft butter.

"One of my many talents," she said. "I could not, you recall, interest you in the others. Perhaps you were repelled."

"Never," he said quickly. "Never repelled, Helga. You're one of the nicest."

"Just nice." She sighed. "When you are finished I want to show you my gardens."

They explored the carefully tended grounds. She rode a German-built trike and kept to the paved pathways. The day was crisp and cool. They talked and the talk continued when they returned to the house. Ed felt relaxed and comfortable for the first time in weeks, and he quickly accepted when she invited him to stay another night.

Over dinner, seeing that he was avoiding the wine, she said, "There's whisky, and American bourbon." He made a wry face and she laughed. "Still suffering?"

"It's better."

"Such is the way of it," she said. "The other suffering will lessen, too. I know."

He looked at her and understood. She had a heart as big as her small body, and, he knew, all the normal desires of a woman, and she was trapped forever in that runted, unbending body. He did not have a monopoly on personal tragedy. Not that it made him feel better, but it did show him that almost anything is bearable.

"Helga, when I've had a little time to pull myself together, I'd like to visit you again."

"I would welcome you, at any time."

"Maybe I'll see if you've been lying to me." He grinned.

"Ha, that would be easy to prove."

For almost two months there was an unreal quiet in the world, but there was much activity in England. War would come to the Western Front. Germany would have to make a move, for all the while Britain was arming, sending men into France. Germany could not hope to win a war of economic attrition. A British and French blockade being set up around Germany would force Hitler to try to decide the issue on the battlefield, where the German was so competent. It would be long, very rugged.

The world had never known a war machine as powerful as that built up by the Germans. People no longer spoke of the "phony war."

Ed did his job, taking it day by day, and sometimes, when he was writing, he could forget that last picture for hours at a time. He began to think that when the United States came into the war, he might enjoy killing a few Germans, but he knew that the death of German soldiers at his own hands would not change what had happened. The men he'd be facing if he joined the army would be very much like him, pawns.

His supervisor liked the articles that came out of the Scandinavian tour. "Good stuff, Ed. I want you to take a day off and get saddled up again. Belguim, France, Holland."

He saddled up. And then once again he was back in London and his mother told him that Bea had called every other day while he was away. He'd come from areas where uncertainties were rampant, where men and women and children faced each day not knowing when the German panzers would move, where they would move, whether or not Hitler would honor his pledges to respect Belgian and Dutch neutrality. In France there was a sort of ignorant confidence as the proud French Army sat behind the supposedly impregnable Maginot Line. He needed something like Bea's cheerfulness. He called.

Later that night, in her flat, he lay beside her on a couch, accepting her invitation to try to curl her toes. His own were beginning to bend a bit.

"Lady," he whispered, "I feel the cad coming out in me. Better tell me good night."

"Oh, I have the utmost faith in you," she said. He tried to pull away only to be held tightly. "Go ahead, do it, take advantage of me. And then you'll have to make an honest woman of me, you know."

"Bea—" he said.

"Go on, deflower me shamelessly, and I promise I shall make you rue it with about ninety-nine years of married life."

He was not sure he wasn't acting half in jest when he disentangled himself, knelt before her, and said, "Miss Bea Goodpasture, I take this opportunity to fall on my bended knees to ask you to do me the honor of becoming my fully flowered wife."

"That was rather nice," she said, beaming and nodding. "Would you care to have another go at it? I think you can get it right."

"We-erd," he said.

"Are you serious, then?" she asked, her face twisted as if she were going to cry.

"With one condition," he said. "You have to promise me that you'll stay where it's always safe, promise me that you won't get yourself killed, that you won't die before I die."

"Please—" she whispered, hearing and seeing his seriousness. "Oh, Ed."

"Promise," he said.

"Yes, yes. Oh, my dear, I do promise," she said, throwing herself at him, bowling him over onto the carpet.

But even as she kissed him, laughing now, a picture formed in his mind, a death's head, Emma. And then it was Bea and he was holding her so tightly that she squeaked. He relaxed, enjoyed the kiss. "Hell," he said, "I think I really do want to marry you."

"That's nice," she said. "But do you think you had much choice?"

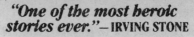